The Diwali Party

A STORY OF FRIENDS, FAMILY AND
OTHER BROKEN PIECES OF LIGHT

The Diwali Party

A STORY OF FRIENDS, FAMILY AND
OTHER BROKEN PIECES OF LIGHT

LEENA SALDANHA

 **Leadstart**

ISBN: 978-81-948043-0-7

Cover design: Girish Rapatwar
Layout: Kshitij Dhawale, Leadstart
Printing: Jasmine Art Printers Pvt. Ltd

Published in India 2020 by
Leadstart
A Division of One Point Six Technologies Pvt Ltd
Building J2, Shram Seva Premises, Offices: 119-123
Wadala Truck Terminus, Wadala (East)
Mumbai 400 037, Maharashtra, INDIA
T + 91 96 99933000   **E** info@leadstartcorp.com
W www.leadstartcorp.com

DISCLAIMER: The opinions expressed in this book do not purport
to reflect the views of the Publisher.

** Gender indicators are neutral.

To Abhijit
… because you see me.

ACKNOWLEDGEMENTS

Mom, your faith in me is what keeps me going. But it is your investment in my stories that makes me truly happy. Thank you for reading every word I have ever written and for being my cheerleader-in-chief.

Dad, you are one of the best storytellers I know. I couldn't become the genius sportsperson you are, but thank you for passing on the storytelling gene.

Siddhant, you inspired me to go on when I had given up. That is one of the greatest gifts I have ever received. Thank you, my child.

Sanaah, my partner, secretary, best friend, motivator, you teach me how to be a better person. Thank you for the gift of you.

A heartfelt thanks to all my friends and family and my team at work. You guys make it easy for me to follow my heart. Without your support, this would be impossible.

Contents

Chapter I

Very deliberately, she poured the nail polish remover onto a large wad of cotton. It was more a ball than a wad. With an unwavering gaze she watched as the astringent liquid squished the diaphanous ball into a limp mess.

Then with hands that were as steady as a surgeon's she unvarnished her nails. First her toes, with their fancy gold and ruby toe-rings. Then her long, slender fingers. A huge solitaire on her left hand sparkled in the muted light of her white and peach bedroom. The plain platinum band on her right hand glinted dully. Her other rings were slightly less ostentatious. But they were there. Each one a little story by itself. The emerald and diamond star on her middle finger, the delicate tiara of diamonds on her forefinger, the precious gold braid of her childhood on her little finger. Aaji had given her that one when she was twelve. And she had only worn it on festive occasions. Her school would never have allowed anyone to wear finger rings to school. But on the day that she got married she had found the ring again, lying hidden and half-forgotten in the pile of ornaments that her mother and her mother and mother-in-law had collected for her over a lifetime. She wasn't sure then why she had reached out for that ring, why she had felt the need to try it on, and why she had felt so relieved when it had fit on the little finger of her right hand. "What are you doing, Rekha??? Take off that silly thing. It doesn't go with any of the other jewellery you are wearing!" her Kaku's slightly supercilious voice rang clear in Rekha's mind after 14 long years. And so did the calmness in her own voice, "I'm wearing it, Meera Kaku. It goes with me." Her Kaku and her Mom had exchanged a quick look. Her Aaji had smiled a sweet smile. And Rekha had never taken the ring off after that.

Today the diluted red of her nail polish ran down her fingers, through her rings. Her hands were messy. But she did nothing to clean the mess. She just let the remover clean the last trace of colour from her nails. She had done this meticulously for the past 14 years. A little bit of cotton, just a few drops of the remover, a clean, precise rubdown of her nails, a thorough cleanse, a clinical manicure and a new coat of nail colour. Sometimes nail art. Her nails were her signature. Always perfect. Even when they didn't have colour, they'd have that fancy protection coat that she ordered in bulk from New York.

But none of that today. Today she drenched herself in remover. And long after the colour was gone, she kept rubbing. As if to remove the artificial colour from her cells. Her soul. Her old faithful enamel tub sat next to her. It was chipped and slightly dented, but she wouldn't hear of getting rid of it. "It's slightly embarrassing, Re. What do you need it for? Let's get you a new one..." Anay had said to her more than once. In his genteel, refined manner. Always restrained, always polite, always suggesting, never insisting. And 'Re' had gritted her teeth and never replied. She had always smiled back. Polite. Always polite.

The warm water with the mild cleanser in the chipped enamel tub was like a little haven of comfort for Rekha. She dipped her hands on which the colour had bled out profusely into that warmth. And let the water and cleanser leach it all away. 14 years of artificial colour.

After the water cooled she again very calmly patted her hands dry. Gently. And brutally chopped off her long, perfectly shaped nails. Only once did her hand tremble. As she placed the monogrammed nail cutter back into her manicure set after she had cut off her nails.

Very neatly she cleared up after herself. She put her arsenal back into its pouches and boxes. Then she drew herself up to her full height and looked into the floor-to-ceiling mirror in her walk-in wardrobe.

For the first time in 14 years, Rekha Jaisingh felt naked. And clean.

Chapter 2

She knew where he would be. He was always there at this time of day. Sitting at the family table. The morning sunlight slanting across his clean-shaven, angular, handsome face. Reading the Express. Drinking his second and last cup of tea for the day. Nothing had caused him to change this routine. Not even the day when her Aaji had died. He had still read the Express that day. With his second cup of tea. She thought of that as she saw him sitting there today. And was unprepared for the bolt of white anger that shot through her at the memory. She had never been angry with him. Or maybe she had never allowed herself to feel the anger. "Too much nail polish" she thought to herself, "I wore too much nail polish; it coated everything in gloss."

She was surprised at how steady her gait was as she walked to him.

He continued reading. Completely unaware of her existence.

"Anay".

He read on.

"Anay", this time a little louder.

And he looked up at her. Mildly surprised. Everything was mild about Anay. His serious brown eyes asked a mild question through his expensive glasses. Everything he wore was expensive. Once, many years ago, Rekha had got him salted, roasted groundnuts. In a newspaper cone. From a street vendor. On an impulse. He had looked mildly aghast at his young wife. But he had accepted her gift. And eaten the peanuts. Politely. He had then neatly folded the cone and dropped it precisely into the centre of the bin in his office.

She had felt miserable that day in the way that she imagined prisoners on death row on their last night before the noose must be feeling. As if there was no hope left. Of course, she hadn't allowed herself to feel the misery for long. "Melodrama, Rekha, melodrama" she had said to herself. And hadn't allowed herself to ask why her own voice in her own head sounded like Anay.

Anay cleared his throat in enquiry. And Rekha jerked back to the present. She was here to say something to him.

"I'm going out to breakfast with the girls" she said in her calm, steady voice.

He nodded and his head turned back towards the editorial he was reading. "The Pillars of Democracy. Are they crumbling?" by Anuja Menon. One of his favourite social commentators.

But Rekha wasn't done yet.

Once again, she interrupted his unchanging morning routine. "And Anay..."

"Yes?" he said with a little sigh.

"I'm getting a divorce."

For just one moment, something glimmered in his brown eyes. Something that gave Rekha a moment of wild hope. Before the shutters came down again.

"Okay."

And without another word he turned to his cup of tea.

As Rekha made her soundless way out of the room, she heard the porcelain cup rattle slightly as her husband of 14 years placed it back in its fine Wedgewood saucer.

Back at the threshold of her own room, her breath caught in her chest and sudden tears pricked her beautiful black eyes. "That look in his eyes. It was happiness. I told him I'm getting a divorce. And he was happy" she said to herself as the tears came in torrents. Loud, melodramatic sobs escaped her heaving chest. And for the second time in 14 years, Rekha Jaisingh felt naked. And clean.

Chapter 3

(FEBRUARY 15, 2016)

No one knew how everyone managed to hear anything in that chaos. But for the past 50 odd years, all the people who thronged to the popular Udipi joint on College Street in Pune had apparently developed temporary superpowers. Because as long as they were in the idiosyncratically named New Coffee House, they could hear like bats. Everyone talked there. Non-stop. Loudly. Large groups of people argued at the top of their voices over just about anything, ranging from which movie was better, the day's headlines, whether dropping Tendulkar from the playing XI would have been possible if he had not retired on his own, whether Pendse should pay today's bill because his son had decided to become a tattoo artist instead of an engineer, who had cheated more in the morning's game of badminton, how one dosa could be split between three people, how many extra sambars were needed between eight people, right up to the fate of Arctic glaciers because of the increasing use of air conditioners in Pune.

And the funny thing was no one minded.

In a city like Pune where people minded if you sneezed too loudly in your own house, and put up official boards announcing that the air in the tyres of your vehicle would be let out if you parked in front of a gate no one used anyway, that was an anomaly. But again, that was Pune for you. Anomalous.

An unremarkable group of seven women in their mid-thirties sat at a table in the centre of New Coffee House that clear February morning. They were unremarkable in New Coffee House because everybody was unremarkable there. Minor stars could walk in and go unnoticed. In fact, they would be pointedly ignored. In New Coffee House, sambar was the star. Uttapam was a celebrity. Strong filter coffee drunk out of tall glasses was the story. Everyone else was simply the paying public.

Waiters treated you with familiarity. They had seen you walk in there with your parents, known before your parents did which boy you were dating, warned you to drop the 'long-haired hippy' before he broke your heart, and then signalled their approval when you walked in with a mangalsutra round your neck, suitably hitched to a suitable boy. They knew who in the group needed extra sambar with their masala dosa, who liked their idli-wada mixed with sambar and who didn't. They knew everything.

Rekha caught herself wondering how soon it would be before Raghu Kaka noticed her fingers. He sauntered over, his pencil on the ready. He knew the order by heart. But every once in a while, one of the women in the group would surprise him with a request for mango shake, instead of filter coffee; or that one time when the tall one had asked for a veg burger instead of her usual medu wada sambar. The mango shake order had continued for nine months, just as he had guessed it would. Rashmi's first pregnancy had been a mango shake pregnancy. Her next one had been a dahi wada pregnancy. And there was that time when Roopa had asked for lime soda, salted. He was sure she was pregnant. But the next time she came, her eyes had looked dead. And she had asked for strong coffee. He was sure she had miscarried. So, he had given her her strong coffee, with an extra warm smile. And she had smiled back in sadness. Raghu Kaka read stories in food choices. He wasn't a waiter. He was a legend. And for Rekha, he was a bit of a Mother Hen. She would have pulled off a major minor victory if she could manage to fly under Raghu Kaka's radar today.

So as Raghu Kaka approached the group, Rekha busied herself in the menu card. Which was her first mistake. Because you don't avoid eye contact with the Mother Hen. That switches on the Mother Hen Radar like nothing else does. He stood there, next to the group, as if nothing were wrong, noting down the well-known order as the girls (for him they were always girls) shouted it out to him all at once. "3 masala dosa, 1 onion uttapam, 1 idli-wada mix,1 idli-wada separate, 1 tomato omelette with extra white butter..." At this old joke there was a rousing yell from the group, "Kaka, no butter, what extra butter, can't you see how we are all expanding, soon enough we won't be able to fit in your narrow chairs!!!" Kaka would continue as if he hadn't heard them, "1 tomato omelette with even more butter, 1 cheese chilli toast, 4 extra sambar, 7 coffee – 3 strong, 4 normal." And the group would wait for his parting shot, "Extra malai in one strong coffee." And once again the 'girls' would rise in protest and collapse in laughter, "Kaka, no malai, she'll vomit right here!!!"

As Raghu Kaka strolled away with his pencil tucked behind his ear,

Rekha heaved an unnoticed sigh of relief. "Why does he even have that pencil?" asked Zoya, all sporty chic in her short, white tee and her dark blue jeans. "I've been coming here forever, and I've never seen him write down a single order. The man has the memory of a... a..." she clicked her fingers as she searched for an appropriate comparison.

"Of an anti-Ghajni" supplied the witty Maya.

It wasn't a particularly funny joke. But everything sounded funnier in New Coffee House. So, the women collapsed in laughter once again.

And the easy banter flowed. It wafted on the unchanged aroma of the coffee and the sambar. Meaningless. But important.

Just when everything was settling into a familiar rhythm, in a flash the energy of the space seemed to shift a little bit. Like a tiny cactus had walked into a gently flowing river. Mixed metaphor. And quite impossible to imagine. But try, nevertheless. Because that is what it felt like when Tilly made her entrance.

Tilly was beautiful in the way a cactus is attractive to some who pot one and keep it in their balcony. Prickly, but with a definite presence. When Tilly walked people naturally made space for her. She was like the eternal Moses, and some Red Sea or the other was constantly parting for her. You see people like that. They seem to occupy more space than their physical bodies do. Arms distance. That was like Tilly's T-shirt line. She bristled her way into the seat the group had kept waiting for her. Because that was Tilly's auto mode. Bristling. She never seemed to feel the need to start a conversation afresh, from the beginning. It was like she was in the middle of this long, unbroken dialogue with a million voices and she expected everyone to be able to hear the chatter as clearly as she did. No 'Hi's' and 'Hellos' from our friend Tilly. Tilly would just continue whatever conversation was happening in her head at the moment and expect everyone to catch up.

Today, apparently, Tilly was agitated about the rickshawallahs of Pune. Which again, was neither new nor surprising. Because agitation was another shade of her auto mode. And rickshawallahs were her natural enemies. Control-freak, cactus Tilly was quite literally terrified of trusting anyone enough to take her safely from point A to point B. And for a woman who abhorred boxes and rebelled at stereotypes, she was very happy to box and stereotype all the rickshawallahs of the world into a callous, rude, rash, brash singularity. Which was not just untrue and unfair, it was also counterproductive. And typically Tilly.

"Not done. One morning I need an auto and this is what happens. Blessed Raju didn't turn up. And there's no place to park here. So, what choice do I have? I have to take an auto. 5 chaps simply refused! What audacity, ya! No one can do anything about it. It's a mafia. And then they expect *you* to carry change. As if you are the one obliged by them ferrying you around like blasted maniacs. And who gives them their licenses, ya? They think they drive some bendable, Ramdev Baba type magic contortionist contraptions or what? Why do they believe they can squeeze into a space between two buses that are belching out fumes and racing one another on a road meant for bicycles and bullock carts?!!"

Zoya handed her a glass of water as Tilly looked up from the giant tote that she had been ranting into. Looking for some typically Tilly thing that she seemed to have found. In one long gulp she drank the water, handed a little parcel wrapped in newspaper and tied with a pink ribbon to Maya, and said, "Where's my Mysore Masala?"

"An old P G Wodehouse!" Maya squealed as she tore open her gift from Tilly. "You are such a darling! Where did you pick this one up from!" she asked, as she held the worn, yellowing pages to her nose. "London. I bought it last year for you. And then forgot to give it to you. Such an idiot I am..." mumbled Tilly, not completely done with her rickshawallah rant in her head. "From one of those places on Charing Cross Road. Love the place, ya."

"I know... no rickshawallahs!" piped up Zoya mischievously.

And for a split-second Tilly's eyes glinted dangerously before she broke into that marvellous Tilly guffaw. Clear, loud, from the bottom of her stomach. She threw her head back and laughed like a conquering general. One of her many exes used to say that when she laughed, she looked like what he imagined Alexander the Great might have looked like when a minion dared to crack a joke in front of him – momentarily surprised, but hugely and unselfconsciously amused at not only the joke but at the fact that someone had actually attempted funny in his presence. Tilly was like that. Fuming one second, laughing raucously at her own self the next. When Tilly laughed, everyone laughed with her. And in that moment, the cactus bloomed. Pretty pink flowers that made the thorns look a little less menacing for now.

"Raghu Kaka!" she called out in her clear, strong voice. "Where is my..." "1 Mysore Masala, beti. On its way" he smiled across the crowd on his way to another table. "I know no one placed my order. You girls are just a bunch of so and so's."

"He knows, Tilly" came an exaggerated drawl from the other end of the long table. "He *always* knows!" Mitali, the wannabe saint – seer of the group could make anything sound like a spiritual secret being revealed. She wore sandalwood paste on her forehead, there was always a new stone or crystal or amulet somewhere on her immense person, and she had the amusing ambition of wanting to become a sort of spiritual handyman. Someone had a minor tiff at home over monthly budgeting, Mitali would rush off to examine if the south-east corner or whatever in their house had sunlight; someone's kid wasn't doing too well in math, Mitali would gift the child an exotic stone to tie around his navel; someone was having team trouble, Mitali would land up in the office and burn some incense. She meant well. But she was yet to establish the clear connection between sitting down and applying one's mind to the task at hand and doing well in basic mathematics.

"Shut up, Mits" tossed back Tilly good-naturedly. "He doesn't *always* know. He'd once got me a Mysore Sada. And remember that time when he almost fainted because Rashmi asked him for a shake instead of her coffee?"

Some more laughter, some more pointless, meandering, conversations, and then the food arrived, balanced magically in the hands of the mythical Raghu Kaka.

"Mysore Masala, served first, because you came last" that was the kind of complete illogic that Raghu Kaka specialised in. Some days it would be "One strong coffee extra, from me, because you are wearing a bindi." On others it would be "Your son said such a sweet 'good morning' the last time you were here, so extra cheese on your onion cheese uttapam." "But I didn't even order an onion cheese uttapam!" the giftee would say bemusedly. "I know" Raghu Kaka would answer over his shoulders as he walked away on his eternal beat.

Today, he studiously avoided Rekha, almost as studiously as she avoided him.

But he was not the great Raghu Kaka for nothing. As he brought the bill folder to the table, he went and stood behind Rekha and said to no one in particular, "Gajju had come in last week. He brought back this. He said I should give it to you girls when you came in next."

The girls all looked towards Rekha as one. And Rekha felt a hot blush creeping up her neck. "Silly" she chided herself. "Just silly. Why should I care? After all these years. Get a grip, girl. 16 years is a lifetime. He probably doesn't even remember my name now."

Raghu Kaka held out his hand and Zoya took the enlarged photograph from him. It was a picture of the gang from college. And at the base, in permanent marker, was a tiny R. In a heart.

"Oh my God!" Zoya exclaimed. "It's all of us, from way back when. This was the summer of '98. Sinhagad trek. We were so young! And so ugly!"

Everyone wanted to see the picture at once. Necks were craned, elbows were shoved into comfortable midriffs. And there was considerable screeching. Enough to get the usually tolerant and accepting cohabitators of New Coffee House to aim a few disapproving glances in their direction before diving back into their own sambar.

Finally, everyone had seen the picture. And it was Maya who spoke the truth everyone had so assiduously avoided speaking. "We were all so thin!" she said in a voice filled with awe and almost unbearable regret. And a collective sigh trembled through the group around the table. For a few moments, the unthinkable happened – no one spoke. Until the always sensible Zoya decided to take matters into her own hands. "So? It just goes to show that we can be like that again."

"No, babe. Not going to happen. That was then, this is now. Best to accept who we are and move on." This from the Mother India of the group – Rashmi. Rashmi had spent the last 13 years of her life on creating the perfect children. Her children were her project. She created schedules for them, researched nutritional charts and planned weekly menus for them, she chauffeured them to all the coaching classes that she insisted they attend - 'A child must be well-rounded.' She 'sacrificed' her own parlour visits for their swimming practice; she 'postponed' her own health check-ups for their study tours; she 'gave up' morning walks for tiffin preparation. She was the first to dismiss the idea of going back to the shape they had all been in, in the days of what she clearly saw as their irresponsible youth. For Rashmi, it was just too time-consuming. And time was the one thing she did not have. All of her time had been given over to her pet project. And even this breakfast was beginning to stretch.

The quietest voice in the group also finally spoke up "I'm not chasing after foolish dreams. I'm already late. Got to go girls. Bye for now. See you soon." And with a small wave of her pudgy hand, the slightly sad Sarika smiled her slightly sad smile and waddled away to her miserable job as an underpaid, completely bored, assistant professor of economics in an all-girls junior college.

The mood around the table was unusually sombre. And everyone looked toward Zoya for succour. Habit is a powerful force. Everyone looked toward Zoya and Zoya delivered. It was just an old habit.

"What rubbish" she said with the full force of Zoya. "What utter nonsense. It is not foolish, unattainable, impossible, or anything of the sort. We can make this happen. It's mathematics." With Zoya, everything was. She, along with her brother Zaid and his wife, Anu ran a very successful accountancy firm. After 2 C-sections, Zoya herself was just slightly overweight.

"It's ok for you to say" grumbled the plump, almost matronly Roopa. "For some of us it is physics and chemistry and biology and history all combined in order to change our geography!"

"I can't diet, ya. That's just not going to happen, Zo" Tilly said, with a look of longing directed at the cold coffee being carried to the table behind theirs.

"Let's get a sexy gym instructor! We'll do personal trainings. I'm all for it!" Mitali trilled.

"No. Let's go swimming!" Maya chipped in.

"I'm not swimming. I look like a flippin' whale!" Roopa groaned.

"Yoga. We should all do yoga!!!"

"You know our neighbour Shalu? She lost so much weight just going on morning walks. Why pay anyone any money? We should just walk every day."

"Zumba."

"Jogging."

"Hypno-therapy."

"Let's give up sugar."

The suggestions flew in fast and flippant.

"Whoa, whoa, whoa! Give peace a chance, ladies! Let's just give this a moment." Tilly intervened. "First of all, who wants to look like those girls in the picture?"

Everyone's hands went up. Except Rashmi's. So Tilly, being Tilly grabbed her hand and lifted it for her with an impish wink. It was impossible to resist Tilly.

"Ok. Now next steps. Zo, go for it." Tilly allowed poor Rashmi's hand to fall down limply.

"Alright then, first things first - let's set ourselves a target. How much weight do we want to lose? And until when?" Zoya began briskly. She grabbed a tissue paper. "I'm making a chart here. Tell me your current weight and your ideal weight. It's a simple calculation. We can figure out who needs to work out how much, on how many days. We can plan out diet charts for everyone, because clearly, we all need to personalise our weight-loss plan for maximum efficiency. We can schedule our micro-planning sessions later, but for now..." she trailed off. "What?" she asked the rest of the group who were all staring at her with mouths that were gaping slightly.

"Zo, you are a little scary when you get like that." Tilly was first respondent. The others were still a little intimidated by Field Marshall Zoya. Then Rekha spoke up. "Let's plan our Diwali party."

Zoya's head snapped towards Rekha like she'd been whiplashed. "What??? You trying to be funny here, babe?"

"No. Seriously. We're sitting in the second week of February. Diwali is the first week of November. We have a good nine months. Let's plan the party. Let's plan what we are going to wear. Let's plan the colours and the theme." Rekha said, her eyes shining for the first time that morning.

Rekha talking about parties and clothes was even more unsettling than Zoya channelling her inner despot.

The group looked at each other, bewildered.

It was Tilly, predictably, who saw sense where everyone else saw the need for psychiatric intervention.

"Genius! Rekha madam, you are a genius! Girls, that's just what we need to do. How long has it been since any one of us cared about what we wore and how we looked? Just look at you, Roopa! What gorgeous hair. And how do you wear it now? Tied up in a bunch! Mad or what you are? And Zo, love the white tee and the jeans, but when was the last time you applied kajal? And Rashmi! God, Rashmi! You, I will yell at later! Rekha, I love it. Let's do this. Let's meet up and plan our Diwali party. Everyone head back, go online, turn to Google maharaj, select what you are going to wear, and let's take it from there!"

The Tilly effect took place almost immediately. Everyone's eyes held a faraway, dreamy look. And smiles started breaking out around the table like the Sun breaking up an overcast sky.

"Let's do this" smiled Zoya as she busily collected her laptop bag and riding helmet. "Next week, same time. Right here."

The group filed out. Talking at the top of their voices, excited like a bunch of teenagers about a party nine months away.

They had almost reached the door when Rekha became aware of a silent presence over her shoulder.

Raghu Kaka was standing in a corner. Lying in wait like only a Mother Hen knows how to.

"He's a good boy, beta."

"Raghu Kaka" gasped Rekha, "How can you say that? Gajju is…"

He raised a firm hand to stop her mid stride.

"Who's talking about Gajju? Anay. Anay is a good boy, beta. People like him are so few, you can count them on your fingers" he said, looking pointedly at her bereft hand with her tonsured nails.

And once again, the tears that had stayed dangerously near the surface shimmered in her beautiful eyes. "Melodrama, Rekha, melodrama" played a familiar voice in her head as Rekha headed back to a life that looked lost. After 14 years.

Chapter 4

Maya Wagh had been on her way to breakfast with her gang of girls when she had remembered that today was the day when she had learnt to make chiffon cake. That was the sort of thing that the pretty Maya milestoned her life with. Others remembered birthdays and anniversaries; Maya celebrated in her own mind the day she had rolled out her first perfect roti. The victory of it had been almost physical. She could still feel that warm, golden glow in the centre of her being. Her virago of a grandmother had decreed that no one in the house would eat any more rotis until the 11-year-old Maya served them up – perfectly round and perfectly soft. Maya's gentle, grey-eyed mother's eyes had watered. "She is just a child, Aai" she seemed to be mutely petitioning through her downcast eyes. But there was no recourse in the tyrannical reign of the grand old lady. Her word was rule of law, her will was set in stone. And the demure Shaila Wagh had removed the well-thumbed novel from the stubborn grasp of her first-born and had shepherded her into the family kitchen. Maya had been furious. "She is so much like her father, and her grandmother" poor Shaila had sighed quietly to herself. To her daughter she had said, "She means well, Maya rani. She wants you to learn to cook early, so that by the time you are married…" "Stop, Ma. Please stop right there!" Maya had intervened in hushed fierceness. In the Wagh household, any form of dissent was unheard of. So, Maya had learnt at an early age to whisper her rebellions into her poor mother's ears. "What do you mean 'by the time I am married'? I am NOT going to learn to make rotis because I need to make them for my husband and his family. I am NOT you, Ma. You keep cooking for them. You think anyone notices? I am NOT going to be treated like that" Maya had rushed on, unheeding of the sharp pain in her mother's eyes, callous as only a daughter can be. "You are too young to be talking like this, Maya Wagh" Shaila had responded, with her unique brand of dignity. And something about her mother's turned back and her use of her full name had caused the little firebrand of a Maya to stop in her mutinous tracks and stand in the middle of the kitchen, wringing her hands a little uselessly. "I'm sorry, Ma. I didn't mean to hurt you. Really. Sorry" Maya had said to her mother's firmly turned back. And in the softening of her shoulders she had seen her instant forgiveness. Many years later, when she had turned her back and stood staring out of a barred window, she had forgiven someone like that – with a softening of her rigid spine. The things we learn from our mothers...

But on that far-away day in the Wagh family kitchen, Maya's mother had given Maya a gift. She had taken her through the entire process of serving up warm, round, soft rotis. First, she had taken copious amounts of the soft, white, wheat flour that was made out of the golden wheat from their farms back in the village. And she had asked Maya to run her hands through it. "Feel the flour, Maya, it talks to you" she had guided her daughter in the first mysteries of cooking with love. No measures and calculations worked there. It was all touch, and feel, and sense. Magic was made with a 'pinch' and a 'dollop' and a 'little bit' and a 'fistful'. That was Maya's first brush with wonder. Other little girls probably felt the same thrill at the thought of stardust; Maya felt it with warm, soft, powdery wheat flour, milled in the little flour mill at the corner of the street, where everything smelled a little like heaven.

Her mother had drizzled a little salt on to the flour, then she had made a little well in the centre of the mound of flour and added a little oil to it. "Just a little bit, Maya, makes the rotis nice and soft." And then she had said to Maya, "Watch, and see how all of this comes together with water." Maya had never forgotten the smell that rose up swiftly from the flour as the water sloshed into it, making rivulets, collecting the stray particles, binding it all up into a soft, warm collective.

Her mother had kept up a monologue. And Maya's sharp, eager mind had soaked it all up like bread soaks up curry. It's like the nature of the bread changes after that. From bland and a little nothing, the piece of bread becomes a morsel you can't wait to consume – its very nature changes.

That's how Maya's mind had changed that day. As she had heard her mother say, "One hand, Maya. Dough is to be kneaded only with one hand. And no messing up the palms. See how easy it is? Nice and neat and clean. That's the way to do it. Your hands can't be messy, and the paraat can't be messy. And absolutely no question of any flour falling out on to the kitchen platform. It's a matter of a couple of minutes. That's how long it should take to knead the perfect dough. Here, you try a batch."

And that's when she had really begun to fall irrevocably in love.

The first soft whispery kiss of her hands running through the powdery flour turned into a fierce embrace as her unpractised fingers tried to emulate her mother's practiced moves and turn flour into dough. It took her only a couple of tries before she got it. And if her mother had thought that it was a minor miracle of sorts, she had kept those thoughts to herself.

Actually rolling out the dough into a perfect circle, thin at the edges, ever so slightly thicker in the centre, then transferring that transparent round sheet on to a griddle that was at exactly the right temperature, then roasting it slightly on one side, flipping it over expertly with a flick of a forefinger and a thumb, then taking the griddle off the fire and roasting the roti directly on the fire with your bare hands. Making the perfect roti out of a ball of dough, from rolling out to roasting is only a matter of a minute or so. But the skill involved is absurdly high. Everything has to happen with the touch and precision of a race car driver. No extra turns, no wasted movements, no wasted time. Roll, flick, flip, roast, repeat. Smoothly. Like clockwork. Or Alonso. And when that roti puffs up in a perfect golden globe atop the blue orange flame... no matter how many rotis you have rolled out in your lifetime, your heart swells with pride and a little smile plays at the corner of your eyes.

Maya remembered how she had had an epiphany of sorts on that day in the Wagh kitchen. Once she had started, she had been unstoppable. She remembered how she had pestered her mother to make more and more rotis until she got it right. For the next few days after she had started, the Wagh family kitchen had generously fed stray dogs and cows and goats in the neighbourhood. The stray cats had turned up their noses at the burnt, thick fare. But it wasn't long before Maya had got it right. Her long, nimble fingers had perfected the art of the round, soft roti. It was like something deep in her muscles had responded to the messages from the sensors on her fingers and palms. After the mandatory singed fingers, burnt rotis, tears of frustration and burn marks on wrists and forearms, Maya had found her genius.

Her grandmother had been unforgiving in her expectations though. "They have to feel as soft tomorrow morning as they are today morning. That's when it qualifies as a good roti. I remember, when I was newly married…" It was a tale all the womenfolk in the house had heard interminably, but no one dared interrupt the old lady in full flow. "They used to take the rotis that the new daughter-in-law had made and burnt by mistake and hang them from trees in the yard, so that people in the neighbourhood could laugh at her. Not one single roti that I made ever made it to the branches of a tree!"

Maya's mother had long suspected that that had been because her in-laws had been very kind people, not because she had been a superlative cook. But she had kept her counsel. Like there had been any other choice. Maya's father would never have heard a word being said against the mother he thought was a saint. And Maya's mother would never have thought of challenging that perception.

"He's a good man, Maya" her mother had explained to her once when Maya grew into her twenties. "And not all battles need to be fought. He has loved me in his own way, he adores you. Now, he also adores his mother. Why should he be penalised for that?"

"But Ma… she is a monster!" Maya had protested.

"To me and you, maybe. But to him, she is his mother. Will you ever stop loving me?" Shaila had asked with her gracious logic.

"Ma, please. You are the sweetest thing on the planet. Aaji is not!

She's this..." Maya had spluttered in rage.

"Leave it, Maya. She is who she is. Just because Baba loves her doesn't mean he loves me any less. Some battles are not even battles. He is her son, my husband, your father. And he has more than enough love to spread amongst us all."

"But *she* doesn't see it that way. For her everything is a battle."

"That's because she is a little stupid, and we are not" Shaila had giggled conspiratorially with her beloved daughter, sealing a secret pact that had everything to do with umbilical cords of the soul and nothing to do with malice.

But whatever her grandmother's intent, Maya had learnt to make rotis that stayed soft overnight.

And she had warmed her grandmother's heart enough to make her want to part with her special recipe for karanjis. No one made them as well as her Aaji. Fresh coconut, pure white sugar, a little bit of jaggery, a hint of cardamom, a tinge of condensed milk all cooked into mouth-watering seduction; then stuffed into a light, thin covering that deep fried into crisp without becoming crumbly and soft without being mushy.

Every Diwali Maya now sent out a silent thank you to her still cantankerous Aaji. And when her own children told their friends proudly, "My Mom makes the best karanjis in the world, even better than Mothi Aaji" Maya's long-held resentment against her draconian grandmother melted just a little.

But today was not karanji day. Today was chiffon cake day. And Maya had planned out a delectable, multi-layered strawberry chiffon cake for the evening. As she had driven to breakfast in the morning, visions of pink cream and spun sugar had played themselves out in her mind.

Not that she was going to bake it. Maya's husband, Arvind Desai was a practical sort of man. A civil engineer by training and a builder by instinct, he didn't have the bandwidth to waste on what he perceived were frivolities.

He had fallen madly in love with a Muslim girl when he had been in college. Saira. Her name was Saira. And she looked like something out of the movies. He still kept a picture of hers. And he was honest enough to tell Maya that he did.

"Why?" she had asked him, before she had agreed to marry the man a matrimonial site had recommended as being the perfect match for her.

"I honestly don't know. I only know that I have tried to throw it away, but I haven't been able to. It's the only thing I have from that time" he had answered with an honesty that had spoken to something inside her.

"What happened with her? Where is Saira now?"

"I don't know. She went back to Raipur. And I never heard from her again. Also, I never tried to find out anything about her. That was more than 6 years ago."

The young, focussed, smart, civil engineer turned entrepreneur had appealed to Maya's sense of uprightness.

And if she had worried about the photograph, she was enough

Shaila's daughter to know that some battles are not even battles; and that there is more than enough love for everyone.

It was only much later that Maya began to think that what she had experienced as honesty was maybe borderline insensitivity. And that Arvind's choice to keep Saira's photo was his spirit holding dearly on to a part of Arvind that knew how to care till it hurt.

Arvind was successful, generous, fun to be with. But throughout their time together he had remained strangely untouched. It was like there was an invisible wall around his heart. And nothing was allowed in or out.

Maya had watched him closely when he planned his real estate projects. They were all children of his almost brilliant mind. Whenever a landscape designer suggested an extra flowerbed instead of a parking space, he dismissed it out of hand. He had no patience for fancy elevations and over-the-top brochures.

Arvind dealt in facts and solidities.

He had neither the time nor the heart for his wife's dreams of spun sugar.

But that's not what Maya was thinking of when she parked her dark blue Mini Cooper under an old tree bang opposite New Coffee House.

She was thinking, "Lucky me, lucky me, lucky me. I got parking space. Who needs strawberry chiffon cake when you have parking space and breakfast with the girls?"

Chapter 5

It wasn't until she had let off the parking brake on her drive to work from breakfast that the chiffon cake made its stubborn way back to the front of her mind.

"Maybe I should make cupcakes. The boys will love them. But maybe Ayush will prefer chocolate. Tuhin I know will love strawberry. How can they be so different? Ayush is like Arvind in many ways. Chocolate. Definitely chocolate cupcakes for him. I'll go easy on the cream though. Maybe just a little drizzle of glazing. Hmmm... that should do it. And a side of whipped cream. Just in case..." Maya day dreamt on as she drove to her job as a pre-primary school teacher in one of the city's best schools.

She worked from 12 to 6, in the second shift of the school. It was convenient, close to her house, she was at home in the mornings when her kids and her husband were leaving for the day. She was back just a little after her kids returned and way before her husband got back. And she was very, very good at her job. The children absolutely adored her. The parents trusted her. She had been offered the post of Principal of the pre-primary section more than once. But Maya had always, very graciously refused. Firstly, there were so many other teachers who could lay claim to the post by way of seniority. But more importantly, Maya was a pre-primary school teacher because she enjoyed the constant interaction with young children. She had no interest in scaling up imaginary ladders. She was a foot soldier, quite happy to leave the paper-pushing to others who wanted to be Generals.

"Good morning, Maya Ma'am!" came a chorus of little voices as Maya, pretty in her white churidar kurta with a floral printed pure silk dupatta, traipsed into school. "Good afternoon, children" replied Maya pointedly, but with a charming smile. "Have you noticed the hands on our big, round clock? The big hand is at 3, and the little hand at 12. So what time is it?" "It's 12.15, Ma'am" said Mohit, the bright-eyed, red-cheeked little imp from her Senior class. "So, we have to say 'Good afternoon, Maya Ma'am'!" he bellowed out in a loud sing-song. And the others followed suit.

Maya couldn't help laughing along as she moved on, flinging a wave over her shoulders to the children who all waved back enthusiastically.

"Hi, Maya!" smiled Neha, one of her colleagues. "How was breakfast? Tummy full?" she patted Maya's slight pot belly. "Ouch! Don't do that!" Maya instinctively sucked her tummy in. But, she noted ruefully to herself, even that was no longer enough to prevent an unsightly roll from appearing around her midriff in her reflection in a slightly dusty window of the classroom she was walking past.

"We were all so thin in that picture. How could I have let myself go like this? The girls are right. We have to do something. Look at me, I'm thinking of chocolate glazing and strawberry cupcakes, when I should be thinking of yoga! And boiled vegetables" the glum look on her usually vibrant face was enough to get a little 3 year old to tug at her kurta. "Good afternoon, Maya Ma'am. Why sad?"

Maya bent down to speak to the little girl in lopsided pigtails, "Good afternoon, bachcha! Not sad, baby. Just thinking."

"Then don't, Maya Ma'am. Thinking bad."

"Wisdom from the mouth of babes", Maya had thought during break that day. She had been talking to her fellow teachers about her breakfast meeting and Rekha's brilliant Diwali party plan.

Most of her colleagues accepted her for who she was. But there were the inevitable few who couldn't suppress their antagonism. Though they didn't say it to her face, she knew she was the subject of many 'builders' wives' discussions. "She doesn't need the job." "Why should she care?" "Has madam arrived in her fancy car?" "Saw the diamonds today?"

That last one had been her fault in part. She had come back late from a fancy builders' wives get together. And the next day she had simply forgotten to take off the statement ring she had slipped on for the evening.

Usually she was very careful to look the part of a pre-primary school teacher, but that Tiffany statement ring had been a major blunder. It had taken the quiet counsel of her Principal to restore equilibrium, "Don't pretend, Maya. It's nothing to be ashamed of. You have a fine husband. And a great life together. You shouldn't have to pretend in order to be accepted. I would think less of us if we judged you for having more."

After that day she had been less careful and more carefree. Most of her colleagues loved the glimpses she gave them into the lifestyle of the have-mores. The others she largely ignored. It was easy. All she needed sometimes were the wise words of random 3 year olds, "Thinking bad."

Today she had walked into a couple of her colleagues sniggering "All that money can't make you thin. We might not have that much in the bank, but less is more when it comes to butts!"

So now they were being a little mean about her few extra kilos. Well, she'd show them.

Tonight she was going to go online and look for a slinky saree to wear for their Diwali party. And then imagine a halter neck blouse to go with it. And then she was going to figure out how she was going to have a less is more butt. She'd show those skinny bitches.

She giggled a little guiltily to herself. "What the heck" she thought as she drove back to her warm, generous, gorgeous home, "sometimes it's ok to be a teeny-weeny bit of a cat. So, sometimes my claws come out. And that's ok."

And suddenly she braked. Almost involuntarily. Her idle mental conversation of cats and claws had stirred something in her subconscious. An image of Rekha's hand as she had held it out to take the photograph from Zoya flashed passed her eyes. "What's with Reks? And how come we didn't notice? No colour. And her nails were gone! I have to call her!"

Maya had woken up early that day. She had had breakfast with her friends and then gone straight to school where a bunch of 4 and 5 year olds had exhausted her almost limitless patience; but her day was far from over at 6:30 in the evening.

There were 2 batches of cupcakes that she just had to bake in honour of chiffon cake day – one strawberry for her dinosaur-mad 11 year old Tuhin, and one chocolate for her junior sethji, her 8 year old Ayush. Then there was the mandatory no cell phone, no TV family dinner that she insisted on. She loved listening to Arvind catch up with the boys over the simple dal-roti-subji-rice fare they usually had for dinner. She was mostly silent during their dinners; she spoke too much during the day. Then there had been that tell-tale look in Arvind's eyes as he had hugged her round the waist before she had left for breakfast; so there was that to follow. And then, after everyone had fallen asleep, she would treat herself to half a strawberry cupcake and half a chocolate cupcake with a chapter or two or maybe five of the new, old P G Wodehouse that Tilly had gifted her this morning.

A deeply sated, comfortably loved Maya drifted off into a happy sleep with her new old book half open on her chest. Arvind, who had slept off much earlier, after a mutually satisfactory biweekly romp in the sheets woke up due to long habit. He gently removed Maya's reading glasses, took her book from her hands, hitched up the sheets to her slightly double chin and switched off the last light in the Desai – Wagh home.

Just as he was settling back down to sleep, Maya caught his hand and in the smooth, velvet dark of a February night in Pune, said "Aru, Rekha cut off her nails, Aru. I should have called her. I just forgot."

Arvind smiled a smile that no one could see. "Good night, Monu. Sleep now."

In their many years of marriage, there had been these strange Aru-

Monu moments. Intimate when least expected. There hadn't been too many of them. But they hadn't been too few either.

The Desai – Wagh family slept that night with nothing to complain about.

Except for the cupcakes. They were not too happy that Arvind had not even looked at them. Not even once.

Chapter 6

Across town in a quiet street in a predominantly cosmopolitan suburb of the fast-growing city, Zoya was anything but happy. And very far from asleep.

It was past midnight and the TV in Zoya and Asif's plush drawing room was flickering away into the darkness. Zoya sat sunk into the oversized coffee coloured sofa and stared unseeingly at the Tamil movie that her remote had stopped at.

She didn't understand Tamil. But at that point, she was really not understanding much of anything.

Her darling brother Zaid. She would never have believed it if anyone had dared to suggest anything of the sort to her even a day ago. She had looked up to him ever since she could remember. Her Ammi would always say, "I have nothing to worry about when it comes to my Zoya. My Zaid will always take care of her." And her Abbu would agree, with a shared pride of a son well brought up.

Zaid had been her biggest support, her shoulder to cry on, her confidante, her guide, her hero. He had never intervened in the childhood struggles against bullies that the frail, delicate-looking

Zoya had had to undergo. He hadn't been the big brother who protected his helpless little sister and beat up the bad guys. He had, instead, taught Zoya how to stand up for herself. He had taught her to draw herself up to her full height and stare bullies in the eye. He had taught her which battles to fight, which to avoid, which to neutralise and which to never retreat from.

Zoya had grown up hanging on to Zaid's every word. Her tall, good-looking, honest, kind older brother had been Zoya's biggest strength.

"He is such a gentle soul. He wouldn't hurt a fly. How can I ever believe he is capable of such a heinous crime? Rape? Zaid is a rapist?" Zoya buried her head in her hands and pressed her face into the oversized cushions to muffle the agonising wails that threatened to escape her. Asif had sat firmly with her through the ordeal of Zaid's arrest, holding her, comforting her. Their two boys were too young to understand anything. And Zoya wouldn't have dreamt of telling them their darling Mamu had been carted off by the police.

What had broken Zoya's heart most had been the tears that had filled and spilled out of Zaid's shattered green eyes. His calm, perfect green eyes had splintered into a million fragments when the rude policeman had said, "Zaid Lakdawala, you are under arrest for the rape of Shireen Shaikh."

"What??? There has to be some mistake. Zaid would never do anything of the sort. He... Shireen... say something Zaid!!!" Zoya had screamed.

Zaid's wife Anu had simply stood there. A mute spectator.

"Shireen? Shireen said I have raped her? Who filed the FIR?" Zaid had whispered hoarsely.

"How does it matter, Zaidu? Tell them it is all a mistake! Shireen is your..." Zoya's eyes had widened in shock born of sudden understanding.

"No, no, no Zaidu! What have you done?!! Oh my God, Anu. I am so sorry!"

And Anu had stood there still, unmoving, white, desperately in love with the man who had betrayed her.

"Inspector sa'ab, wait for a moment please. He is diabetic, please let me give him his pills. He can't miss even a single dose" Anu had said in a voice thick with pain and strained with the effort of remaining dignified in the face of complete disaster.

That was when he had cried.

"Forgive me, Anu. Please forgive me" his despair had matched hers, beat for damned beat.

And then the police had taken him away.

Only to set him free the moment they reached the Wakad police station.

Because Shireen had withdrawn her complaint, dropped all charges and insisted that the whole thing had been a giant misunderstanding.

The rest of the day was a blur. Anu had gone home without saying a word to anyone. She had hugged Zoya, patted her sadly on her cheek and walked away, head held high, but staggering slightly. Zoya had wanted to go after her, talk to her, weep with her, do something. But her Asif had stopped her. "Leave her be, Zo. This is not the time. Give her some space. We'll go over tomorrow."

"What if she does something terrible?" Zo had whispered, all of her famed logic flying out of the nearest window.

"Don't be silly. Get a grip on yourself, Zo. They are both strong, mature people. Shit happens. We deal with it. It's as simple as that. Anu knows it. Zaid knows it…"

"Don't" Zoya had shuddered. "Don't talk to me about Zaid. Not right now."

Asif had looked a little reproachfully at her "That's not fair, Zo. We all know that he didn't do it. He needs us to stand by him just now. He has always stood up for you, and the first chance you get to return the courtesy you do this. Not cool, babe."

"But he didn't say that he didn't do it! He apologised. If he had been innocent, he would have been angry and shocked. But he just sat there. Asking who had filed the FIR! I want to stand by him, Asif. I swear I do. But what if…"

"Don't you what if me, kiddo" Asif had sighed. Her Asif was turning a becoming gray at his temples. It suited him. The suave, wise lawyer, a gaping 8 years her senior. He and Zaid had been close friends since school. And no one had been surprised when Zaid's best buddy and Zaid's little sister had announced they were getting married. It was such a natural progression. Her whole life had been like a charm. The perfect family growing up. The perfect husband. A great group of friends.

The first hiccup had happened when she just could not conceive.

At first, they thought it was because she had been on oral contraceptives for a while. And she had been so young when they got married. Just 20. And he a strapping 28. She had yet to complete her education. The strong-headed Zoya wanted to be a successful CA as much as the mushy-hearted Zoya wanted her happily ever after with Asif. So, for a few years they didn't think about kids. And when they had started thinking about kids, the kids hadn't happened.

Zoya shuddered even now at the terrible memories – the agonising wait for two lines to appear on the home pregnancy kit, the despair when only one appeared, the endless tests, the deadening visits to doctor after doctor; and absolutely the worst memories were of the planned sex – the ovulation charts and the fertility calculators and the clipped, business-like conversations between her and her beloved Asif.

Then suddenly, after they had all but given up hope, they had had 2 kids, in the span of a year and 10 months. 12 long years to the day after they were married, Zoya and Asif had become parents of their second boy – Samar, a spitting image of his favourite person on the planet after his Mom and Dad, his Zaid Mamu.

Tonight, as Zoya had gone into her children's room to kiss them goodnight, little Samar had clung tightly to her and then pulled away slightly to look deep into his mother's eyes with the green gaze that was his Mamu's and said, "Mama, he is the best man in the whole wide world after Abbu. You have to believe that. Tell him I love him, ok?"

Zoya had asked through her tears, "What are you talking about Samster?"

And the child had only smiled his angelic smile in reply.

"Good night, Mama. Tell Zaid Mamu I love him very much."

Today had been crazy in the way a Dali painting is. It had elements that were so familiar, but the arrangement made no sense. First breakfast with the girls, then a carefree drive to work, then meetings over mundane but happy stuff, then Zaid, rape, Shireen, Anu, police, arrest, FIR – separately she knew the meaning and relevance of each. But together they were quite simply absurd. Surreal. That was the word she was looking for. It was not a word she had found need for very often in her own life, ruled as it was by the unvarying mathematical certainties that lived in her mind. Zaid's unassailable integrity had been one such certainty. And now it wasn't.

Zoya had simply no idea how to deal with it.

Zaid hadn't spoken a word to anyone after his return from the police station either. He had walked with weary shoulders into the smallish room he used as a home office and had shut the door, quietly, but firmly on the rest of his life as he knew it.

Until the last time she had checked, he hadn't emerged from there.

He had sent a text to Asif, though.

"I'm not going to put anyone through any more agony by doing anything dramatic or stupid in here. I deserve nothing, but yet, I am asking this one thing of all of you – could you give me some time to sort this out in my head? I will speak to all of you tomorrow. Please, Asif."

Some curly haired, hairy-chested, heavily moustachioed villain in the Tamil film playing on the flickering screen in front of her threw his head back and laughed a big, jiggling belly laugh.

Which reminded her of Tilly.

And a small smile crept into Zoya's heart quite in spite of herself.

The now plump but still gorgeous Tillly would have killed her for the comparison. And then she would have thrown her head back and laughed just like that.

"Dear, dear Tilly. Dear God, how arrogant I was this morning to believe that I could simply draw up a chart and micro-plan everyone's way to losing weight! Nothing can be micro-planned. Nothing is simple. Life is the crap that happens outside the neat charts. I'm never going to lose any weight. Tomorrow I'll call the girls. And tell them I'm out of all this Diwali party nonsense. What's the point?" sighed a bone-tired, soul-weary young woman who had aged suddenly and sadly.

For the first time in for as long as she could remember, Zoya Quettawala went to bed without the one thing she had held close to her heart like little girls clutched warm, oversized teddy bears – the comfort of certainty.

Chapter 7

The group of 20-somethings on the table next to theirs was moaning loudly and earnestly about everything – from exams, to how stupid their profs were, to how badly some of them (the professors) dressed, to how beastly the hostel was.

Tilly leaned across the almost non-existent gap between tables at the outdoor canteen and said cheerfully, "Love listening to you guys. But this stuff that you are groaning about is the stuff of your 'good old days' stories. Just saying. This – all this" she said, gesturing with the wide open Tilly body language, "the crappy food and the bed bugs and the chai that you think twice before buying because you are not quite sure you can afford it, and the T-shirt and chappals at 3 in the afternoon... this is what will go into your' good old days' folder. Enjoy" she signed off with a Tilly flourish as she rocked her plastic chair back into position and nonchalantly continued her earlier conversation with a bemused Zoya.

The group of young students gaped at her open-mouthed. And a particularly scruffy jeans and torn tee stereotype smiled at her weakly. But Tilly had long gone from their midst. She was back in another capsule. Completely immersed in that moment.

"I remember Reks telling me once that Tilly was a goddess. Maybe she is. We just don't pay close enough attention. That table next to ours was like a different world, adjoining us, within touching distance, but separate. How effortlessly she just stretched her neck into their bubble, freely dispensed some profound life truths, and then just pulled her neck out of their bubble, and came back into ours. That's serious goddess stuff." Zoya quietly sipped on her cutting chai and thought some very un-Zoya thoughts. Fanciful. And pointless. That was how the pre-rape-accusation Zoya would have smilingly dismissed such musings. But the post-rape-accusation Zoya was a significantly different animal. It's like the loss of certainty had been a double-edged sword. She constantly found herself second-guessing even the simplest of choices – should she give the kids sandwiches for break, or should she actually make parathas; was the green dupatta working with this outfit, or should she just change the entire outfit. The simple things, stuff that she had never even thought about, Zoya caught herself agonising over it. But on the other hand, it was also like a wall had crumbled and if there was no more safety, then there were also the stunning vistas that she had never seen before. Zoya found her mind wandering down unaccustomed alleys; peering, at first cautiously around corners that she hadn't known existed; then going boldly where no Zoya had ever gone before.

"You look like a poet. Or a painter. Imagining your canvas. Creating a world in your head" said Tilly with the sharp insight of a person who lived her life inside out.

"Tilly" smiled a tired-eyed Zoya, "you say the weirdest stuff. For the longest time I had no idea what you meant when you said stuff like that. But now, I think I do..." she trailed off.

Tilly and Zoya were sitting at a narrow, hardwood table, which had an even narrower hardwood bench on one side and a couple of plastic chairs on the other - chairs that had at some point in their respective personal histories been cream coloured, but were now just residual mud; under the cool, green canopy of an old, old tree in the outdoor canteen at the University. The mild February sun filtered through the green and cast dappled shadows on the many chai-samosa conversations that it suffused.

"Thanks for meeting me like this, Tilly" Zoya said through downcast eyes. "I know it mustn't have been easy, Thursdays are always busy for you."

"Hmmm... let me think" replied Tilly with a smile in her voice, her eyes the colour of warm honey. "You have dropped everything and rushed to be with me for everything from my first period to my middle name crisis to my last heartbreak. With all the intervening episodes between those milestones that would make it a grand total of four thousand eight hundred and twenty-two times. So yeah... it was tough for me... leaving all the important stuff I do, and heading out to meet my best friend for chai when she had shattered like glass; but what to do, I am generous that way." Tilly, to state the obvious, had a gift for exaggeration, and an absolute genius for injecting sunlight into dark spaces.

"Come on, Zo. It IS the end of a world. Don't let anyone come and tell you it isn't. That it's no big deal and that you are overreacting..."

"I overheard Asif's Mom talking to him. She was being oh-so considerate, all warm and gooey. Ugh," shuddered Zoya. "Can't stand the woman. Never have been able to. I've just been sensible Zoya for so long now that I haven't ever acknowledged my feelings about her. But last night she had no idea I was standing outside the room, checking my phone. You know I never check my phone on the go, I need to stand or sit in one place. I can at most talk on the phone when I am moving. If I have to read, I stand in one place."

Tilly waited patiently for Zoya to work herself up to saying what she really wanted to, what she really needed to. She quietly observed the workings of Zoya's mind – how out of long habit, her mind sought comfort in stating facts, and how it balked from any indulgence in ostentatious emotion.

And she saw how Zoya had changed. She saw it in the storm in Zoya's tired eyes, in the nervous folding and refolding of the tissue paper in her hands, in the way her face was mobile, alive with the new movement of unfamiliar emotions.

"She said to Asif, 'It's her age, beta. She must be reaching an early menopause. She's probably just being hormonal'. The bloody woman" she ended, with feeling that seemed to come straight from her belly button.

Tilly grimaced, but couldn't suppress a Tilly laugh.

"What are you laughing about?" Zoya looked up from the many times folded, unfolded, refolded tissue paper in her hand, a rueful, self-deprecating smile playing on her full lips.

"What an item she is, that mother-in-law of yours. Hormonal, my left foot!" another laugh from Tilly. "You should have burst into the room, sobbing and hugged her tight, wailing 'Mummyji, I don't know what is happening to me!!! Mummyji!!!' It would have freaked the fake honey out of her. But I'm guessing you just tiptoed out and sat at the kitchen bench, and stared at the blinking lights on the microwave."

"How do you even know that, you weird woman!' Zoya laughed for the first time in 3 days. Really laughed. Like she meant it.

"Witchcraft, my dear Watson."

"I'm going with magic. You are my wizard, Tilly. In a Dumbledore meets Lily Potter and then the two of them melt into Sapphira the blue dragon way."

"My, my, my. Look who's waxing all eloquent and Eragon. What did Zaid do with my Field Marshall Zoya?" Tilly uttered the name that had remained unspoken and Zoya's throat quite literally closed up. She couldn't swallow. She couldn't speak out. The ferocity of her own physical reaction to even the mere mention of Zaid continued to take Zoya by surprise bordering dangerously on shock.

"It's ok to feel like you are dying, Zo. You kind of are." Tilly said. "Like all of us are, honey. We are all dying a little every moment until we finally die" she added in her own mind.

"It's been 3 days" Zoya said, after a valiant struggle to find her voice. "And I can't forgive him. I don't know how Anu is handling it. I know it must be so much worse for her. But I can't find it in my heart to forgive him, Tilly."

Tilly reached across the narrow table and hugged her best friend from school. Sometimes there were no words. Only time.

Zoya's perfect brother Zaid had turned out to be not-so-perfect after all.

He had stumbled and slipped and fallen.

What had been perfection was now blemished.

And Tilly knew with the same certainty that Zoya had lost that her friend had a long, hard struggle ahead of her.

She knew that the fair, balanced Zoya; the non-judgmental, live and let live Zoya; the Zoya that always had solutions; that Zoya's foundation had been shaken. She knew that that was the danger when your foundations lay in someone else's fragile hands. She knew that what Zoya was finding so impossible to forgive was not the furtive affair that he had supposedly had with the delectable Shireen, but the crumbling of the solid pillars on which she had built her entire life.

She knew that it was the most dangerous thing to do – hand over your moorings to a flawed, fallible another.

She knew all of this.

And yet, she simply hugged her best friend.

Zoya would realise her big mistake in time. And she would rebuild. Tilly wanted to believe that she would, so under the setting February sun, she did believe it.

She had no idea whether her best friend would ever truly forgive Zaid or not; she didn't care at that moment that Zaid's indiscretion was not Zoya's to forgive. On that briskly cool evening in the University, Tilly was being Zoya's friend.

And just for a moment, Zoya's shattered sense of self had hope that somehow the pieces of her would come back together. Not in the same order perhaps. But that's the beauty of kaleidoscopes.

Chapter 8

"Table for 7. We've got a booking, Manu Sheth!" Chotu, the 55-year-old University outdoor canteen major-domo laughed as he shouted across the late evening canteen bustle to his boss.

Manu Sheth, his bald head bent over the day's English crossword in the Times looked up and asked, "Tilly Madam?"

Chotu smiled back through every pore of his body, but mostly through his jewel-bright dark brown eyes and answered, "Who else! They are coming here for breakfast tomorrow. She's told you to make sure the poha don't have more stones than peanuts. Proportion maintain karo, she has ordered."

The two old friends shared a mock long-suffering look, did a coordinated eye-roll and went back to their respective work.

Neither of them noticed that they continued to smile for a while – Manu Sheth at his crossword and Chotu at the tables he was busy wiping down.

'Tilly Madam' was a bit of an institution at the University outdoor canteen. She had come here to do her MA in English Literature. Which she did in signature style. But in her 2 years at the University, she had just seemed to fill up the space; a habit she had sort of carried over into her life outside and after University.

She hadn't been cactus Tilly then. Then, in the best days of her life, she had been as vulnerable and tender on the outside as a cactus is on the inside. University Tilly lived raw. The bristles had come much later.

But even then, she had been a little mad.

She was the only local who had chosen to stay in the hostel. The reason she gave everyone was that her home was in Talegaon, a sleepy village halfway to Mumbai and that staying in the hostel made more sense than long-distance-bus-hopping twice a day. Which was true to an extent, but more than marginally a Tillyism. Because although Talegaon was sleepy, and it was little more than a town, it was a mere 50 odd kilometres from Pune. And Mumbai was about 150 odd kilometres. But by the time Tilly was done with her glorious 2 years in the University, almost everyone who knew her, knew of her, knew of someone who knew her, had come to believe that Talegaon was a suburb in Mumbai, that Manna Dey was the world's greatest singer, that it was reasonable to eat Maggi at 3 in the morning and that chocolate could cure anything.

The world was sprinkled with people from the batch of '99 who unknowingly comforted crying kids with a bit of candy, hummed along to 'Zindagi kaisi hai paheli' with a little spot in their heart going soft, and had vague memories of 3 am rituals. They didn't quite realise the umbilical connection of their little quirks with the pocket-sized mad girl that they knew or knew of in a time far away. But then, that's the magic of the human network. We are all connected with invisible strands, thinner than the ones suspended from your balcony grill, woven by the genius of a spider. Thinner. Also, stronger.

So when Chotu reached the canteen early next morning and made sure his 2 new underlings wiped every glass clean from the outside and in, specially at the rims where lipstick marks remained, he didn't quite realise there was a strident Tilly voice in the back of his head, yelling, "Chotu, if I ever see another lipstick mark on a glass in your canteen, I will personally apply my red lipstick on your lips and take pictures of you and blow them up into posters and paste them across the city! Just you watch, my friend!"

But that lovely morning at the tapering end of February, every glass gleamed at the University outdoor canteen. And Chotu herded grumbling, complaining, hordes of students away from the table he had 'reserved' for the special party of 8.

It was no mean feat, 'reserving' a table when irate University students were hankering for their morning cuppa. There were the bleary-eyed Chemistry majors who clearly needed a smoke and endless chai to make sense of a crazy night at the lab. Then there were the Theoretical Physics nerds who always looked like they were at the edge of a breakdown. And the gregarious Political Science group who seemed to come to the University with the sole aim of sitting and arguing in the canteen.

There were always more people than there was space at Manu Sheth's canteen. So, they had to come up with a crazy plan to 'reserve' Tilly Madam's table. And they did. Anything for Tilly Madam. They had simply turned the big table upside down, piled a couple of chairs on it and had told the other students that the table had a bad leg, and the University Mistry was coming over to fix the wobble. Considering that all tables in Manu Sheth's canteen soldiered on valiantly with various stages of the same affliction, most people treated the upturned table with incredulity and the Mistry story with disregard. But there were more important things for University students to do on chill February mornings than discuss the health of a wooden table. So, they grumbled a little, but moved on quickly to more important matters like special chai and bun maska.

Manu Sheth and Chotu might not have been Theoretical Physicists but they knew, better than most the Theory of Relativity of Importance.

Which is why, when Tilly arrived with a pale-faced Rekha for their very important Diwali Party Summit, their table awaited them. Upturned. But available without a moment's delay.

Completely ignoring the protests from surrounding students, Chotu's minions set the big table on its magically unwobbly legs and Tilly and Rekha settled down to wait for the others.

The breakfast conclave was to have happened over a week ago. At the New Coffee House. With all 8 of them in attendance.

But for many reasons it hadn't.

First of all, Sarika had quit the group. The witty Maya had named her Paperweight Sarika. "She seems to weigh us all down." In 2016 it was very easy to quit a group. One simply had to exit a Whatsapp group and everyone got the message.

"I have always loved being with you girls. You have been my friends since College. But I feel unable to carry on like this now. I think a boring Assistant Professor at a boring Junior College has nothing left in common with the rest of you beautiful, vibrant women. I'm going nowhere, friends. And I'd like to go there all by myself. It's time to discover me. Bye. I will always love you. Sarika."

Sarika had said more in her farewell message than in the past many years put together.

And her sudden exit had rattled the rest of the group.

"We should have paid her more attention. We never seemed to have ever noticed her in the past few years." Rashmi had typed in the group.

It was called The MuskEighteers, their group. A rather clever name, they had all thought at the time.

"We'll have to change the name of our group!" Tilly's dismay was as real as it was unpredictable.

"Rashmi, you and I should go and talk to her today. I called her the moment I saw the message. She didn't answer her phone! Is it something we did? Or said?" that from Roopa. The plump Roopa, the Rashmi of the mango shake pregnancy and Paperweight Sarika all lived in the same sprawling complex.

And Roopa and Rashmi had indeed gone over to Sarika's house that evening. Sarika's ageing, grey mother had opened the door, led them into the grey and brown drawing room and told them that Sarika had quit her job and had left that afternoon for a trip to Ladakh.

"Ladakh? In February? Aunty, it is so cold in Ladakh right now.

When did she plan this trip? And why travel in these conditions?"
Rashmi and Roopa had been befuddled.

"She said she wanted to live in white for a while. And that she was
learning how to breathe. And, it's cheaper now than at other times,
she said." Aunty answered their puzzled expressions as best as she
could.

"But how...? So last minute..." Roopa had wondered aloud.

"There was this group from her pottery class..."

"She goes to a pottery class?!!" Mohini had interrupted.

"No beta, she conducts a pottery class. Twice every week. She's
been doing it for a couple of years now. "Aunty had said with a
small smile.

"But... she never said a word..." Roopa had whispered.

"She always says you girls have so many interesting things going
on..." Aunty had shrugged her shoulders in explanation.

Rashmi and Roopa had walked back home in silence that evening.

Paperweight Sarika took pottery classes. On the spur of a moment
she had quit her job and headed off to a white retreat to Ladakh
because she wanted to learn to breathe.

"We were so blind. I wonder if she will ever forgive us" Maya had
sighed over the phone as she spoke to Rashmi that night.

Mitali, of course, had a plan.

"We'll go over to her house the day she is back and burn black candles as we sit in a circle under the open sky, holding hands. That will burn off all the negativity and Sarika will be back."

Zoya had hugged the adorable Mitali and said, "Let's. Because clearly, that's what Sarika needs. A group of friends sitting in a circle, joining hands." "Linking hearts" she had added silently to herself. The new Zoya was finding new insights into the world of feeling with every passing day.

But that plan hadn't quite worked yet. Sarika had returned from Ladakh and taken off for Madurai. "Saree shopping" her mother had beamed at Roopa who had stopped by to enquire. "Her Dad has left her quite a bit of money. And plus, with the Pay Commission her salary wasn't very bad. And then there were her pottery classes. And quite a bit of money that she made selling her pottery pieces to some art galleries or something in London or somewhere."

Roopa had posted these updates on the Sarika saga on the group and Maya had replied "Paperweight Sarika is now officially Heavyweight Sarika – big, strong and packs a punch!"

Then of course, there was the epic Zoya-Zaid falling apart. Not everyone knew all the details. But everyone knew that something was terribly wrong. And that the least they could do was give Zoya some time.

Then Maya's older son had fractured his leg. "Fractures are a sign of rebellion against authority" Mitali had ponitificated. "He should attend some art therapy classes…"

"Thanks, Mits" Maya had smiled in genuine appreciation of her friend's love and dismissed her suggestions as being pure Mits Madness. There would come a time when Maya would turn to

Mitali for advice on her own art. But that was later. For now, she took Tuhin under her own protective wings and stayed back from school for a few days to heal her own heart that had broken when she had seen the silent suffering of her child as he had been wheeled into surgery to repair a shattered ankle.

Through all of this, Rekha and her stark nails had gone largely unspoken of.

Maya had never got around to making that call to her best friend. It was only last night that she had mentioned her niggling worry about Rekha's nails to Zoya. And as Zoya and she drove to breakfast at the canteen that morning, Zoya said, "Let's check on her today, Maya. It might be nothing. What can be wrong with her life? You've not been calling her Perfectosaurus Reks for nothing all these years!"

Chapter 9

It looked like The MuskEighteers were going to have to plan their Mission Weight Loss, their Big Opposite-of-Fat Diwali Party with only 7 people instead of 8.

But all their phones pinged as Zoya, Maya, Rekha and Tilly sat at the reserved table for 7 under the fattest tree in the campus.

"Sorry girls. Can't make it. Kids exams." Rashmi had typed.

"What exams?" Tilly rolled her expressive eyes. "Her kids are barely out of their diapers. She's going to ruin them!"

And in quick succession, there were 2 more 'Sorry girls'. Roopa and Mitali, who never missed a chance to catch up over food, suddenly had very important reasons why they could not make it to a meeting to dedicated to losing weight.

"So wada we doing now? Wada sambhar? Or wada pav?" Maya asked, trademark wit present in full force that morning. "Looks like we're not losing any weight today, so might as well eat wada-eva" she laughed.

"Nothing doing. Nothing changes. We go ahead and plan our way back to health and fitness" Rekha said with newfound resolve. "So, it's just the 4 of us. So what? I don't think we should lose focus of what is important" her voice shook just a little and her naked nails tapped a dissonant rhythm on the hardwood table.

For a very long moment no one spoke. And then Zoya said quietly, "I know I'm not being much of a Field Marshall right now. But I think I might have died and my spirit went and possessed somebody else here..."

There was some nervous laughter around the table before Zoya asked, again very quietly, "You want to tell us what's going on, P Rex?"

That had been Maya again. If Tyrannosaurus Rex could become T Rex, then the journey from the Perfect Rekha to Perfectosaurus Reks to P Rex was an almost obvious one to her lightning quick sense of funny. For her closest group of friends, Rekha had become P Rex; a name that always elicited a quick smile from her.

But not today.

Today she was grim. And in response to Zoya's quiet query she did nothing more than shake her head slightly. She wrapped her hands around the tall glass of steaming special chai that had almost magically appeared at their table. No one remembered actually asking for the chai. But it was there.

"I wish life functioned like this everywhere; as if it were run by a wish-fulfilling genie' sighed Tilly, mirroring Rekha and wrapping her own hands around her glass.

Soon all four of them had their chai and their hands in communion, as if the warmth from the glasses was seeping into somewhere deep in their souls. So much can be learnt about how a person is feeling by simply observing their relationship with their tea.

There was control and rigidity in the way Rekha's husband Anay silently sipped his two cups of tea in an unvarying sameness. There was lightness in the two fingered grip on the cutting glass of the student who held a smoke in the other hand. Then there was the strong full cup grip of the business person making a point. Also, the lazy, rainy afternoon two-hand lift and drink move of a contented tea drinker gazing out a window. And the pure joy of tea being slurped noisily out of a saucer.

But when you see people wrapping their hands around their tea and holding on as if for dear life, they usually need the warmth to reach their soul, not merely their hands.

"Girls, where is Field Marshall Zoya when we need her the most, ya?" asked Tilly in mock outrage. And just like that the mood of the group changed. Their hands loosened around the glasses, they visibly relaxed, fell back into their chairs and Rekha's face lit up a little with a smile. So what if it didn't quite reach her eyes.

"I'm taking over for the time being" Rekha announced. "I've never even been Lt. Rekha, forget Field Marshall. But I think enough is enough. I'm taking charge. We are going to lose weight, in style, and have ourselves a Diwali party that will knock the socks off the bloody world!" she sat upright in her chair, her pale cheeks gaining more colour with every word she spoke.

"Chotu, paper please. And also, pen. Big paper. Not small and crumpled. Please" Rekha's sudden ascension to the rank of Field

Marshall did nothing to diminish her ingrained politeness.

But then, if bristling was Tilly's auto mode, then polite had been Rekha's. For at least 14 years now. And it was going to take a lot more than temporarily replacing Zoya as the autocrat of the group to make even the slightest dent in that.

Manu Sheth looked up from his new crossword and glanced at the table for 7 and saw 4 lovely women busily hunched over what looked suspiciously like a notepad that belonged to him. Their chai had gone cold, no food was in sight, they didn't seem to be looking around to ask for any. So he signalled a question to Chotu. In response, Chotu merely smiled and gestured a 'hold on' with his left hand.

The order for food would come, there would be a couple of rounds more of chai, Manu Sheth knew that. But this was unusual. This looked like they were planning something. "And if a group that contained Tilly Madam was planning something, then the world should look out. Because if she is anything anymore like the girl who planned the University's first and biggest inter-University student fest, then God save us all. She won't stop until she makes this whatever it is happen" Manu Sheth smiled into his own glass of chai as he went back to his crossword, quite happy that what looked like a big plan was being hatched at one of his own tables.

30 years of running a University canteen and you learn the fine art of living vicariously.

Chapter 10

April in Pune is one of the worst months of the year if you happen to be anyone but a school student. It's hot, it's barren, the relief of the monsoon is still a whole May and half of June away. The school kids love April, of course. The exams are done, the summer vacations have just started and the whole of the sweltering season is all about mangoes and ice creams and cool, shady afternoons.

"Remember how we used to hang out under trees in the afternoons in our vacations? These kids nowadays do nothing more than watch TV or play their stupid computer games. I don't know how to put a stop to it. And they can't seem to exist without blinds and air-conditioning!" panted a sweating Zoya as she, Maya, Tilly and Rekha completed their 4th round of the huge University ground. They had been brisk-walking here almost every day since Rekha had taken over temporary command of their Diwali party campaign almost a month and a half ago. It had been difficult at first. They had all been terribly out of shape and had been able to manage only a couple of rounds for the first few days.

But P Rex had bullied and badgered them into persisting when it looked like the plan would crash and die even before it had taken off.

And in the middle of April, all 4 of them were positively happy that she had been such a monster.

They were managing 5 rounds easily. And next week onwards they had promised themselves they would try and jog at least 1 round of the ground.

"We had a watchman who lived in our society with his family. His kids and the rest of us kids, we were all friends. And in the summer holidays we would steal raw mangoes from the big mango tree outside old Mrs Gokhale's window. She was such an ogre! Didn't have the teeth to eat the mangoes herself, but she would guard the tree like that blessed dragon who guards the Golden Fleece. What's that dragon's name, Maya?" Rekha tossed the question over her shoulder to the group's resident expert on everything bookish.

"No name. Poor chap was just called The Colchian Dragon, because he was from Colchis. It's like calling your Mrs Gokhale The Ratnagirian Ogre" Maya half laughed and half panted.

"Good one, M! Rekha's childhood tormentor now has an official genre. 'Ladies and gentlemen, on your left is The Ratnagirian Ogre. It looks fairly harmless, until you do anything to disturb its afternoon sleep. Anything like, for instance, breathe. And by no means should you try and play cricket under its balcony. Or near its windows. And never, ever laugh loudly at a joke in its vicinity. As long as you barely breathe, stay still, are never seen, most definitely never heard and well, basically dead in its presence, you should be fine. But show even the slightest signs of life and The Ratnagirian Ogre will breathe fire and extinguish whatever little spark that might have dared to exist in you. Found in quiet, leafy, well-to-do neighbourhoods. Which is why they remain quiet. The neighbourhoods. ' I can do a whole Night at the Museum scene with your Ratnagirian Ogre, Maya!" Tilly rattled on full speed, unmindful of the effort her lungs had to make to keep up with her.

For another full round the women threw around stories of childhood summer vacations.

Tilly's lovely mountain vacations with her kind, wrinkled maternal grandparents who lived in a small village at the foothills of the magnificent Dhauladhars.

Maya's own sweltering summer vacations in the narrow coastal strip between the majestic Western ghats and the Arabian sea. Her vacations were also with her maternal grandparents. She rarely went to the wheat-growing village of her paternal family on the Deccan Plateau. Now that she looked back on her childhood, she wondered how her otherwise meek and docile mother had pulled that one off – sending both of her daughters off to her own parents' for the vacations, instead of her in-laws' huge extended family.

"My mother is strong in the most surprising ways" she mused aloud as the group wound down under their usual banyan tree, fiddling with the new solitaire on her finger; absent-mindedly slipping it on and off. It had been Maya's 13th wedding anniversary last week, and Arvind Desai had gifted Maya Wagh a mid-week surprise break to a coastal resort in Sri Lanka and a solitaire the size of what Tilly joked was an eyesore. Maya, on the other hand, had baked him a melt-in-your-mouth peach and passion fruit three-layered dream. She had planned it for months, she had hand-picked the ingredients, and she had lovingly constructed it, decorated it and presented it to him at the stroke of midnight. Both her children had quite literally danced with excitement; their eyes shone and there was a very real struggle for the boys to keep their hands decently by their own sides until Baba came downstairs and Mom and he cut the cake.

Arvind had jogged down the stairs, his green-tinged tawny eyes alive with intelligence behind the clear lenses of the black-rimmed glasses he wore. And he had grinned at the sight of his children bouncing off of walls; he had given a one-armed hug to his wife of 13 years; gone and touched the feet of his parents and his in-laws who had all descended on their home for the event. But even when he cut the cake, he didn't really look at it.

Photographs would show that Arvind Desai was happy and smiling broadly as he celebrated the beginning of the 14th year of his married life. They would also show his wife Maya smiling along. What they would not show was how Maya felt.

She couldn't explain the disappointment.

The entire celebration that followed had felt flat to her. The exquisite resort, the breath-taking views, the signature Sinhalese hospitality, the ring, the sex... she felt like Arvind had planned it all to perfection. And yet, something inside her simmered.

"What is wrong with me, Zo?" Maya asked, turning to Zoya out of sheer habit as they all settled themselves down to stretch on their colourful yoga mats under the tree. "He is perfect. I don't have a thing to complain about. And yet, I feel like I want to scream. Am I going all first world here?"

Maya stretched to touch her toes. And almost managed. Barely a month ago she would come short at a point midway between her knees and her ankles.

"I want him to just notice, for once! How can he do this? I'll be talking about a Victoria sponge and he smiles like I'm a child. If I talk about sports, or the economy or what makes Mutual Funds the safest investment option for people starting to create a nest-egg, then he listens. But I don't really care about that stuff. I talk about it because he cares about crap like that. I don't! How is it okay for him not to care about me?" Maya was quivering with anger, her eyes flashing with indignation.

As she saw the collective surprise on the little group's faces at her uncharacteristic outburst, she quickly doused the fire. "I'm just PMS-ing, maybe. Maybe, Zo, that mother-in-law of yours is right. Maybe it's just hormones…" said the usually bright-eyed Maya with a quick, self-deprecatory shake of her head.

Tilly and Zoya and Rekha exchanged a quick look as Maya bent down to the ground again. And in unspoken agreement to talk later, the three others bent down to reach a little closer to a stunning Diwali party.

Chapter 11

In the period leading to the end of April and the beginning of serious mango season, three things of varying importance happened.

Zoya Quettawala spoke to her lawyer about ending the partnership between her and her brother Zaid. Zaid had been trying for months now to have a rational discussion with Zoya. But she had nothing to say to him. She was tired of feeling angry all the time. And she thought ending the work relationship might be the best thing for everyone.

Maya resigned from her job at school. The school was dismayed, they thought it had something to do with her thinking that the job was too insignificant for her. So once again they offered her the position of Principal. She had refused ruefully. And had stuck to her decision. Arvind had been quite happy, "Now you can focus on doing something really important. Start coming to the office, Monu. I really need you to head marketing and sales!" And the fire inside Maya had just dialled itself up a notch from simmering to seething. It was only a matter of time before it went to roaring and then raging out of control.

Rekha Jaisingh packed her bags and moved with her two young

children in tow back to her parent's home in Sahakar Nagar. It had all been very quiet. No fuss. Her children had thought they were going to their grandparents' home for the vacations. They were mildly puzzled as to why Mom had come with them. But her explanation of, "I need a vacation too, you know. Why should you get all the pampering and I get none?" had worked and they had all driven over from the posh Koregaon Park to the old-world charm of conservative Sahakar Nagar in customary calm. No one had seen Anay Jaisingh watch them leave from the shaded windows of their first-floor bedroom. No one had heard his heart explode. No one had noticed that Anay Jaisingh, in the first time since anyone could remember, had asked for a third cup of tea and had drunk it standing up in his bedroom, staring straight out of the window that had shown him the quiet, dignified exit of the woman he loved with a passion that made his insides feel like molten lava.

No one, that is, other than Laxmi Tai, the cook who made the tea and asked the new boy, Ashok, "A cup of tea? Just now? What has happened to sahib? All ok, na?" But Ashok was new. And all he really cared about was keeping this job, his entire family back in the village depended on it. "Laxmi Tai, just give me the tea, please. Who am I to ask sahib whether all is well or not? He asks me to get him tea, I get it. We servant folk shouldn't get too inquisitive, no? Who knows what these big people think about? Some days they want to starve and eat leaves and berries; some days they want to eat mangoes with fresh cream; and some days they want 3 cups of tea. Why should poor people like us worry about them? They are just fine. What problems could they have?" Ashok asked aloud the poor man's eternal question.

But Laxmi Tai had worked in the Jaisingh household for 24 years.

She had seen Anay sahib grow up. The greying, portly, kind-eyed Laxmi Tai who single-handedly ran the huge Jaisingh kitchen smiled with an insight born out of long observation as she said to Ashok, "You will be surprised, beta. You cut them and they bleed red, just like you and I. They are people too, Ashok. And don't you ever forget that. The only difference is that they have a little more money than people like us do. And what good is that money when you can't sleep at night because your stomach is full but your heart is empty?"

"What rubbish you speak, Laxmi Tai" Ashok had laughed out loud. "I would sleep like a king if I were to sleep in a palace like this!"

Laxmi Tai nodded her head a little sadly in agreement, "That, I am afraid, is exactly how you would sleep, Ashok beta. Now go and give sahib his tea."

As Ashok walked with a light step out of the large, airy kitchen that opened out into Rekha Madam's vegetable patch and garden, Laxmi Tai heaved a sigh and turned back to her stove. Today she was making lunch only for sahib's tiffin. Rekha Madam had told her, "Pumpkin, carrot and tomato soup, palak paneer, 3 rotis, mixed dal, and cucumber. Please slice them into perfect thin, round slices, Laxmi Tai. You know how sahib likes them."

"And for you and the children, Madam?" Laxmi Tai had enquired.

"Nothing, thank you. We are leaving today" Rekha had answered, dignified smile firmly in place, nothing of the inner heartbreak showing on her unlined face.

"Like kings. That is exactly how these people must be sleeping. Their heads full of worry, their hearts full of sorrow. What good is their money if their eyes are so full of pain?" Laxmi Tai wondered to herself as she remembered the look in Rekha Madam's eyes as she had looked out of her kitchen into the little garden she loved like it were her own baby. As if she were saying goodbye.

"She's just going over to her parents' for a vacation. We married women become like that. We fall in love with the home that we are married into. And although we love our parents' home we never really want to go back. We miss our parents and our childhoods and we would give anything to have our mothers pamper us with their hot food once again. But when we are leaving our own homes, we, just for a small moment, we don't want to go back. Women" she sighed to herself, "we live in little pieces. It's like we are born and straight away start breaking ourselves up – one little piece for our father, one tiny fragment for our mother, a whole chunk that belongs to our husbands, then a little piece for our in-laws, and our heart and soul for our children. And we feed our own selves with the leftovers of our selves. It's the exact same thing that we do when we feed the family. The best portions are reserved for the children, then comes the husband, then there are the others in the household, then the pets of the family, then finally we serve ourselves. It doesn't matter how rich or poor we are. When we portion out food, women everywhere are the same. Happiest with leftovers."

While the venerable Laxmi Tai was ruminating on the condition of Being Woman, Anay Jaisingh was slowly disintegrating.

In the calm of the bedroom he shared with the woman he loved with an intensity that made him slightly afraid even after all these years, Anay Jaisingh thought, uncharacteristically, "This is probably what it feels like to be a stick of chalk. All white. And brittle. And turning to dust." Then his phone rang. It was his secretary, the obsessively loyal Aparna Dutt. "I'll be in for the 3 o'clock with the Japs. Keep Boardroom 1 ready. Please make sure the tea is on time. And has Prashant got the changes done in the ppt? I told him I needed him to pull out more stats on migration into the city and compare with migration patterns across major cities globally? Hope he's done it all..." Anay breathed a little easier as the old, familiar mask of control slipped over his troubled soul. And in the relative comfort of a calm surface, he stepped away from the window that had held him captive for so long now and headed towards his study; where order prevailed, lines ruled and everything fit into neat boxes.

"She's never going to fit into a box, dammit. Why does she try? If she needs to go away from me for her to become the Rekha that she really is, then fine. But why can't she be Rekha with me? What great lack exists in me that my wife turns into an unfeeling automaton when she is with me? I have seen her in her blessed garden, she lavishes love on bloody plants. I have seen her with the kids. She laughs out loud with them when she thinks no one is watching. Why can't she be like that with me? With me she is like a porcelain doll. Perfect. And dead. Why???" fumed Anay. There were no more safe places for Anay Jaisingh, no more sanctuaries that he could lock himself into. Rekha's absence finally invaded even the aseptic serenity of his study in a way that her presence could never have.

And Anay stood reeling under the brutality of the invasion.

Business wiz. Scion of an old business family. Ruthless negotiator. Refined art collector. Astute investor. Responsible father. Affectionate son. There were so many labels that Anay Jaisingh carried off with unassuming ease. But the one thing that he wanted most had eluded him for 14 years – the privilege of being Rekha's person. Not merely her husband. Or even her best friend, or go-to-guy or bff or mvp or whatever fancy-shmancy new abbreviated relationships the social media junkies thought up. He wanted to be her person. Like Mama was their family dog Bruno's person. There was this look that Bruno, the aristocratic, staid, almost debonair greyhound reserved for Meghana Jaisingh. It was a heart-twisting mixture of puppy love and telepathy. It was like he was saying to her, "I know you know how much I love you. And I know you love me right back." So much in just one glance that he directed at her every time she entered a room. That came close to what Anay had wanted to be for Rekha for so many years now.

And now she had just packed her bags and quietly walked.

No hysterics, no accusations, no melodrama. He should have appreciated that. "So why do I feel so terribly let down? It's not like we are the first couple to go our different ways. It happens. And she didn't make a fuss. It was all dignified. So why does that hurt so much? Why do I wish she would have thrown a tantrum, a fit, or at least a bloody glass at the bloody walls? Why is this the worst thing that could have happened? Why is her calm so bloody painful?" Anay allowed the mask to slip for an unguarded moment and he bent over in pain, raking his long fingers through his thick hair.

It had been about 10 in the morning when Rekha had driven off with the kids. It was 1 in the afternoon now. And Anay still sat in his study. Laxmi Tai had packed his tiffin and then realised that he was still at home. "Ashok, go ask him if we should lay the table. It's lunch time."

Ashok had returned with a strict order, "Don't disturb me, Ashok. I'm working. Go way. Shut the door. I am perfectly capable of asking for anything if I need it. Do NOT disturb me."

"You go and get your head bitten off the next time, Laxmi Tai. Sending me into the lion's den all the time. You ask him if he wants to eat or drink or dance or whatever. I'm not going back there. For no reason at all he is yelling today. Barking. Even our Bruno baba doesn't bark like that" Ashok complained, feeling all righteously aggrieved.

"This is not good. Anay sahib has never been anything but polite. Mark my words, Ashok, something is not right. I wish Rekha Madam comes back soon. Only she can handle him." Laxmi Tai began to worry. And that was not good. Worry is not a flavour one wants cooked into our daily bread.

Chapter 12

(May 15, 2016)

"How many kgs have we all lost?" Rekha asked the question that Zoya would once upon a time have hounded them with.

"Give us a break, P Rex. It's only been a couple of months. And this is mango season. Eat the mousse. I didn't make the mango mousse with the best mangoes from Konkan to have you come over and obsess over weight, did I? Eat, eat. It's good for you. There is very little in the world that mango mousse can't set right!" Maya laughed with her eyes as she served up her light, airy, fragrant and almost unbelievably delicious fresh mango dessert at the end of what had been a hugely successful dinner party for four.

She had spent 3 days planning the menu. And after oscillating happily between Thai and Mexican, North Indian and South Indian, Pizza and Puran Poli, she had finally settled on a delicate, flavoursome South Indian vegetarian meal.

The gang had arrived at varying points between 7 and 8:30 in the evening. Tilly, being Tilly, had swept in last and when Maya had opened the door, she had simply continued her mental conversation, "Who says 4 cups of coffee is too much coffee? I think people just make up all sorts of crappy data to make our lives miserable. Last

I heard, my Uncle Ronnie was absolutely fine. These guys are all funded. I'm sure there's some green tea brand that's funding all this 'research' against coffee."

Tilly had hugged each one of her friends, rid herself of her giant handbag, draped her latest scarf on the back of one of Maya's high-backed chairs so that the chair looked like something from a catwalk in Milan, and taken several pictures with her new phone, all while continuing this monologue about coffee.

By now the girls knew her too well to ask what had set her off. So they had simply imagined a back story to Tilly's coffee catharsis. Maya had imagined that her Uncle Ronnie was probably some Ranjit Mehta or Verma or something and that he drank copious amounts of coffee but was still fine. "But then again" Maya had thought, "he might well be Surjeet Khurana, he might be drinking copious amounts of brandy, and have no connection with coffee. This is Tilly we are talking about, who knows what dots she can join in that mad head of hers."

Rekha had mused silently that Anay should turn to green tea. He only drank 2 cups of tea in the morning. And then worked so hard all day long. A little green tea at 4 in the evening might not be a bad idea. "But maybe he should drink something stronger" she had thought uncharitably. "It might make him lose a little bit of that horrible control. Maybe he'll behave human for once." For a woman who said she wanted a divorce, Rekha spent ungodly amounts of time thinking about Anay.

Zoya had looked at Tilly taking pictures and thought, "She should do this for a living. I think she takes amazing pictures. "

Dinner by Maya Wagh had been simply divine.

The rasam had been to die for. The light, fresh avial; the ladies finger in tempered yoghurt; the homemade fried papads; the sambhar that was made with Maya's own sambhar masala; Maya's love for food shone through the simple fare.

Even the lime pickle was a story. And Maya had been happy to share it.

"My Aaji's sister was married into a big family near Hyderabad. And every summer she used to send us these huge earthen jars of pickle that they made from the produce of their own farms. Aaji had once taken me and my sister Mandira along with her to her sister's village, just to learn how to make pickles. I will never forget those few days. From slicing the raw magoes just right, to drying out the spices under the harsh sun, to mixing up the masalas with your fingers... and the lime pickle with the whole limes is just a sleight of hand that those women have perfected!" Maya's eyes told her stories when her stories were of food.

"Don't know about those women, babe. But you sure have magic in your hands. I don't even like vegetables!" Zoya had exclaimed with a laugh and a rueful pat of her no longer slim waistline. "If my mother ever finds out I have done everything but actually pick up my plate and lick it clean without once missing my staple chicken, I am going to get the lecture of a lifetime!"

The others had exchanged a quick look after Zoya's reference to her mother. For the past many months, Zoya had gone almost silent on anything related to her family. Not once had she even mentioned Zaid, Anu, her parents. Considering that they met almost every day to exercise, this radio silence had been deafening. But no one had pushed her. They knew their Zoya. And they had given her the time that she had so desperately needed.

 And now they were all sitting in contented silence, polishing off a dreamy concoction of fresh mango, fresh cream and pure Maya.

"These mangoes are from Ratnagiri. Alphonso from Ratnagiri tastes completely different from the Alphonso that comes from Devgad..."

"Shhh..." Tilly cut Maya off. "Don't speak. Just don't say a word. This" Tilly whispered dramatically, "this is magic. And you are the magician. And we are the wide-eyed audience, gaping in awe at some trick you have performed. And this, this is..."

"Maya!" laughed Zoya out loud, breaking the spell. "This. This" she said, holding her dessert aloft, "in a cocktail glass is Maya!"

And as the others laughed along she continued, "No, I'm serious, google the meaning of Maya. Tilly, google Maya."

"The supernatural power wielded by gods and demons to produce illusions" Tilly read out with a hoot.

"You are the god of good food, Maya!" Rekha smiled broadly, giving Maya a one-armed squeeze; her other hand was busy cradling the divine mousse.

"No she isn't. She's a demon! Feeding us like this when we are supposed to be losing weight! Demon Maya!!!" Tilly sang out with her childlike enjoyment of her own jokes.

"I don't care. I'm eating some more mousse. We can walk an extra round tomorrow. But tonight, Zoya eats!"

"It's good to see the light back in Zoya's eyes. So what if it's mango mousse that has put it there." Rekha mused to herself. "Anay eats his mangoes diced into neat little squares. Not like Gajju. Gajju used to eat mangoes like a child. He used to mess up his hands and face and clothes and even his hair" a fond smile crept up into Rekha's features as she thought of a young man, his long untidy hair falling over his laughing eyes, his face smeared with mango. She remembered how she had picked out bits of mango from his hair and had tried giving him some of the tissues she always carried in her bag. "I'll just wash all this mango off in a minute, after I've finished eating. Then I'll use your dupatta to wipe off the water, what use is this tissue-vissue to me?" Gajju had grinned at her.

"What are you grinning about, Reks?" Tilly dug an elbow into Rekha's ribs.

"Nothing, just thinking about how good this mango thingie is. And how happy I am that Zo is smiling again."

"And...?"

"And nothing!" Rekha protested.

"Aaaannnddd...???" Tilly had a dangerous glint in her eyes.

"Tilly Mata. And nothing. What can boring old Rekha be thinking about?" Rekha tried to head Tilly off.

"Reks, you know you've got to talk, right? I mean, we've all been very polite..." Tilly began, until Rekha cut her off brusquely.

"Be whatever you want to with me. But for God's sake don't be polite" Rekha said with a savagery that shocked the room that had gone silent suddenly.

"I'm done with polite. I want rude, and brash, and stupid, and childish. I want to giggle over a couple of drinks. I'm done with smiling over cognac. Anyone wants to get drunk with me?" Rekha asked the room, a little wide-eyed and out of breath, as if not sure that she had actually spoken out loud, and unaware of how to continue.

"But you don't even drink..." Tilly said a little weakly, finding herself in the unusual position of not being the craziest person in the room.

"I know" Rekha exhaled, like she had been holding her breath for long. "I know I don't drink. But maybe I should. Just once. Drink and get drunk. And laugh loudly and cry loudly and get up on some table and dance."

"You dance beautifully" Tilly ventured hesitantly.

"I know, Tilly. I KNOW. But that's not the point. I want to dance like a mad woman. I want to scream. I want to take a long, sharp knife and stab polite. Repeatedly. I hate polite! I hate polite! Polite kills. That should be printed like a statutory warning on every marriage certificate. We warn people about all sorts of dangers of married life. But we haven't noticed the silent killer. Politeness is like diabetes. Silent. But deadly. We've all got kids. We should be teaching them at a young age the dangers of polite. I want him to hate me, if he can't love me. It's the polite that I can't stand!"

And there it was. Like the vomit of a drunk. Vile. With undigested bits of her 14 year long marriage floating in the bile. No one wanted to look at it. But no one could take their eyes away.

Maya quietly cleared away the dessert. And signalled to her maid to bring in the coffee. She handed out the steaming mugs of authentic filter coffee, gently got Rekha to fall back into the comfortable, stuffed armchair, settled herself down at Rekha's feet and said, "Talk, Rekha. We're listening."

Chapter 13

"I don't know what to say" Rekha whispered miserably.

"Say what you never have." Maya answered with the quiet equanimity in times of disaster that she had inherited from her mother.

"I don't know." Rekha's agony was heart-breaking.

"He gave me everything. See. Look at all these diamonds!" Rekha held out her fingers. Still no nail polish.

"And cars. And vacations. And clothes. Oh my God, the clothes!!! Sometimes all I wanted to do was rip them into tiny shreds."

Maya reached out and held Rekha's hand in her own. Rekha continued, unseeing, uncaring, lost in her own world of bewildered hurt and anger "He gave me everything. But I don't have Anay!"

"Is that asking for too much? Is it asking for too much to be the single most important creature in your husband's life? Is it too much to want to feel like there is a special place in his soul that nobody else has access to? Nobody except me? I have spent the past 14 years waiting to meet Anay. I'm not a stupid romantic child!" Rekha glared around the room in defiance, as if daring her friends to contradict her, asking only for understanding, too proud to seek validation. And then the tears sparkled their way into her beautiful eyes, all her pride melted away as she asked the one question that had haunted her for years.

"Am I?" she asked through her tears. "Am I just stupid and childish and stupidly romantic? Is this all my fault? Am I a bad person?"

Tilly jerked upright from her place at the far end of the room and strode across the Persian carpets to haul Rekha up from her chair and give her a big, fierce Tilly hug.

"Don't you ever think that! It's not all your fault. And you, you Rekha Jaisingh, are easily one of the best persons that any one of us has ever met. I want to go right over to your place, right now and shake your precious Anay by the scruff of his well-bred neck! Don't you ever dare to doubt yourself! The bloody sod!"

There was no one quite like Tilly when it came to standing up for one of your own.

But Rekha was not so easily mollified. 14 years of pent up emotion had finally breached her dam of self-control and the tears kept cascading over the broken walls of her heart. She cried and cried and cried her deep sorrow out. And her best friends let her.

In the silence that was broken only by Rekha's loud sniffs the four young women sat huddled together, arms around each others' shoulders and waists, quietly willing strength and love and hope into the wide open wound that was their P Rex's heart.

"It's easy to dismiss another's pain. What could Rekha Jaisingh have to complain about, much less weep so copiously about? Was it melodrama? Was it indulgence? Was she overreacting to a minor coldness on her husband's part? Just look at her..." the newly sensitive Zoya thought to herself as she stared at the unvarnished truth of Rekha's unpainted nails. "Just look at this beautiful woman, torn apart by a grief that she doesn't even understand. Is her pain any less real just because she is wealthy? Sure, it is easier to survive when you are rich, but is it any easier to live?"

"What are you thinking, Zo?" Rekha asked in a halting, hiccupping voice, through very undignified sniffs, breaking Zoya's reverie.

"Nothing, P Rex, nothing at all. Just wondering at how we are going to get you out of this mess." Zoya answered with a small, tight smile.

"Liar" Tilly nudged Zoya playfully in her ribs.

"Mind-reader" Maya nudged Tilly in her ribs.

"Clown" Rekha nudged Maya in her ribs.

And just like that, in the healing energy of genuine friendship, a collective smile broke out over the tight group of women in the middle of a large room. Rekha's pain eased a little and the other 3 relaxed back into their seats around Maya's plush living room.

It took Tilly's brand of insouciance to ask the question that needed to be asked.

"What now, Reks? What do you want?"

"The kids are very attached to him..." Rekha began hesitantly.

"Wrong answer, babe. You know I'm not going to let you give yourself pretend answers, right?" Tilly intervened, gently but firmly.

"What's a pretend answer?" Maya had to ask.

"You know, when someone asks you if you want to buy this new dress that is way too expensive and you say that you have to attend a party that is going to be full of diplomats and their well-dressed wives? Or when someone asks you what you want for dinner and you reply saying your husband loves Chinese...? We are all masters of the art of the pretend answer. We think we have answered, the person asking the question thinks we have answered, but in reality all we have done is skirted the issue. The pretend answer is the result of mastering the fine art of Being Crab" Tilly finished with a flourish, looking impishly and with great expectation at Maya, who was most likely the first one to possibly get it.

"Side-stepping! The fine art of side-stepping!" Maya delivered, on the money as always; and Rekha pulled a face at the two of them.

"Shut up, Tilly. Shut up, Maya. And just for good measure, shut up, Zo." Rekha flung her heavy and aching head back into the soft comfort of her stuffed chair.

"I'm being such a drama queen" she groaned from somewhere deep inside the chair.

"Good for you" she heard Maya's voice, muffled by the acres of billowy cushioning around her ears.

"Take all the time you need, honey; but you are not going to get anywhere until you answer the question. You can leave the room, you can run off home, you can take off and head to the Himalayas, but you will not get anywhere without the answer to what you want. You can go, but not get anywhere. Got it?" Tilly asked, making her point repeatedly, as if some of Rekha's intelligence had been washed away in the flood of her emotions.

It took the usually sharp Tilly's floundering, meandering, failed attempt at making a point that got Rekha to finally emerge from her hiding place inside the armchair and give Tilly a good, long glare.

"I'm heartbroken, not stupid. Also, I'm throwing a fit!" she snapped at Tilly before diving back into armchair oblivion.

Maya and Zoya burst out laughing at the look on Tilly's face. It was usually she who would be doing the irrational Diva routine.

"Presenting Rekha. Pulling off a very convincing Tilly!" exclaimed Maya with a dramatic sweep of her comfortably plump arms.

And they all laughed. Tilly with her characteristic head-thrown-back demon laugh, Rekha with shaking shoulders and a jiggle of her little pot belly, her head still hidden in a vast ochre cocoon.

Rekha didn't answer the question that day.

But no one minded.

It was enough that the question had been asked. Sometimes it really is enough to open up a conversation, to throw a pointed question into the chaotic ring and wait and watch how all the dangerous animals in the ring arrange themselves around it.

It's a favourite ringmasters' trick – create a situation that has to be addressed, a fire that has to be jumped over, a ring that has to be jumped through. The wary animals can take their time. But the ringmaster waits there, patiently. Knowing full well from the look in the wild animals' eyes that they will have to decide to jump, sooner rather than later.

Sometimes, questions are like that. Like the fire in the ringmasters' ring. It doesn't go away by itself. And you have no choice but to jump, or get burnt.

Rekha Jaisingh didn't jump that day. But ringmasters are patient. And the fire wasn't going anywhere.

Chapter 14

(May 25, 2016)

"I think you should wear pink more often, Mama" said Tilly's four-year-old daughter Riva, with the all the solemn wisdom of her four long years on the planet.

"And why do you say that, angel?" Tilly asked, looking back at Riva's serious face reflected in her dressing mirror.

Tilly and Riva were sitting that summer morning as they often did, in front of Tilly's ornate white dressing mirror, on matching white stools that had fuchsia cushions, embroidered with thin gold flowers.

It was a mother-daughter routine.

They would sit there, side by side, as Tilly dressed up for the day. Riva would rifle through Tilly's giant box of earrings and neck pieces. With her mother's unerring eye for beauty, she would pick out random pieces that went together and hand them to Tilly.

And every day, Tilly would wear jewellery that her little daughter had picked out for her.

She had gone into important meetings wearing one pink jhumka and one silver stud. And when a slightly antagonistic client had tried to score a point over her mismatched appearance, she had answered into a boardroom avidly listening in to the gladiatorial contest, "My four-year-old daughter Riva handed these to me in the morning as I was getting ready for the day. And when you receive a gift with love, you accept it with love. That's partly why my clients trust me. Because I know stuff like that. And I bring it to my work." The whole room had smiled. And Tilly had won yet another round in the interminable sparring contest that was her work at one of the country's biggest media houses.

Tilly always took Riva seriously. That was one of her gifts to her child. So today, when Riva gave her sage advice on the colour pink, it was only natural for Tilly to ask her the why behind the what.

Just as natural as it was for Riva to elaborate, "Mama, have you seen the rose plants in our balcony. Come with me!"

But Tilly wasn't yet dressed to go out into the balcony. So Riva grabbed her phone and said, "I'll take a quick picture and show you, Mama!"

Tilly was gazing absent-mindedly into her mirror as she applied her kajal, thinking about what a blessing Riva was, when she heard her daughter squeal, "Mama, you have to come here. NOW!"

"Riva, you know I can't do that. I'm getting ready for work. I have to be there in time" Tilly yelled back.

"But Mama, a bud is blooming. And you have to see it..." Riva rushed wide-eyed into Tilly's bedroom, barely able to speak with her excitement.

"Riva, work, office... have to go" Tilly tried staccato explanations with her young child when she thought there were no other options left. And usually they worked. But this time, Riva didn't let her complete her broken sentence. She walked up to her mother, took a deep breath, looked deep into her mother's eyes with eyes that were a reduction photocopy of her mother's eyes, lay a chubby palm on her mother's shoulder and said, "I understand, Mama. But this is IMPORTANT!"

Tilly couldn't explain the sudden tears that prickled into her eyes and threatened to ruin her freshly applied kajal, or the lump at her throat that made it impossible to speak. She threw on her dupatta, ran into the balcony with her daughter's palm clutched tightly in hers and crouched down in front of the lone rose plant in her little patch of green. Riva's face crumpled when she saw that the bud had already blossomed into a flower by the time they had reached. But to her absolute delight, a butterfly landed on the newly blossomed rose and settled there, frozen in time. Tilly gently plucked her phone from Riva's hand and took a quick picture – her angelic four-year-old daughter, staring wide eyed and open mouthed at a bright blue butterfly perched on the perfect deep pink rose, on an early end-of-May summer morning.

Riva glanced at the picture her mother had taken, and said casually, "See, that's why you should wear pink more often, Mama. It makes the perfect picture."

And then she was gone, that little girl on a summer morning, busy in a make-believe world of pictures and crayons and rag dolls made out of her grandmother's old cotton sarees.

Tilly uploaded her summer picture on her Instagram account, titled it #LoveStories and went to work, her mind still stuck on the ease with which her little daughter had been able to point out the importance of important.

"Maya, that's the thing you know, we just lose sight of what is really important" that was her opening line on the phone call she made to her friend as soon as she was settled in her cabin, her first mug of black coffee in her hands, her laptop switched on and her air conditioning beginning to kick in.

Maya smiled to herself "When is she ever going to start with a 'Hi'? And when is she ever going to realise that we don't live inside her head, and that we generally have no idea what's going in that crazy space!"

Tilly in the meanwhile was rattling along, "Who says setting an alarm, rushing to the rooftop and sitting in silence to watch the sun rise over the same horizon every day is less important than rushing to beat a deadline for filing tax returns. I'm not saying we shouldn't file our returns. God, no! That we must do. I remember once I hadn't filed my returns for 3 years straight. I didn't even know we were supposed to. It was mayhem when I wanted to apply for a home loan. But sunrises and watching butterflies in silence and walking barefoot on grass and taking the time to make love instead of just having sex. Who said these things are not important?"

"Love you, Tilly. Good morning" Maya smiled down the phone she was cradling in the crook of her neck as her hands busied themselves icing a blueberry and vanilla sponge she had just tried out.

"What are you doing just now, Maya?" Tilly asked.

"Nothing much. Only icing a cake. Just baked it. You tell me. You were saying something..."

There was a long silence on the other end, so Maya asked, "Tilly? You still there?"

"You didn't hear a word I just said, did you? I was saying we just lose sight of what is really important. You cut the call right now" Tilly's voice was deadly serious, enough to alarm Maya.

"Of course I was paying attention to you, Tilly! Why are you upset? I heard every word you said..."

"Maya" Tilly voice was fierce "cut the call and get to your icing. You don't get it, do you? You. The cake. The icing. That's important. Do it. We can talk later. You go do your important, Maya. " Tilly had rung off before Maya could so much as get in a word.

And for a long, long moment, Maya Wagh stood still, her neck still cradling the now silent phone, in her kitchen flooded with the summer sunshine, a new light reaching into an unexplored corner of her soul.

"She's right. That mad woman is right. This is important. How have I not realised this? In all these years that I have spent on the planet, how has this simple truth eluded me? This is important! This feeling of dough under my hands, the colours, the fragrance, the bite of the blueberry, the hint of vanilla that will float through my nervous system for the entire day. This is important. Oh my God. I have to call Mom and tell her. I have to tell Arvind!"

But, she didn't.

She wanted to. She picked up the phone to call Arvind first. She almost pressed 7, which was her speed dial number for him. But she didn't. She told herself that she would probably be disturbing him in the meeting that he was scheduled to be having with some investors from Australia. "He told me they were originally from Mumbai, but they've been living in Australia for the past 25 years. Some family called Gupta or Maheshwari or something. I don't know what I should do with my memory. Can't seem to remember a thing nowadays" said Maya to herself, the same Maya who could remember in the middle of the night the exact recipes, with measurements of over a hundred cakes; and the names of random dragons from Greek mythology.

She didn't stop to ask herself why she couldn't remember the names of the Guptas or Maheshwaris or Somethings that her husband was meeting today. The answer was simple – it just wasn't important to her. But she wasn't even asking the question. No wonder that so many simple answers had eluded her.

Maya Wagh, doting mother, happy wife, ex-teacher, avid reader, devourer of random facts that she could reproduce at will because of her eidetic memory, and exemplary cook had just wasted a moment of blinding insight.

Because it had never occurred to Maya Wagh, long time keeper of peace, inheritor of the role of the perfect family woman, unconscious follower in her mother's selfless footsteps that her important was important.

She didn't call her mother either. At least, she didn't call her to talk about her moment in the Sun. "Mom, we need to plan Dad's birthday. We are less than a month from his 65th. It'll be fun to get the whole gang together." The idea was to meet up with her Mom and sister and detail out the big party. They got on a conference call instead. And spoke for the better part of 2 hours. It didn't occur to Maya Wagh that she had spent more than an hour out of that time discussing her ideas about food. And about half of that time talking only about the cake that she had all planned out in her head, down to the smallest detail – a rich, dark chocolate layered cake, with 4 different types of chocolate, a ganache frosting instead of a cream frosting, and tempered chocolate shards to add drama. It wasn't just a cake; it was her Dad and his life on a plate. "Dad is this iconic man. He has depth and richness of heart and character. We can't have a vanilla bean pudding for his birthday; or a red velvet; or anything with fruit. And this cake is not very sweet. In fact, it's slightly bitter. That's how he is. Awesome, but not too sweet. Sophisticated. That's the word I'm looking for. He is sophisticated. And there is nothing quite as sophisticated as a dash of Angostura Bitters. I'll maybe add a little white chocolate on the ganache just to lighten things up a little bit. But that's about it."

Maya ended the call feeling ridiculously happy.

She was humming to herself in the evening when Arvind came back home.

She was humming as they gathered around the table for dinner that night.

She smiled benignly as the boys ran through their litany of woes for the day – how school was so boring, and how vacations seem to fly and the school year dragged, and how teachers were ogres to give them holiday homework, which by the way should be banned, and how it was monstrously unfair that Mom made them eat salad at all meals.

Then Arvind turned to her, his eyes tired from the day's negotiations, and asked her, "So what did you do today, Maya?"

She answered, a little smile still tugging at the corner of her lips, "Nothing. I did nothing important today."

Her husband believed her. Her kids believed her. She believed her. And therein lay the problem.

Chapter 15

(June 6, 2016)

When climate change was yet to happen, when Delhi wasn't choking under smog, when the world was a better place, the monsoons would arrive in Pune in the first week of June. On the dot. But those days were soon fading into the dog-eared albums of Punekars who remembered the time when fans used to be completely unnecessary even in the peak of summer.

The Pune of Zoya's worst summer ever was a different Pune.

People could no longer imagine life without air conditioning, winters were non-existent, no one needed warm clothes anymore, and the monsoons, if they arrived at all, did so grudgingly by the end of June.

"I'm not liking this at all" Asif said to her as they drove to work in the silence that had become a sad habit over the past few months. "Zo, you are going to have to get this sorted, once and for all. I know you are mad at him. But isn't this a bit excessive. You haven't said a word to your brother in over 3 months now. He made a mistake, Zo. He admits he did. He and Anu are trying to work things out. You haven't asked after them. You haven't gone in to the office. For how long are you going to keep this going, darling? And why?"

Pune was still hot. The morning traffic was sluggish. And overhead, a sullen yellow sky waited for the first clouds of monsoon. Respite, however, seemed a long way away.

In uncharacteristic but matching sullenness, Zoya stared straight ahead out of the slowly moving car. But then, most things about Zoya nowadays were out of character.

She had not gone in to her own office even once since the showdown with the police. She couldn't get over that day. Right up until that moment when the two policemen entered the reception her world had moved along in an orderly, well-oiled fashion. She was always on top of situations. It's not like there had been no problems. Zoya Quettawala had had the most idyllic upbringing. The Daudi Bohra community that she had been born into had loved, protected and nurtured her in ways that are almost unheard of in the world outside the community. There had been a strong sense of belonging, a rootedness that gave her stability. So even when the storms came, as they must in everyone's lives, she had remained largely unshaken. There was that time when her Abbu had faced a huge loss in his hardware business. He had had a partner, and the partner had one night simply vanished, leaving behind huge debts that her Abbu had not even known existed. The shock had been debilitating, but the whole community had rallied behind him. And within a few months Abbas Lakdawala had been back in business. Both literally and figuratively.

Then there had been another time when her Mom had met with a terrible accident as she was coming back home from the Masjid on her two-wheeler. Zaid and Zoya were just little children then. Their Abba had been distraught and Mom had been in bed for 6 months. Once again it was the community kitchen and their huge network of family and friends from both within and outside the community that had seen the family through. Zoya remembered how Mrs Patil, Zaid's classmate and best friend along with Asif, Rajesh Patil's mother, or Patil Kaku as everyone called her, had unfailingly sent breakfast for the family every single day for all the time that Fatima Lakdawala had been immobile.

Then there had been the usual and largely acceptable annual flus, biennial fractures, broken hearts, exam anxieties, teenage rebellions, and petty politics of the extended family variety.

But none of it had rattled Zoya. She had always had the certainty of Zaid.

When Zaid had come home one day and announced in that liquid, quiet, clear and warm way of his that he had fallen in love with Anuradha Deshpande and was going to marry her with the permission of his and her parents, Zoya had danced around the house like a mad woman.

Anu, Zaid's closest friend other than Asif Quettawala and Rajesh Patil, had been practically family for as long as Zoya could remember.

Abbas and Fatima Lakdawala had merely exchanged a look, Abbas had shrugged as if to accept the inevitable, and then they had both smiled and embraced their son. They had always hoped that he would marry within the community, but they had also always known that Zaid and Anu were a match meant to be.

"Mom and Abbu are frantic" Asif's gentle voice broke into her flashback routine. It was getting to be one with her. She found herself obsessively playing back the past, digging out old albums, running her fingers along the creases that had formed in ancient black and white pictures of her grandparents and parents and of the days that had led up to the now.

The more that Zoya refused to acknowledge her brother and her family in the present, the more that she engaged with them in the past.

The past was safe. It was certain. And Zoya had fled there. For reasons that those who loved her could simply not fathom.

"You can't continue like this. I think, Zo… please listen to what I'm saying" Asif took his hand off the steering wheel and reached across the comfortable luxury of their new sedan to take Zoya's listless hand in his.

"I think you should go see somebody…" Asif said hesitantly.

"Like who? A pir or baba or jhaduwala?" Zoya shot back, some of her personality seeping back into her eyes as her riposte raised a laugh in Asif's throat. He gave her hand a gentle squeeze before he let go to change gears in the gap that had just opened up on a hitherto clogged street.

"No, Zo! You know what I mean! I think you should talk to somebody. Maybe we don't get what you are going through… You should have someone who you can talk to…" Asif struggled to use the word.

"I have tons of people who I can talk to. I have you. I have the girls. I have Mom and Abbu. I have…" Zoya's voice caught and ripped, like a piece of fine cloth on a barbed wire. Consciously she kept out all references to her beloved Zaid. But her subconscious was a different animal. When she least expected it, a Zaid connection would crop up. She no longer had Zaid, the gash in her voice told Asif, and he sighed a long sigh.

"Honey, you are going to have to talk about this. About him. Zaid has no idea what to do with you."

And it was as if the air in the plush car solidified at the mention of his name. Zoya's eyes hardened, her spine stiffened, and with a deliberate effort at callousness she asked Asif, "So, how's the new girl in your office? Pretty thing she is. Quite friendly also, no? What's her name, Kavita or something, right? She seems to looove working with Asif Sir!"

"Don't do this, Zo. It's not fair. It's not you. And it's not working. You can try and head me off, piss me off, stonewall me, but that's not going to change anything. You need help. And either you can get it for yourself. Or I'm getting it for you. I think you need to see a therapist."

There it was. Out in the open. Zoya's worst nightmare had raised its fearful head over the breached wall of her certainties. And she was feeling the beginnings of real terror stir somewhere inside her stomach.

"I feel sick, Asif. Like I need to throw up. God, don't tell me I'm pregnant!"

Chapter 16

"You're such a kook! Where have you learnt your physics, chemistry and biology from? Hindi movies?" Tilly's laughter pealed across her mobile into the quiet cabin in Asif's office that Zoya was using as her own office.

"Don't laugh, Tilly! Vasectomies fail. I've read it up on the Net" Zoya whispered back fiercely. "What am I going to do? I can't have a third kid! I can barely manage two!"

"Take a test, you ninny. Go buy a kit, pee on a stick and then we'll talk!"

"I can't do that!"

"Why can you not do that, may I know?"

"Because I don't have a home pregnancy kit" Zoya almost hissed into the phone.

Tilly's laugh was a roar, "No one does, Zo! What do you think the rest of the world does? Order three home pregnancy kits along with 4 packs of Maggi in the monthly groceries? Go to the chemist and buy one!" Tilly couldn't stop laughing.

"But... but... surely I can't do that! What will the chemist think?" Zoya spluttered.

Her friend's very real agony communicated itself to Tilly who was now wiping away tears that were streaming down her round cheeks. So she took some pity on the distraught Zoya and said, "Fine. I'll get you a kit. But I can only see you in the evening. Late. Very late. After 9. Have meetings until then. Back to back." Tilly lapsed into staccato mode not only with a distressed Riva but with a distressed anybody. It was as if she was acknowledging that the person at the other end of the conversation already had so much going on that she was not going to add to it with long-winded sentences and too many words.

Tilly had a million ways of delivering comfort. And all of them were a story in themselves.

Like ginger tea. She herself drank only coffee, but she had soothed untold numbers of people with wounded, broken, bleeding hearts with her trademark cup of ginger tea. There was something about the aroma that wafted out of her open kitchen, the collection of rhinestone pottery mugs that she served her tea in, and more importantly that warm two-handed grasp of hers as she pressed the tea into the hands of the injured soul that made people feel comforted immediately.

Or her favourite one – the trek to Sinhagad. The fort of Sinhagad was a short drive from Pune. And every fortnight or so, Tilly would clamber up its well-worn trails. Sometimes she would go alone, sometimes in a group. But on special occasions she would take along a beaten up creature, and lead him or her up a path that somehow led to salvation. She had a special routine for those treks up to the fort. She would pack sandwiches from home, along with two flasks – one with coffee for herself, the other with tea. Not ginger tea, plain tea. In her opinion, ginger tea tasted a little off when it came out of a flask. Maybe it did, maybe it was just a Tilly thing, but for whatever her reasons, she'd carry along plain tea. They'd go by bus, get off at the base of the fort and then Tilly would drag the poor soul who was with her on a long walk to freedom. There was a tree on the trail, at a bend that overlooked the valley. She would stop there, pull out the two flasks, pour out the tea first and then her own coffee, and then sit down, her legs dangling off the little projection, invite her charge for the day to sit down next to her and they would drink serenely from the cups they held in their hands. Tilly believed there was something about that place, with its view of the valley, the breeze that was always blowing, the rustle of the evergreen leaves. "Sometimes, you have to turn your back on life, dangle your legs over the edge of everything you know and stare into space. Sometimes, that's all it takes." Tilly had a poet's imagination and a pragmatist's legs. They both worked very well for her. And surprisingly, almost all of the people who had had the privilege of a Tilly-special Sinhagad picnic had come back from the fort with some knot untangled.

So Tilly went over to Zoya and Asif's house late that evening with a big bag full of diced watermelon for the boys, a paper bag of his favourite samosas for Asif, and a big favour in the form of a home pregnancy test kit for Zoya.

"Go, pee" Tilly's eyes laughed.

"What if it's too early? Sometimes pregnancy doesn't show up on these stupid home pregnancy things..." Zoya held up a stick that spelt out a negative.

"I feel so sick in the mornings. I'd rather be pregnant than have intestinal cancer or something!"

"Ok. That's it. Your time is up. I'm calling an emergency meeting" Tilly was already typing out a message on their whatsapp group – Fit 4 Diwali.

"Tomorrow no walk. Meeting at New Coffee House. Need to talk. Important."

"Think we should ask the others also?" Maya typed back.

"We never have breakfast without them. It's not nice to leave them out just because they don't exercise with us, no!" Rekha agreed.

"Girls. Just this once. Can we call them the next time? Please?" Zoya knew she could no longer put off the inevitable chat; but she wasn't up to facing the well-meant mystic meddling of Mitali, or the 'what-are-your-poor-kids-doing' uber motherhood of Rashmi; or Roopa's unintended flippancy.

This was the one time that she would have actually liked to sit down and talk with Sarika; but last heard of Sarika had taken up a 6 month teaching assignment in some institute in Ladakh. She was expected back only in the first week of October.

"I miss Sarika" Zoya said as she took her first sip of sublime coffee from the tall glass at New Coffee House the next day.

It was nearing the end of June. And the rains were still nowhere in sight. The monsoons had covered Kerala and south coastal Karnataka, but they had stubbornly refused to budge from there for almost two weeks now.

"It's still so hot here. And she's probably wearing woollens. I didn't really notice her much when she was around. But now she's gone, and I find myself thinking of her all the time" Zoya mused, almost to herself.

The others looked at each other in a peculiar code born out of old familiarity. And as if by an unspoken consensus, it was the unofficial, if temporary ringmaster Rekha who opened fire.

"Zo, what's been going on with you? You know I am a complete mess. And you've seen me ugly cry. I mean, really ugly. I can't get over the fit I threw at Maya's the other day. But you have been sitting in mad silence for too long now. You have to tell us what you are thinking. We love you. And you know that, right?"

Zoya lifted her eyes from the glass of coffee that she had been intently staring at to meet Rekha's piercing gaze. And her little group's genuine desire to help her out of the hole she had dug herself into reached some recess of her soul. Her light brown, honest eyes filled with tears and her voice shook as she answered, "I know you love me. I love you guys too. It's just that I don't know what to say. It's like I have nothing left to say. I know he didn't cheat on me. But it feels like he did. And I know how that sounds – all incestuous and sick and horrible. But I feel betrayed. And I have no idea why..." she tapered off, her eyes heavy with a misery she clearly could not comprehend.

Tilly cleared her throat and said, "Zo, you want to tell us exactly what happened? None of us knows, to be honest. You've spoken in bits and pieces about how you feel about what happened. But we are not really sure what you are speaking about!"

A liquid mixture of warmth, love and respect for her closest friends flooded through Zoya. These were her people. For over 3 months now she had been moody, irascible, unreasonable and out of character. And for all that time, these amazing women had stood by her, walked with her, listened to what little she had chosen to share with them. But never, not once, in all this time, had they tried to go behind her back to find out the details of what had happened. In a world filled with people who mistook gossiping behind someone's back for caring about that person, Zoya had found a precious few who spoke to her about her; and that too only out of love.

"I love all of you. I really, really do" Zoya smiled into the eyes and open hearts of her girls.

Raghu Kaka descended just then, balancing their regular orders in his well-practiced arms. His keen eyes had consistently scanned Rekha's face and her nails for any improvement since February. He gave a little sigh at the sight of her still-naked nails and her still-tortured eyes. It was as he passed Zoya her idli-wada sambhar, mixed, that he noticed Zoya's plight.

As he sauntered back to his usual place at the head of the section, he was nodding his head and muttering under his breath, "They were all just fine for years and years. And now all of a sudden everything seems all crazy. That Zoya. What can be wrong with her and her perfect life? These girls, I tell you, they know how to make an old man worry."

"You've got the Mother Hen clucking, Zo" Maya smiled at the nodding head and retreating back of their old guardian angel mixed with fierce watchdog blended with co-conspirator and harbinger of all things good in the form of masala dosa and filter coffee in tall glasses.

Zoya looked back over her shoulder and smiled a little sadly, "Let me tell you what happened that day."

Chapter 17

(JUNE 27, 2016)

"It was an absolutely ordinary February day. I had started the day so well, we'd met up for breakfast, right here. And Rekha had come up with her brilliant Diwali party plan. I remember floating a little on the drive back to work, dreaming of wearing a very slim pair of cigar pants and a sequinned crop top for the party after I had developed dreamy abs. Then I reached office; Zaid and I were worried about the impending year end; there was so much work, so many new clients. Bad economies are always great times for CAs – all our clients were panicking and everyone wanted us to do some magic with their figures. As always, Zaid and I were spending most of our time explaining to clients that we could make sense out of their figures, but the figures were untouchable. I had just walked into the reception area to ask Sapna, our good-looking front office girl to call a certain Deorukhkar & Co on their landline, when a couple of policemen walked in, arrogant, full of themselves.

'Where is Zaid Lakdawala?' the younger one asked.

'He is inside. What would you like to meet him about?' Sapna asked with a courtesy that had endeared her to us from the first time we saw her.

'Tell him to come out. Or we will go in.' I was beginning to feel severely irritated by the attitude of the policemen. Who did they think they were? They had barged into our office, and now they were behaving as if we were all criminals!

It just so happened that Zaid came to the reception at that point, wondering where I had got lost.

'Zaid bhai, these gentlemen want to see you' I had been super polite, given a special emphasis on the 'gentlemen', to show the boorish policemen a study in contrast."

Zoya had always been a gifted storyteller. While Tilly was the magician and the sorceress, it was the straightforward, simple, easy-spirited Zoya who could make a story come alive in front of listening eyes.

The listening eyes that day could picture clearly Zoya and Zaid's sunlit office, the vibrant Sapna, the disrespectful policemen.

"I will never forget that moment when they said, 'Zaid Lakdawala, you are under arrest for the rape of Shireen Shaikh'. I will never forget the look on Zaid's face. He looked guilty. I will never forget Anu's face. She just stood there, in the corner, under that big painting of daffodils, her eyes looked like a ghost's eyes, her face like a ghost's face. The rest of the day is a blur. Someone called Asif. I don't even know who. And Asif reached the Wakad police station before Zaid. By the time Zaid got there, Shireen had withdrawn her complaint. Zaid didn't say a word to anyone that day. He went into his room, sent a text to Asif, begging for time until the next morning. And then... that's that. I haven't spoken to him since" Zoya sighed miserably.

Rekha cleared her throat, reached out and put a steady hand over Zoya's trembling one and said, "Honey, this much we sort of already know, because you told us. What actually happened?"

Zoya looked around the group with a slightly vacant look in her eyes, as if not quite understanding the question.

"Oh, you mean between Zaid and Shireen? They had a brief affair. Shireen... all of you know the gorgeous journalist friend that was always Zaid's spokesperson and all-round sycophant, no?" The girls nodded. They had all heard of Shireen, even seen pictures of her – all peachy skin and almond eyes.

"So, this Shireen had apparently been in love with Zaid for almost like forever."

When Zoya lapsed into the 'like' and 'so' cadence, you knew she was seriously upset.

"And when he married Anu, she like made an oath never to marry, ever. Ever. And Zaid knew. And he kept telling her that nothing was ever going to happen because he was in love with Anu. And this continued for some 15-16 years. I can't believe he was so stupid!" Zoya almost spat out the 'stupid'.

"I mean, who stays friends with someone who is openly in love with them; and thinks it is never going to cause a problem? Who did he think he was? The Buddha?" Zoya's eyes were a little wild now, her nostrils flaring just a little. She looked around her little group, as if daring anyone to challenge her. When no one did, she continued "He knew!!! Just imagine that! He knew the bloody woman was supposedly in love with him. And get this. So did Anu! Looks like the whole bloody world knew. Except me."

She caught Tilly shifting in her seat a little uncomfortably and Maya picking up a menu card. It was the menu card that gave it away. Because no one used a menu card in New Coffee House. It was clear her closest friends were hiding something.

"You girls also knew!" Zoya exclaimed, her voice sharp in a mixture of shock, surprise, accusation and indignation.

"You knew! And you never told me! Why? How could you have done this!" Zoya didn't say any of this, but her girls heard it loud and clear.

So Maya moved slightly forward and spoke in the particular brand of calm that was her mother's gift to her, "Zoya, we just presumed that you knew. It's not like we sat down over coffee and discussed the Shireen angle. We all just presumed it. And presumed that you saw it too. It seemed so obvious."

"Yeah, Zo" Tilly bristled a little at a memory. "Remember that time at the reception, Zaid's reception... Shireen was singing all those melodramatic songs. And there was no alcohol. So she wasn't drunk."

"I don't remember, actually. Come to think of it, I never paid her much attention." Zoya said, thoughtfully scratching at a little mole on her chin.

"And, to be honest, what Anu told me is that he slept with her once. I have called it an affair. She calls it a mistake. The woman is a saint. Or just stupid!" Once again, the 'stupid' came out as spit and a hiss.

"Just let me get this clear in my head" Rekha shook her head full of soft brown curls from side to side; as if to shake her wayward thoughts into order.

"You are so mad at Zaid because he slept once with Shireen. Mad enough not to have spoken a single word to him in over 3 months, moved out of the fantastic office that you shared with him, and considered a legal split in the business? Am I right in my understanding?" The first hint of a dangerous glare from Rekha was beginning to find its way into her eyes, that had so far held nothing but support and genuine concern.

"When you put it that way..." it was now Zoya's turn to squirm uncomfortably in her chair.

"Is there any other way of putting it that I have not understood?" Rekha had her calm voice on. And everyone knew that spelt danger. She wasn't called P Rex for nothing. In her own quiet way, Rekha Jaisingh could be quite a monster.

"Give her a moment, Reks" Tilly intervened lightly. "Is there something you aren't telling us, Zo?"

"No. This is it. He slept with that bitch of a Shireen. He says it was only the one time. But I don't think I can trust him ever again." Zoya knew it sounded lame, even to her own ears.

It was unnerving to see the calm, steadfast Zoya groan and hold her head with her smart, short bob in both of her strong hands, "I don't know how to stop feeling like this! I am so angry. And so hurt."

It was Maya who used the right word. "You feel abandoned."

Her mother had taught her well.

The word hit Zoya like a meteor striking the earth. She felt punched in the gut, the air rushed out of her in a gasp.

"Dear God. That is exactly how I feel! But why? Why do I feel like this? How can I make it go away? I want to stop the pain."

"I don't know if I am right in thinking this way, but I have known you longer than anyone else here has. So here's what I think" Tilly spoke up.

"I think you made a Horcrux" there were loud groans all around the little table. Tilly's love for the absurd and her obsession with Harry Potter were legendary.

"No, no, no... listen. Hear me out. Fine, let's not go with the Horcrux. Let's talk about the giant from the stories we heard as kids, the fellow who kept his soul in a parrot. Or Ravana. His soul apparently was in his navel. Which is not too bad, at least he kept his soul inside himself. And I think the giant was plain stupid to trust a parrot with his soul. But our Zoya is not stupid." How much of a person's mental state can be discerned just by listening to their use of words. Where Zoya had been spitting out her 'stupids', Tilly was gliding over them, the sibilant a soft whisper.

"Noooo" she continued, "Our Zoya is one of the smartest people I know. So she took her soul and entrusted it to the one person she thought could never, ever do wrong – her perfect brother Zaid. And here's where it gets interesting. Who told her Zaid was perfect? Her parents!" Tilly gave a dramatic flourish, like a magician whipping a rabbit out of his top hat.

"Good Zoya, smart Zoya, clever Zoya, intelligent Zoya gave her soul to the safe-keeping of her brother. Because he was perfect. And now he is not. So what does that make smart Zoya?" Tilly asked with an arch of a perfectly shaped brow.

"It makes me stupid Zoya." Zoya's 'stupid' came out harsher and fiercer than before.

"And therein lies the problem" Tilly slumped back into her chair. She was no longer worried. This was a relatively simple one to solve. Nothing that a trek to Sinhagad and tea on the trail wouldn't solve.

"You are coming with me this Sunday" she announced to Zoya. "Be ready at 5:00 in the morning. I'll pick you up."

"Girls, thank you for breakfast. This meeting is officially over..."Tilly was already half out of her seat, before Rekha stopped her.

"Not so fast, Madam. I'm carrying our Diwali Party diary. This is the 16th week. I'm not letting anyone go anywhere until we record how much weight we have lost, and how far we still have to go."

There was steel in Rekha's voice. And if she had started her leadership of the group as a reluctant ringmaster simply to fill in the gap that Field Marshall Zoya's temporary absence had created, then 16 weeks into the program she had progressed dramatically from Lt Rekha to at least Brigadier Rekha.

The diary was a disappointment. No one had achieved anything spectacular in more than 3 months of walking regularly. Rekha, Maya and Zoya had all shed between 1.5 and 2 kilos. Tilly, on the other hand, had put on 3 kilos.

"What are you doing, Tilly?" Brigadier Rekha asked Tilly, her chin jutting out in challenge, pre-empting any flippant answer from Tilly.

And for once, the whiplash smart Tilly had no idea.

Chapter 18

(June 30, 2016)

"What a lovely way of doing things" Shaila Wagh said to her daughter Maya as they packed the return gifts for her husband's 65th. "I just love how you girls all got together and planned to lose weight for a Diwali Party. And then you picked out and bought the outfits you are all going to wear in the first week of November this year. I think that is very, very smart. Nothing works quite as well as incentive. I always think you girls have got it right. Look at all these people rushing about, going on crash diets, looking haggard, running like maniacs. But you girls are putting so much joy into this. I love the way you think" she smiled her warm, generous smile at her older daughter.

"It hasn't worked all that well, Ma" Maya laughed back at her. "We've lost only a very few kgs and a very few inches. And that madcap Tilly has gone and put on 3 kilos. I don't know how she does it. But then, that's Tilly, I guess. When everybody else is losing weight she just has to go and gain some!" Maya's laugh was infectious.

Maya and her Mother sat in Maya's huge bedroom, surrounded by acres of wrapping paper, and ribbons and pretty things to decorate the wrapped boxes with. It was her Dad's much awaited and superbly planned 65th birthday today. And some 200 of their closest family and friends were invited to the party in the evening.

Now, Maya Wagh, wife of successful builder Arvind Desai, could have hired the best teams in town to professionally wrap all the return gifts. Who are we kidding here, she could have got them pre-packed and hand delivered to her destination of choice from just about anywhere in the world.

But that was not her style. She and her younger sister Mandira had hand-picked the gifts, as well as all the wrapping material. And they had gotten together every evening for the past week to pack the gifts and stick personalised notes on each one of them.

There were only a few remaining to be packed. So Shaila had offered to help out. She was the undisputed queen of all things pretty. And as Mandira breezed into Maya's bedroom she pulled a face at the little pile that her mother had collected on her side, "We spend a whole week slaving like bonded labour and you come in for one morning and make all our work look like it's been done by a bunch of particularly challenged kids from kindergarten!"

"Meet Mandira, official maker of mountain out of non-existent molehills" Maya threw a fistful of red gelatine paper on Mandira's head. Shaila merely smiled indulgently as only a mother can.

She had two daughters. Both beautiful. Both happy. Both very well off. What more could she ask for?

"I was just telling Ma about the progress on our Diwali Party plan" Maya said to Mandira.

"Yeah. I love the idea. Ma, these girls will look all stunning this

Diwali and we will look like potatoes!"

"Mandy, don't be silly. How you can make everything about you God only knows..." Shaila smiled at her younger firebrand.

"Shut up, Mandy. So Ma, I was telling you... the plan isn't working out all that great. We have less than 4 and a half months to go. And when we started out, we had all planned to lose 10 kgs each. No logic" she directed that towards Mandy who had opened her mouth to argue. "There was no logic to the 10 kgs, we just picked that out randomly. And none of us is anywhere closing to achieving our goal. I need to lose another 7 and a half kgs in less than 5 months. Never going to happen" Maya shook her head good humouredly.

"And did you tell her Tilly has put on weight?"

"I did. She's just mad, Ma. The things she gets up to, I tell you."

"I don't think so, Maya. I think she's sad. You should talk to her." Shaila spoke almost absent-mindedly as she looked closely at the photograph that Gajju had sent for Rekha. It was now in Maya's house. Rekha had left it there on the night of her great meltdown.

"See how her eyes are sparkling here. Her eyes are different now, Maya..."

"Ma, you are getting fanciful in your old age. Tilly's eyes are like light bulbs even now. They flash and sparkle and light up a room. What are you saying!"

"I don't know, beta. I'm just telling you what I think. I think her eyes sparkle with unshed tears nowadays."

For a few long minutes there was complete silence save for the rustle of the wrapping paper and the snip, snip of scissors as they cut ribbons and sticky tape.

It was Shaila who broke the silence, "Maybe I'm just imagining things. You are right, Maya, I'm getting my old head full of fancy thoughts. Here. All gifts done. Now we are all set for the evening!"

The evening, set on the sprawling lawns of Maya and Arvind's home was an unmitigated success. If Maya's Dad was the hero of the party, and Maya's Mom the blushing, beautiful female lead, the undisputed star of the party was the birthday cake.

Maya had planned, tweaked, refined and redefined the menu many times before the party. But her cake had remained unchanged from day one. She had personally overseen the preparation of all the food, while her personally groomed team of cooks had prepared it.

But the cake was all hers. She hadn't allowed anyone anywhere near it.

It had taken her the entire day before the party to bake it, set it, decorate it, and wheel it into the cold room that she had added onto her large house after she had quit her job.

When the stewards had wheeled the cake out in the late evening, her eyes had sparkled brighter than any jewel in the gathering. Her heart had thumped like a teenager's gazing across a room at first love. Her cheeks burned with a fire that started somewhere in her heart. And instinctively, she looked around for her husband. This was a moment she had to share with him.

There he was. Surrounded by her Dad's friends. He was so good with her parents. He knew her Dad's friends were important to him, so he always made special efforts to make them comfortable.

He was busy listening to an old story about an old cricket match played in Belgaum when Maya's cake made its appearance.

And he didn't notice.

Maya kept waiting for him to turn towards her.

But he didn't.

Once again Maya's heart sank. And only Shaila saw the stiffening of the spine in Maya that spelt danger in the Wagh-Desai household.

Chapter 19

(July 12, 2016)

The deluge was unrelenting. Massive banks of clouds had rolled in from the angry Arabian Sea and were venting what felt like a whole year's worth of pent up fury on their hapless first port of call – Mumbai. While the coast was being battered and life was being drowned to a grinding halt, Rekha Jaisingh sat in the coffee shop of a sea-facing five star; staring unseeingly at the melodrama of the Mumbai monsoon that felt like it was being staged exclusively for her on the other side of the huge toughened glass picture windows.

On her right sat Gajendra Chauhan – Gajju from the picture that had sparked off the Diwali Party plan. It was a table for four. And Rekha and Gajju sat at right angles from one another. She was constantly conscious of her jeans clad right knee. She kept fearing it would brush against Gajju's long, muscular legs under the table that was suddenly seeming too small.

"I can't tell you how good it is to see you after all these years." He still looked at her in that direct way of his that had made Rekha Patankar – she had been a Patankar before she had become the Rekha Jaisingh – fall hard for him in Junior College.

"I wish he had turned fat and bald and just a little ugly. All this time

I had been imagining him leading a sad, boring life; with a paunch that hung over his belt, and bags under his eyes. What business does he have, turning up like this, looking like a goddamned Greek god? Who knows what Greek Gods actually looked like? Maybe they were all round cheeked and fat bottomed. I should check with Maya. Goddamn this Gajju" Rekha's internal dialogue was as fast and furious as her surface was calm and untroubled.

"I was out in the Andes last month. And took this photograph of a mountain sunrise. It reminded me of you. So I framed it and I thought you should have it..." his strong, shapely hands held a rustic, wooden frame. And in the frame was the most beautiful photograph that Rekha had ever seen. There was a line of tall, sharp peaks that were still in the shadows and over the tallest peak the sun had suddenly risen so that it looked like the beginning of new time. There was so much drama in that frozen frame. The power of the sun to throw light on what was thus far cowering in the darkness, the majesty of the Andean peaks, the failing struggle of the dark against the light, hidden valleys, golden mountain tops. Gajju had always had this power – to capture the essence of a moment.

With a sudden prick of tears in her eyes Rekha remembered how they had once been walking home from college, she hugging her books as if afraid that if she unlocked her hands they would find their way into his; he swinging his arms in that carefree manner of his. They had spotted a kitten mewling pitifully under a pile of garbage. They had stopped, looked around for its mother, and then Gajju had just stepped into the steaming, stinking pile, lifted the kitten out of the filth and held it close to his chest.

"Eeeks. Don't do that Gajju, it's so dirty!" Rekha remembered the stench of rotting eggs and cabbage.

Gajju hadn't even noticed. He had smiled back at Rekha with that wide-eyed smile of his. "Look, it has blue eyes. It's the most beautiful kitten ever! I'm calling him" he had checked quickly "I am calling him Mowgli."

"You can't do that! Where will you keep him? Pets aren't allowed in the hostel. And it's so dirty!" Rekha had been unable to see beyond the grime coating the kitten.

Gajju, on the other hand, hadn't even noticed. He had carried the skinny, dirty, bag of bones close to his heart all the way back to Rekha's house. The quivering kitten had quietened down next to the comforting, steady beat of Gajju's heart. Gajju hadn't cared about how dirty his T-shirt had got, or how his hands smelled vile. He had just taken Mowgli back to the hostel with him. Where he had sweet talked the guy who ran the Mess into adopting him. Mowgli had been cleaned, fed and seamlessly adopted into the daily life of Fergusson College's ancient boys' hostel.

For almost 4 years Mowgli and Gajju had been inseparable. He would follow him to class and curl up on a window and go to sleep. He would climb into his room through the bars on his window and sleep on his pillow. He would be sitting proprietarily on Gajju's study table and fixing his blue eyes unwaveringly on anyone who popped in to borrow a book or exchange notes. They were the best of friends. Until Gajju decided to go to the States.

"What happened to Mowgli?" Rekha asked out of the blue, her eyes swimming with tears as she gazed at the Andean sunrise in her hands.

"Huh?" Gajju's face revealed an amusing mixture of perplexity and disappointment. Here he had travelled halfway across the world to meet the one woman he had not been able to get over; he had just, in the manner of a grand gesture, handed over one of his best photographs ever to her, after telling her that the sunrise had reminded him of her; and she was asking him about a tom cat!

Rekha looked back at him with liquid eyes. She hadn't thought of Mowgli in many years now. To her that felt like a betrayal.

From the look on Gajju's face it looked like he hadn't thought of Mowgli in the longest time too.

"I don't really know" he said slowly; his eyes travelling back to his years as a student in Pune's best college.

"For a few years Ranga" Ranga was short for Ranganathan, the long name of the tiny chap who ran the boys' Mess at Fergusson College, "for a few years he sent me pictures of Mowgli; and then one day he simply disappeared."

"Ranga?"

"No, madcap, Mowgli!" Gajju laughed with his eyes. That was another thing that had made her heart do little handsprings when she had been a young girl. Rekha was dismayed at how her breath caught once again at Gajju's laughing eyes.

"You could have..." Rekha struggled to complete her sentence. "Mowgli must have..." Once again words failed her.

There it was. The cloud that had hung over their last conversation was back. It felt like the storm that had been playing itself out on that side of the glass windows had made its way into the cosy coffee shop.

"I could have what, Rekha? Mowgli must have what? Let me hear it, Rekha. I should have done exactly what?" the air crackled with tension, but his voice was soft and low and rich.

"Dear God help me. His voice is like a whole orchestra. So much feeling, so many vibrations, I can hear his pain, his confusion, his frustration, his..." Rekha was not ready to say the four-letter word, even to the solitary listener that was her own head.

"You should have asked me to wait."

It was a bald statement. And the simplicity of it ripped into Gajju.

His head, still full of his crazy hair, but graying, fell into his own hands. And he sighed, "I know that now. But then, I thought I was doing what was best for us."

Rekha waited in patience. She had waited 16 years for an explanation. She could wait a little longer.

"It was impossible to move Mowgli with me. I was just about 21. I was just about starting out in life. I didn't even know what I really wanted to be. I had to go and find myself. It was so tough..." Gajju looked at Rekha with eyes that begged for validation.

Many years later, when Rekha looked back at her life, she would see this moment, this plaintive moment, as the turning point. But on that stormy Mumbai afternoon, she only experienced the very first, slight healing of her heart as Gajju continued "I left Pune with no clear ideas about who I wanted to become and what I wanted to do.

It was a matter of the rest of my life. You know that Dad was never a big supporter.”

Gajju’s non-equation with his strict industrialist father had been the point of many lazy afternoon discussions under the flaming Gulmohar tree outside the English Department. Gajju’s father had never been able to accept that a son of his, bearing his illustrious name, coming from his fine stock, would opt for something as lame as a major in English Literature. “Couldn’t he have at least tried for a B.Sc.?” the socially traumatised Raghavendra Chauhan would growl at his wife every few days. “You know he could have walked into any IIT or IIM if he had wanted to. He wants to study Literature!” the pretty and petite Mrs Chauhan would soothe her grizzly bear of a husband just as often. “But he could have gone to Oxford! What is this Pune that he wants to stay in? It’s all the fault of that Rekha girl that he has met...” Mrs Chauhan knew that there were only two ways in which this conversation could be headed off. And she used them both brilliantly. Gajju didn’t know it then, and he would probably never find out, but he owed the 5 years that he had managed to spend in Fergusson College, Pune, to a mother who knew how to use fine scotch and great sex to distract her husband from interfering in her son’s happiness.

“I wanted to take you with me. But I couldn’t have. What could I have offered you? What guarantees could I have given you?”

“Mowgli was a good cat. He didn’t deserve to be abandoned.”

“I know that! Do you think I haven’t hated myself for leaving like I did?”

“But how does that help Mowgli? Would you have taken Mowgli

along if he had been a better cat?"

"What? No!!! How can you even think that! He was perfect!"

"But you still went away..."

"What else could I have done?"

Their coffee had gone cold a long time ago. They sat there, drenched in a misery that was as old as time. Missed opportunities. Broken promises. Roads taken. Roads not taken. So many words that had been left unspoken. They all sat there together. In a while, the sea outside calmed down. The clouds cleared up.

Rekha pushed her chair back from the table "I should leave. It's a long drive back to Pune. And the kids are waiting."

Gajendra Chauhan, ace photographer, global bohemian, award-winning photo journalist, high-flier, over achiever watched Rekha walk calmly into her waiting car. And he knew with complete certainty that nothing had been worth that retreating back.

Chapter 20

(July 15, 2016)

"You did what???" Maya almost screamed into the phone.

"It's no big deal. We had to meet some place. At some time. We couldn't have not met ever again." Rekha's voice smiled down into Maya's unbelieving ears.

"So you drove to Mumbai in these mad rains?"

"Of course not. Mane Kaka took me." Mane Kaka was Rekha's Dad's old trusted Man Friday. He was driver, electrician, plumber, vegetable shopper, keeper of secrets all rolled into one.

"In these mad rains? You have any idea what a stupid thing to do it was? Who drives to Mumbai when the whole world is telling you to stay away? Don't you know how dangerous it can be? Rekha, that Gajju has always had this effect on you. You are so sensible otherwise. Why can't you just stay away? Remember the Mumbai floods? What would have happened if any such thing would have happened again this time? And you in Mumbai? Driving? It's a death trap!"

"It wasn't raining that heavily when I went..."

"What do you mean when you went? When did you go?"

"I went a couple of days ago..."

There was an ominous silence on the phone. And Rekha recognised it correctly as the calm before a Maya maelstrom.

"I do not like the sound of this, Reks. What are you not telling me?"

"Nothing, I am trying to tell you everything. If you will let me speak, that is. You freak me out when you go into that tailspin of yours."

"I'm not going into any spins. And this conversation is not about me, Reks. So your smartass misdirection is not going to work. I'm almost done with this coffee walnut thing that I tried out. Should take me another 20. Then I'm coming over. Let's go for a walk. I need to clear my head. I've spent too long cooped up in this stupid kitchen."

There it was. A classic Maya move. Caring, selfless and firm all at the same time. Shaila would have been proud of the way her daughter had drawn out the reticent Rekha in more ways than one. Prevarications and evasions are relatively easier on the phone. It's almost impossible to lie when one of your best friends is walking close by your side and sensing your truths, spotting your lies in the cadence of your breath.

The park was relatively deserted. It had been raining for the past few days and the well-worn jogging trail was a slushy red mess. It was impossible to stride briskly on the slippery mud, but a brisk walk wasn't on the agenda for the two slightly out of shape women in their mid-thirties, friends for a lifetime, now walking in an unconscious rhythm, deep in conversation.

Anyone looking at them from a distance would've thought they were discussing matters of state, or the state of the rainforests. Thoughtful and animated in turns.

"You are right. I shouldn't have gone, Maya. Nothing is ever going to be the same any more. He gave me a photograph that he had taken somewhere in the blessed Andes; said it reminded him of me."

"I cannot believe you fell for that line. It's the oldest one in the book."

"It's not a line." Rekha blushed at her own hurried defence of the indefensible Gajju. "No, really, Maya...!" Maya directed a look of pure disbelief at the harried Rekha who rushed on, "Maya, really, I know him. I've seen him try a line, and I've seen him when he means it... There's this look that he gets in his eyes, and his voice sort of trembles."

"And so it wasn't a line. And maybe he meant it. So?"

"So... nothing, I guess" the sheepish shrug was in Rekha's voice more than in her shoulders.

"It's just that... it felt nice; for a change. Someone actually expressing his feelings. He didn't say it out loud, of course. I mean, what are we, 16? But I could see it in his eyes. It's been so long since I felt like I mattered. Anay" Rekha's foot caught on a protruding, half-hidden root of a tree and she stumbled; Maya had to reach out and steady her, or she would have fallen face first into the slushy red mess at their feet. "Anay" Rekha continued after she was back on her feet and they were once again on their way, "I think Anay never sees me. Not like that, anyway. I can't imagine him taking a photograph on a mountain somewhere and telling me that the way the sun rose majestically from behind a long line of mountains reminded him of me."

"Gajju said all of that?"

"No, but he meant it. He only said the moment reminded him of me."

"Hmm…" Maya was thoughtful as they walked on.

"What?"

"Thinking."

"Thinking, what?"

"I was thinking that you might not like what I think, but if I think of myself as being your friend then I have to tell you what I think, no?"

Rekha laughed out loud at her friend's simple honesty "Please tell me what you think, M. It's very important to me!"

"Reks, this is what I think. I think you read too much into one man's silence and too little into another's."

There was pin drop silence in that little nook of their park. They had walked into their corner, and were now sitting on a damp wooden slab that had been artistically arranged as a bench. For a moment, there was nothing – no birdsong, no damp whispers of wind, no feet squelching in the mud, nothing. Until Rekha exhaled, "Go on."

"I think you need to get to the bottom of this one. Why do one man's eyes tell stories and the other man's eyes tell nothing? I've seen how Anay looks at you. And it's heart-breaking."

"What are you saying, M?" There was genuine surprise and hurt in Rekha's voice, her beautiful eyes opened wide as she heard Maya speak in such warm tones about Anay. "Anay doesn't look at me like that! He is so cold. It's like he doesn't even know that I exist!"

Later that night, as Maya Wagh settled down into bed, her well-thumbed copy of Little Lord Fauntleroy in her hand, she found her mind wandering back to the conversation in the park. "She really thinks that Anay doesn't care. Who am I to judge? Maybe he doesn't. "

She couldn't shake off her unease about the Rekha-Anay stand-off even after she woke up the next day. "Arvind, you think Anay really doesn't care about Rekha?" she asked her husband as he prepared for another day of making his dreams come true. He looked at her with distant eyes. But he didn't dismiss the question. Arvind Desai held his wife of so many years in too much regard to treat her questions with indifference. "I don't know. I've seen them together so many times" his brow furrowed as he tried to make sense out of a question that he had neither anticipated, nor prepared for, nor, quite frankly, was he terribly interested in contemplating.

"I think he cares. Very much. But who am I to say? Maybe he just finds her very sexy even after all these years, and can't take his eyes off her. And that's why he looks like he wants to kill any man who even glances at her..." a smile was playing itself out around a corner of his lips at some memory and he hadn't registered the surprise on Maya's face.

"He does?"

"Who?"

"Arvind! Anay, of course! You just don't pay me any attention! Sometimes I swear I think I could dance naked in front of you and you wouldn't notice…"

"Oh, that I would!" his eyes were wicked and Maya made a mental note to wear her new powder blue thong for the night. There was that about losing even a little weight. Her butt, she thought was looking just a little better. And she was planning on testing her theory. With the most reliable source of feedback she had.

The morning had passed quickly in mild sexual banter and the promise of a long night. So it was mid- afternoon before she got around to her regular call with her Mom. And it was Shaila who, as she did so often, put her finger on the pulse of Rekha's turmoil. "Anay is mad about that girl. He always has been. But Rekha, bless the child, has never seen it. She is so smart and kind and wonderful, but she is blind to Anay. And nothing is quite as scary as that, nothing has worse consequences, Maya. Being blind and not even knowing that you are blind. Poor Rekha. And poor, poor Anay."

"But Ma, can't Anay make her see!!! He does behave so cold and aloof. I've seen it myself. To be fair to Rekha, Anay does behave like an automaton around her."

"It's in the eyes, Maya. Watch his eyes."

"Ma, sometimes I think it's all in your head. First it was Tilly's eyes that were saying she is sad; now it's Anay's eyes saying they are desperately in love with Rekha. What kind of books are you reading nowadays? I should come and check out this library that you have joined!" Maya laughed at her mother. And Shaila, knowing that love so often took the form of good-natured teasing, laughed along.

As she headed to her own kitchen to make herself a cup of tea to drink along with her latest Nora Roberts, though, Shaila Wagh said to herself, "But both those things are true. Tilly IS very sad. And Anay IS hopelessly in love with that mad child, Rekha. God help them all."

Chapter 21

(July 20, 2016)

This time it had been the Rain Gods who had frustrated Tilly. Her plan had been simple – she was going to cart Zoya up her favourite fort, sit under a lonely tree, and over a cup of tea and coffee watch Zoya untangle the knot called Zaid. But it had been raining consistently over the past month. And even she wasn't foolish enough to try and trek up a treacherous mountain in the season of landslides. There had been stories of mountain sides simply vanishing under the torrents that were sweeping across Western Maharashtra. And Tilly had no plans of getting washed away. She still had Riva to live for.

Even if she felt like that was about all that she had to live for.

Some days it was a struggle to get out of bed. But it was the thought that Riva had to be woken up, bathed, fed and hugged off into her waiting school bus that brought her to her swollen feet. Tilly took joy in the small things that Riva needed from her – packing her tiny snack box, smuggling a surprise treat into her backpack, brushing and neatly plaiting her long, curly hair, finding matching socks from the magic pile of washed laundry that never decreased in size...

Tilly was Riva's chosen mother. That is how she thought of herself. She had walked into that cold, bleak orphanage in Nashik 4 years ago. And there had been this tiny waif, her arms stick thin, her curly hair matted, her eyes wide open. The formalities had taken forever. And Tilly shuddered even now at the red tape and paper work that had hardened the arteries of what should be one of the most joyful experiences on the planet. But first there had been disbelief from her family. "Who will marry you with an adopted child? Must you always think like this? Haven't you already made our lives more complicated than anyone else? For just once in your life will you think of anyone besides your own self? All the girls are married and settled and doing well. But look at you! Forget about us, we are all old fuddy-duddies and conservative and close-minded. We know that. You've said it a million times. Forget about us. You look at your own friends. Rekha, Maya, Zoya - all married and settled down, with their own children. What is this thing inside you that makes you do all these weird, horrible things? You went and shaved your head off after your MA, we kept quiet. You decided to stay in Pune all by yourself, we allowed it. You kept turning down every single proposal we got for you, we never argued. Maybe we were wrong. Maybe we should have insisted. And now look at what you have gone and gotten yourself into!"

It had gone on and on. TIlly's poor parents had drafted in the services of aunts, uncles, cousins, family friends. And the personal space that Tilly had so fiercely guarded all through her adult life had not merely been invaded, but trampled upon, torn apart and ravaged mercilessly.

Through it all the tempestuous Tilly had remained ominously calm. She had confided in her closest friends. They had driven with her to the orphanage – the car crammed with the hand-me-downs of Maya, Rekha and Zoya's babies. Little Riva had 6 big brothers. And her earliest memories were of wearing blue rompers and playing with miniature cars. She would be many years older before she realised the wearing Tuhin's old T-shirt, strutting around in Samar's Roger Federer cap or running around in Rekha Mausi's Rishu's old yellow sneakers was not how most little girls spent their growing years.

If Riva's adoption had caused a major storm in Tilly's family, her upbringing had brought about nothing but love. And the credit for that was all Riva's. She was simply irresistible. Tilly had taken her to meet the family, and they had all just instantly fallen in love. Even as a baby, Riva had that direct, open-eyed gaze of wonder and love. She looked at you like you were her best friend. And then you were. It was as simple as that.

Riva was Tilly's sunshine. But lately even the pure joy of Riva wasn't reaching some dark recesses of her heart. There was no way that Shaila Wagh could have known why Tilly was sad. But she was right in her astute observation. Tilly was sad. She was sad in the way that makes every bone ache, and the air around you quiver with pain. When she lay down to sleep every night, she felt like her body was a giant pin cushion, everything hurt; her feet hurt, her toes hurt, her calves hurt, even her hair follicles hurt.

But she told no one. She spoke incessantly and yet she said nothing. She had always been a private person. Her friends had respected her privacy. She had poured her heart out to them after she had broken up with Prof Aman, her married, handsome, soulful professor during her MA days. She had loved him with a passion and a madness that she had not known even she was capable of.

And she had hated herself almost as much. She could never forgive herself for being involved in deceit. Prof Aman's wife Najma was a pretty, simple, happy young woman from Satara. She had no idea that her handsome husband had fallen hopelessly and irrevocably in love with a student of his. Campus romances were no big deal. They happened. They were not supposed to happen; and maybe that was why they happened in the first place. The thrill of the forbidden.

But both Aman and Tilly knew that theirs was no run-of-the-mill campus affair. They both fought it for as long as they could. But on a rainy day in September, in the last semester of Tilly's MA, they had both lost the fight and succumbed to the overwhelming force of their passion for one another.

And then Tilly had gone through the toughest three years of her life. She couldn't stay away from Aman, he couldn't stay away from her. Aman and Najma had had their first daughter – Mehzabin – in that period. Tilly would gaze for hours at pictures of Aman with his daughter. She would physically ache to have her child in his arms, his eyes fill up with love for children that they had brought forth into the world. For months she could think of nothing else. All she wanted was children. Aman's children. On the rare nights that they managed to spend together she would imagine what it would be like to wake up every day next to the regular breathing of the man she loved beyond all good sense. On all the many other nights she would hug her pillow tight to soothe the pain that she felt somewhere deep in her stomach. She was ravaged, tortured, rent asunder by her monstrous love for a married man. And for three years she had been helpless against the ferocity of their feelings for one another. He read poetry out to her. She told him stories of her childhood. He wrote poetry for her. Many years later he published a volume of poems written in that period. It went on to become one of India's first bestsellers in the genre of poetry. 'Till I die' was the name of the book. No one knew that he was the only person on the planet who called her Till.

But it had ended. She had ended it. One extraordinarily beautiful December day, Tilly had walked up to her Aman and said, "Never again. We will do this no more. I will not see you. You will not try to see me. Goodbye."

She had turned her back on the silently slumped Aman, and was walking away with the resolve of Titans, when she heard him say quietly, "I will love you forever. Every night, at 9, know that I am saying 'I love you' to you. You will not see me. I will never even attempt to see you. But I will love you forever, Till."

She hadn't looked back. She had merely given him the slightest shake of her head to show that she understood. In the dark, dimly lit corridor leading away from Aman's brilliantly lit staff room, cactus Tilly had been born. She had ventured forth into the rest of her life with all softness, all vulnerability hidden deep inside a prickly exterior. What had followed was a long litany of meaningless flings. She flirted with men that she took a fancy too. They fell head over heels in love with her. She even slept with one of two of them. But no man was ever again allowed close enough to Tilly to hurt her. No other man had mattered to her since Aman. And even now, after all these years, her heart lurched a little at 9 in the night.

"Mama, Maya Aunty taught me a prayer today. 'Thank you God for Mama. Thank you God for my family, my friends, my house. Thank you God for making my life beautiful.' She said I should say this every night before I go to sleep. What do you say just before you go to sleep, Mama?"

Tilly kissed little Riva's forehead fiercely, and clamped her eyes shut to stop the tears from spilling out. "Maya Aunty is such an angel. She teaches us the nicest things!"

There it was. A pretend answer. She saw it for the prevarication that she knew it to be. But she was too much of a coward that rainy night to call her own bluff. It was 9 pm according to the giant panda clock in Riva's pretty bedroom. And Tilly's heart squeezed painfully. Yet again.

Chapter 22

Finally, it had cleared up. There had been a couple of days of bright sunshine. And the Met department had announced that the monsoon had taken a break. Tilly had mustered up enough strength to drive Zoya up the fort and up the wall. Zoya was in her drawing room that evening, back from a mind-bending trek with Tilly. She had called her Mom and then Asif on her way back. "I want to talk to the three of you. Can we meet at home at 4 o'clock today?"

"Just as I was about to hang up, she said, '4 o'clock sharp, Mom'. After months she sounded like herself. God be praised!" a visibly moved Fatima Lakdawala had said to her husband. And at 5 minutes to 4 that evening, they had rung the bell of their beloved daughter's house with hope in their aging hearts.

"I want to talk to Zaid." Zoya had got straight to the point. It was the first time in many, many months that she had uttered his name. And through the hammering of her heart and the rush of blood in her ears, Zoya sensed that his name had felt different as she had said it out loud. If we pay close enough attention, all things are very physical. Our skin crawls when we see something we hate, like cockroaches, or blobs of cream floating in tea. Our heart leaps when we hear great news. Our stomach clenches when we live in fear. But there is nothing quite as ephemerally physical as the way a name feels when we say it. Try it. Say the name of a loved one out loud. A mother calling out to her child has the deep, intractable, unknowable knowledge of knowing the child at a cellular level in the way her mouth forms the name of the child. New lovers taking each others' names have little blushes creeping into the sounds the uttered name makes. For all of her life, every time Zoya had said 'Zaid' there had been a ring of ownership to it. She had said, 'Zaid', but it had always felt like she was saying 'My Zaid'. This time, however, his name felt different. Zoya Quettawala, long-time CA, princess of her parents, dearly loved wife of her husband, adored Mom, cherished friend, for the first time ever, relinquished the manic grip she had kept on her brother.

Zaid had been the teddy bear of a little child, the comforter, the protector against the nightmares, the one thing she insisted on having by her side so that she felt safe. He had been many things to Zoya. But, for the longest time, he had not been a person.

In the way that Zoya uttered his name that evening, she paid him the respect of acknowledging him for what he was; not her Zaid, just Zaid. Person. Human. With his own stories, his own feelings, his own frailties, his own being.

No one noticed it, of course. But Zoya knew.

"I want to talk to Zaid" she said again. "But before that, I want to talk about Zaid. I also want to hear about him. Tell me about him."

"He has been so worried about you, Zoyu. For months he hasn't slept well, he isn't eating well. Anu keeps telling him that things will work themselves out. God bless that child. She is a saint…"

"No, Ma. Tell me about Zaid…"

"But that's what I'm doing, beta…" Fatima looked a little bewildered with the fierceness with which Zoya had cut her short. Zoya was direct, strong, bold, but she was never rude. And this sounded like rudeness.

Zoya shook her head, "Ma… no… not about this…" she had gestured helplessly. "Not about this thing. Tell me about Zaid. Tell me what you think about him. From the beginning."

"But that you already know…" Fatima trailed off at the restraining touch of her husband's hand on hers.

"I'll tell you a story you probably haven't heard before. Zaid was only 3 years old. Or maybe a little older, I can't remember. I had taken him to Monu Chacha's house. And when we left, I saw some coloured paper peeking out of his pockets. I asked him what it was, and he had very happily taken out a fistful of sweets, hardboiled sweets, and held them up to me."

"Did Chachi give them to you?" I had asked." First, he said yes, then his bright grin had faded a little, and then he just started crying. 'They were there, on the table, so I took them…' he had blubbered. I didn't say anything to him. I just picked him up, made him stand in front of me on the scooter, and then at a traffic signal, where we had stopped, he pulled out the sweets and gave them to a beggar boy."

"So he was always a little hero, right?" Zoya could barely manage to keep the bitterness from her voice.

"No, he was a good kid. He made mistakes. And then he did what he could to set them right" Asif entered the conversation lightly; settling himself comfortably on the arm of the stuffed sofa that Zoya had perched on, putting a casual arm around her shoulders as he weighed in on behalf of his oldest friend.

"What I don't get is how all of you are so okay with what he did..." Zoya shrugged in feigned indifference.

The three others in the intimate huddle looked at one another, not knowing who was going to state the obvious, hoping someone would take the lead.

It came down to her Abbu again.

"Beta, it's not that simple. We are not judging him..."

"Since when have we decided to become saints, Abbu!" Zoya's indignation flashed dangerously through her eyes that had lived bereft of kajal for months now.

"Zo, reign it in. That's no way to talk to Abbu." Asif's quiet reprimand did little to douse the fire in her eyes, but Zoya hadn't been brought up to talk back; so her throat closed up against any further sounds of bad-mannered rebellion.

Abbas Lakdawala soldiered on, "Zoya, we've talked about this. In your absence..."

He was just saying all the wrong things. And the poor man knew it. He flashed Asif a look that clearly said, "Help!" But Asif wasn't risking losing the first chance that Zoya had given them all to finally open a conversation about what was tearing them all apart to clumsy man-talk. He simply shrugged as if to say, "You're on your own here, Abbu!"

It was then that Fatima Lakdawala stood up and delivered. Quite literally. She stood up, stretched herself to her full height, all 4 feet 11 inches of her; and delivered the finest lecture of her whole life.

"Enough" she started. "Enough with the hemming and the hawing and the talking behind Zoya's back about what we need to say to her so that she can finally grow up!" Zoya looked at her mother with more than startled eyes as Fatima opened hostilities.

"I have always been a grown up...!" Zoya spluttered.

Fatima held up her tiny hand like a General would to quell the first sign of rebellion, "I said, enough, Zoya! You will listen. I will speak. And no one will interrupt me. You have been our princess. Your every whim and fancy has been indulged. No. Don't..." she shook her head in serious warning as from the corner of her eye she caught her husband trying to reach out to their daughter. "Don't pat her head just now. All of us need to respect Zoya a little more than this."

At this surprising pronouncement Asif and Abbas both spluttered a little in their own right.

But Fatima Lakdawala was in full flow. And she was in no mood to pander to anyone's egos or sensibilities. Her family was her biggest pride, and she begged God's forgiveness for harbouring pride; her children were her greatest loves. She had watched first in mute horror, then in hand-wringing despair as the insane drama between Zoya and Zaid played itself out for months on end. But now, she had decided to take matters in her own little hands. And no one was getting in her way. Tiger Moms had nothing on Fatima Lakdawala when it came to keeping her little brood together and happy.

"Yes, we have all been wrong. And we've been wrong for about 30 years now. Zaid slept with that bitch Shireen. Zoya imploded. For months now we have been talking about how to make Zoya see sense. As if it is all her fault. As if she has suddenly gone a little mad. For all of her life, we have said that Zoya is strong, smart, sensible. Then how come this smart, strong, sensible girl is now suddenly so incredibly stupid that she can't see what is obvious to us all? So who is really stupid here? Zoya? Or the rest of us? Or Zaid? Or all of us?" she glared around at their little gathering as if to dare anyone to answer her. No one did. They were all looking at her with their mouths hanging open a little.

"You said 'bitch' Ma..." Zoya said in a voice of hushed wonder.

"I know what I said" Fatima snapped back. "I know exactly what I am saying... Look at us, just look at all of us. Our beautiful family is falling apart and we are not even asking the right questions! Ask the right questions. And then see how the answers will simply fall into place! So let me ask some first -Since when did Zoya start believing that Zaid was her safety net? Who gave her the idea that Zaid existed for the *sole* purpose of making Zoya's life perfect? Why did she believe that Zaid sleeping with *her*", she almost spat that 'her' out, "was a betrayal of Zoya's faith in him? Why did we not correct her when as a six year old she came home from school and said, 'I told Rhea that she was no longer my friend; who does she think she is... she was saying that Zaidu wouldn't be able to beat up that Aamir from the 10th.' I remember that I had said that Aamir was so much taller and bigger than Zaidu, and Zoya had simply asked, 'So? Aamir was teasing me, I can handle it, Zaid has taught me how to... but if I told him to beat up Aamir he would. And he would win. It's Zaidu, Ma!' And I had hugged her close and told her what a good girl she was to have such faith in her Zaid. Her Zaid. Her Zaid. Her Zaid. We all kept telling her he was her Zaid."

Tears swam into Fatima's kind, brown eyes.

"My beautiful boy, first he was 'my Zaid', then he was 'Zoya's Zaid'; it's a wonder he built such a strong relationship with Anu. But then, credit to Anu for that. She lovingly accepted all our claims on him. Stupid child. Maybe she should have yelled and screamed and thrown a few tantrums – maybe we would have seen the error of our ways a little earlier. But no... our perfect Zaid went and married the perfect woman. And all of us carried on blissfully, claiming for our own what by rights no one can claim – the person that Zaid is. I love you for asking us to talk about him, Zoya beta. I understand what you were trying to ask – You were asking us to talk about who Zaid is, independent of our claws in him. And the answer to that is that I really don't know. I have, for the longest time, built up an image of our perfect Zaid Lakdawala – and I have no idea who he is outside of that image. I, his own mother, the woman who has claimed loudly and publicly for the longest time that no one can love him more than I do, I have no idea who he is. What terrible injustices we heap upon one another in the name of love!"

And here the tears finally trickled down her cheeks. She didn't bother wiping them away. She let them flow.

"Zoya, I'm sorry. I'm sorry for all those years of teaching you, encouraging you, practically brainwashing you into believing the story that we scripted about Zaid. It was our job to bring you up to be a strong, sensible, smart woman. And we brought you up to be a little girl with a big brother. That's what you have been. For all these years. Just a very lucky little girl, with the perfect big brother who was your rule measure for all right and wrong. And now that measure is broken, your ideals are shattered, and we are all asking how come you are so silly that you can't see what is obvious to us?"

Fatima reached out and did what she had expressly forbidden her husband from doing - she patted her daughter's cheeks and continued, "Zoya, Zaid IS perfect. But not inhuman. He is perfectly fallible. And that's what makes him special. Just like all of us. We are all ordinary; some of us are just a little less ordinary than the rest of us. He owes you nothing, beta. No explanations, no justifications, no apologies – nothing. What he did with *her*" there it was again, the expletive in the pronoun, "is something that he should talk about with Anu. And he already has. Many times over. He made a mistake. And he betrayed Anu's trust. God knows how sorry he is about that. But that's it. That's all there is to it. He has apologised to Anu, many, many times. But we have not apologised to the two of you. We were the adults. We were your parents. We should have set things right. But we didn't. It seemed to have worked so well for all these years – you, Zoya, the girl who always won at everything; and Zaid the strength behind her. But we were wrong, Zoya. You are perfect in yourself. Just like Zaid is. You don't need him to be some larger than life creature. You are enough. By yourself..."

And just like that, Fatima Lakdawala ran out of steam. She looked completely bewildered by her own tirade and she looked around at the other three, "Am I making any sense?"

"Perfect, Fatima. Just perfect. You are making perfect sense. I am so proud of you!" Abbas Lakdwala's voice was thick with emotion. The past months had been impossibly difficult for this mild-mannered patriarch. He had desperately wanted everything to be fine once again. But this wasn't some torn knee that he could bandage up and say a prayer over. This was an unimaginable, unthinkable, unfathomable gash that had just opened up in the fabric of their lives. And his Fatima had just stepped in to start knitting it back together.

It would take time, perhaps. But Abbas Lakdawala was a man of both patience and faith. He said a silent, but heartfelt prayer. And for the first time in months he smiled a smile that reached his eyes, "Asif, get Ma a cup of kesar milk. And let me make all of us some chai. Then we'll call Zaid."

"Not yet" came his wife's tired voice. "Not just yet. We'll call him when Zoya tells us to. And she'll tell us when she tells us."

Zoya sat there. In complete silence. She wanted to speak to Zaid. But she had no idea what to say to him. So for now, she chose silence. And a cup of tea.

Chapter 23

(July 30, 2016)

The girls were going shopping. And it was Rekha who had marshalled the troops. "I don't like this online shopping thing. We sit in our own rooms and stare at our laptops. Where's the fun in that? We should go check out the stores, try stuff on, plan the colours for the Diwali Party!"

By now the party had become the Party. You know you are serious about stuff when you start capitalising it in your own mind. Rekha Jaisingh had decided that this Party was going to be the most fun thing any of them had done in forever. And if all the others had been surprised about her sudden, newfound love for shopping, they were all wise enough to hold their counsel.

"Has she met Anay at all in the past few months?" Zoya had asked Tilly. Tilly had replied with a rueful shake of her curls, "She's been talking a little about this with Maya..."

"I know, I know... the whole Gajju bit. He's come chasing after her from Antarctica or something..." Zoya cut in, more of her old spirit seeping back into her with every passing day.

"Not Antarctica, idiot, the Andes" Tilly had guffawed.

"Yeah, yeah…"

Gajju had been the village idiot, main villain, cad and general black sheep for the girls for the better part of nearly two decades now. And a fancy career and one photograph of the mountains was not going to do anything to change that.

"No, I don't care about that clown. I'm asking if she has met Anay any time recently…" Zoya persisted.

"Let's ask her when we meet her today. Before the others show up."

The plan was that everyone who could manage it was to head out to shop. And although Mitali, Roopa and Rashmi had never shown the slightest interest in the sweating and running around till it hurt, they had all loved the idea of a day long shopping trip.

"That was NOT easy" Maya said at around 7:30 that evening. The girls were all slumped around her beautiful family room in various stages of exhaustion. Maya's immaculately trained staff had provided them all with succour in the form of endless rounds of masala chai and nimbu pani and just plain water.

"We're getting too old for this" groaned Roopa.

"Who thought ankles could hurt so much" Mitali poked her head out from the mound of oversize cushions that she had heaped on her monumental self.

"Don't be silly, we haven't had so much fun in the longest time!" Rekha's eyes were shining, and her cheeks were glowing. She was the only one still pacing the room with nervous energy. She was poking into everyone's shopping bags, clicking pictures of the evidence of a day full of fun for Instagram, she was egging the rest of the girls to try on some of the stuff they had bought, and comprehensively irritating Tilly.

"Re. Stop. Sit. Now!" Maya and Zoya exchanged a quick look. Tilly in staccato mode was a signal that someone was in distress. And Rekha was seeming the opposite of distressed.

But in an instant Rekha stopped in her relentless tracks and shimmered into the nearest chair, like a silently deflating balloon.

The room became oddly silent. Mitali and Roopa were still there. Rashmi had rushed back home with an "I can't believe I've let the kids spend an entire day doing nothing!"

And it was the Mitali who spoke up, "I think we should be heading home. It's really been a very long day... let's move, Roopa."

Maya wasn't letting any of that happen. They were all friends, and all in her house. She was not letting anyone feel like outsiders. "Don't be silly. Dinner is ready. Rajma chawal. Simple stuff. And then I've done this new cheesecake that I want your feedback on."

"We can't eat a morsel. We've eaten so much all day long!" Roopa was already settling back into the couch she had half risen from at Mitali's nudge.

"I think Rajma chawal is a great idea. You have dahi? Of course you do." Rekha's voice was suddenly tired. And Tilly walked across to her chair, perched herself on its arm and cradled her old friend's neck in a gesture of pure love. "You're right, P Rex. It's a great idea."

The moment passed and the air around the room shifted in some tangible way. Everyone was smiling again. And genial, big Mitali decided to do a little ramp walk in her one size too small Diwali Party outfits.

"You girls will lose tons of weight. But I'm going to drop a size. Just you watch. Take pictures, Tilly! These beauties are going to be hanging off me in just a couple of months!" It was a little hard to believe that the sequinned red dress that stretched alarmingly across Mitali's generous hips and bulged with her stomach would do anything like hang off her in the near future. But no one was going to rain on Mitali's parade that day. If these girls were anything, they were supportive of one another. In a world full of people tearing others down, these girls did what they could to build each other up. They were friends. And proud of it.

So, when Maya asked for their honest feedback on her new baked cheesecake with tarragon they outdid each other in the generosity and loudness of their praise.

"When are you going to do this professionally?"

"I think I just died and went to heaven!"

"Will you marry me?"

"You HAVE to do something with this!"

Maya just laughed and laughed and laughed. "Stop! You are all so ridiculous! Thank you, glad you like it, but OTT much?"

"Sorry babe, but we're not going to stop raving about this!" Tilly's lovely eyes had glazed over, her lips were slightly parted; she had the look of a blissfully drunk person. "You HAVE to take this to the next level. And you HAVE to do it now. I'm sure Arvind will agree."

And just like that the air around the room changed again. Maya's spine stiffened. The laughter leached out of her eyes though her lips still smiled. She began clearing up the dessert dishes. Completely unnecessarily because one of the maids had been hovering around to do just that.

"Can I get you some more, girls? I've got another one baked. Or some coffee?"

So many little dramas played themselves out in that plush family room that day. There was Rekha who had swung ominously from nervous excitement to a slumped-shouldered listlessness; there was Maya who had baked yet another miracle but shrunk from seeing its possibilities; and then there was Tilly watching them both through half closed eyes, allowing them their silence, but storing away the information from angles of shoulders and spines for a later day.

It had been a brilliant day. A milestone in their journey toward the Diwali Party. They had actually shopped for it. They had tried on ridiculous outfits, tottered around in impossible heels, bought make up they didn't need, eaten more than defensible, and just generally been indulgent, spoilt and a little entitled.

"It's been a great day, girls. But now it's time to call it a night, I'm off." Zoya marched around the large room, revived by the coffee, collecting her bags from the colossal heap they had managed to accumulate.

One by one they all left. Happy with the day. More than a little in love with the shoes and bags and the clothes and the food. Until it was only Maya still sitting in her favourite corner, drinking one last cup of coffee as a special treat to herself. "They loved the cheesecake! They loved the cheesecake! Tomorrow I'll bake the banana bread that I have been meaning to try. The kids will love it. I'll send some over to Tilly too. No. Maybe I'll bake a whole separate loaf for Riva. She'll take it to school, or maybe she'll invite friends over for a tea party. She's such an angel, and she loves my cooking."

That was when Arvind walked in. To see his wife surrounded by the debris of a day with her girl gang, an empty cup in her hand, a smile on her lips and a faraway dreamy look in her eyes.

"Hi sweetie, how was the day?" He took her hand and pulled her gently to her feet. And without really expecting an answer he pulled her into him, nuzzling her neck.

For the first time, Maya pulled back. She straightened her shoulders, looked into her husband's eyes, and said, "I had a really good day. Want to hear about it?"

Arvind Wagh was a good man. But he was also a little tired at the end of a long day. He had walked into the room expecting a quick, relaxing roll in the hay with his always acceding wife. So he was more than a little surprised when she said she wanted to talk. Which explains why he made a classic mistake, "Now?"

And Maya Wagh smiled her mother's smile at Arvind, patted him on his cheek and said, "It's late, Arvind. Go to sleep. I'll come upstairs in just a bit."

She couldn't explain the tightly controlled fury in the whites of her knuckles as she gripped the railing on a verandah that led out of the family room. But Maya stood there. Letting the cool night air fan her face, getting her breathing back under control, regaining the equanimity she had been trained into before her fingers finally unclenched and she walked silently upstairs to her bedroom.

Arvind was already asleep. His back turned to her. Maya felt a huge pang of unease. She had refused her husband for the first time ever. She didn't even know why she had done it. But every day she was growing angrier and angrier at Arvind. In the quiet dark of her familiar bedroom, inside the familiar presence of her husband's regular breathing, Maya Wagh was suddenly afraid. "I have to make this up to him. I'll make him his favourite biryani tomorrow. But then, he never notices." And just like that, her fists clenched again.

Arvind slumbered on. Blissfully unaware of knuckles and fists and the simmering fire building up silently inside his sensible wife.

Men.

Chapter 24

It's strange how we don't generally notice how many things are constantly happening around us. Maybe it's a good thing we don't. Because otherwise we'd have to make sense of the vegetable vendor on the footpath who is staring blankly into the clouded August sky, the flies that buzz around that heap of rotting tomatoes next to her, the newly married couple examining potatoes at the stall next to hers – the young woman pretending an expertise she neither has nor really needs to buy potatoes, the young man absentmindedly twisting his long fingers into his new wife's hair. We'd have to process simply too much. So maybe it is a blessing that we register very little of what happens around us. Because, honestly, too much is going on.

The first week of August was like that. It was just too much. Zoya met up with Zaid. Tilly had a fainting fit. Rekha and Gajju went out to dinner. Rekha and Anay went out to dinner. Rekha and Tilly went out to dinner. Maya took off with her sister for an unplanned trip to Varanasi. All the kids decided to go completely mad at the same time. Zoya's older one had a bout of the stomach flu, Riva went on this 'I-want-a-kitten' trip, Maya's sons both decided to rebel against the institution of homework, Maya was off traipsing around the gullies of Benares, so Arvind had to go to school and face some pretty loud music. But it was Rekha's boys that had everyone well and truly worried.

Rekha had been staying with her parents for almost 4 months now. And she refused to speak about it with anyone. Her poor parents kept trying, but Rekha stonewalled them. They had fallen into a sort of a pattern. Anay would come over every two or three days, pick up the kids, and take them home for a while. The kids spent all weekends with Anay. Or 'at home' which is how they referred to it. And poor Rekha didn't even realise that she hadn't thought of correcting them even once.

So, that Sunday, when Anay called her and asked if the kids were with her, she had replied without a moment's thought, "Of course not! They went home with you on Friday!"

"They are not here, Rekha" Anay's voice was desperate with worry and fear.

"What do you mean they are not here? Where can they be? Have you checked with Laxmi Tai? She takes them with her to buy fresh fruits sometimes. Or the attic? They play chess there. Have you looked for them in the garage? Where is Bruno? They are generally somewhere around him. Have you checked, Anay!" Rekha was almost screaming by the time she ran out of breath.

"I've checked everywhere. I only called after I had done everything else" Anay's voice was like the shutters had come down again. All animation had left him, and with a calm bordering on coldness he ended the call, "I'll update you when I know more."

Rekha, dressed in a pair of blue jeans and an old T-shirt she'd left behind at her parents' place when she had got married, ran out of her parents' house and practically flew back to her home of 14 years.

The gate was opened by a worried looking watchman, and Rekha ignored the new young man's tentative smile. She rushed into the open front door and saw Anay standing there, calmly talking into his phone.

He looked up to see his wife in their home for the first time in 4 months and he stopped speaking. Very carefully he said to whoever was on the other end of the phone, "I'll call you back."

And with unsteady fingers he put his precious phone on the table next to him.

Rekha just stood there. Frozen. A million conflicts rising in her turbulent heart. She wanted to run to her husband, fling herself into his arms and wail. She wanted him to hold her close and tell her that it was all going to be okay, that the kids would be just fine. She wanted to crumple onto the floor of the house that she had no idea she loved so fiercely. She wanted to run into her little vegetable garden and meet her old friends. She wanted to run her fingers along the polished surfaces of her old life to check for dust. She had never realised how much she had missed being home. This was home. She wanted to hug her home. She wanted to shout out her children's names, in the manic, insane belief that they would simply appear in front of her if she only called out to them. But she did nothing of the sort. She just stood there.

"Hi" her voice sounded breathless even to her own ears. "Melodrama, Rekha, melodrama" warned a familiar voice inside her own head.

By the time she got out a stilted "Any news?" Rekha Jaisingh had valiantly regained her composure.

Anay, in those few moments, had simply stood there too, rooted to his spot. His eyes had hungrily drunk in the dishevelled hair, the stained, old T-shirt, the perfect jeans, the wild eyes of his dearly, dearly beloved wife. His heart was filled to bursting. The sheer brute force of his unbearable love for her hit him anew. But he wasn't Businessman of the Year Anay Jaisingh for no reason. His poker face was the stuff of legends. "We've checked the security camera footage. They were last seen running out of the main gate…"

"Why did no one stop them?" Rekha cried out in anguish.

"The watchman had come inside to pick up his cup of tea. He was gone for only a few minutes. Don't hate on him, Re" Anay tiredly pre-empted a tirade from Rekha with a raised hand. "He's good at what he does, he just stepped away for a bit, it's human." His hand went into his hair and as he clutched at the back of his head Rekha saw a worried, harried father emerge from the mask of a controlled, composed tycoon.

Rekha's voice softened. She didn't notice it. He did. "But then, why aren't we out on the streets looking for them?"

"I've looked everywhere, Re…" there was entreaty in his voice, and something that Rekha couldn't quite place. Any half-baked idiot could have told her it was love. But the things that we are deaf and blind to can fill up entire data clouds. "I've been on the streets, roaming around like a mad man. Calling out their names… I don't know where they could have gone!!!" And he sank down into the nearest sofa, his head in his hands, his shoulders sagging in despair.

Rekha Jaisingh swallowed all the recriminations the mother in her wanted to fling at the world. "What were you doing? How come no one was keeping an eye on them? How could you let this happen?" She said nothing of this. Instead, she sat down next to her husband and tentatively reached out a hand to soothe his hair. At the touch of her hand Anay's head shot up as if he had been struck by lightning. He turned to look at her with widened eyes and her hand fell back, as if of its own accord.

"Have you found them?" Tilly burst into the moment, and the spell broke.

The next few hours were a blur.

It turned out that Anay had informed Rekha's friends. "He said he knew you would need us more than anyone else" Tilly had supplied this piece of information as she handed out tea to everyone.

Anay had also informed the police, the society office of the bungalow society in which they lived, his own group of trusted aides and both sets of parents. Everyone had been out, searching, shouting.

It was getting dark now. And it had started raining. Anay had called Tilly and told her to get Rekha back home, "It's no good all of us blundering about like this. Get her to stay put at home, Tilly. And stay with her please."

Maya, Zoya and Tilly had convinced a distraught Rekha to go back to the Jaisingh home. And it was there that Laxmi Tai handed her phone to her, "Madam, you left it here when you went out. It has been making ting-ting sounds all the time."

Rekha didn't really care, but in the vain hope that there might be some news about Rishabh and Mrugank, her darling boys aged 12 and 10, she unlocked her phone.

It was Gajju. He had been texting her all evening. And the messages became more and more loving and caring and desperate as she read them all.

"Heard about the boys. Any news?"

"Talk to me, Rekha. Tell me how I can help."

"I know how terribly worried you must be. All I want to do is hold you and tell you it will all be fine. Because it will. Don't worry, my love, the boys will be just fine."

And it went on and on in this vein. He had heaped endearments on her, whispered loving encouragement to her, told her everything she needed to hear, given her hope, given her courage, told her what a wonderful mother she was.

Rekha couldn't stop reading. The others sat around her, silent. Waiting for her to look up from her phone.

But Rekha couldn't tear her overflowing eyes away from the lit up screen. She read and she cried. She wiped her streaming eyes and re-read the messages filled with love. She cried like she had never ever cried before. She cried like she had wanted to all day long – like a child who was afraid and a mother who was afraid and a woman who was desperately afraid of losing what was most important in her life.

She held her phone close to her heart and rocked back and forth, all pretence at dignity forgotten, all veneers of sophistication stripped away. Rekha Jaisingh had been doing a lot of crying over the past few months, but this was not crying; this was disintegration. It was the first 'my love' from Gajju that had undone her.

And her closest friends watched in silent awe as their Perfect Rekha dissolved in front of their eyes into a woman who was simply torn apart by the most savage weapon known to man – love.

Chapter 25

(August 7, 2016)

The boys had been gone for 8 hours now.

"Stuff like this doesn't happen in real life. This happens in scary TV serials. And if it does happen in real life, it happens to *other* people. This simply can't be happening to *us!*" Zoya anguished to herself silently. She had only recently reunited with Zaid. In fact, she had planned to call all her friends and their families over for an impromptu dinner tonight to celebrate. All the food she had hauled home from their favourite grocery that morning still lay in complete disarray in her kitchen. She and Anu had just entered the house weighed down by the bags, buoyed up by their return to their favourite Sunday morning grocery shopping ritual after months; when her phone had rung. Her own happiness had receded far into the background as she sat in Rekha and Anay's home, sick with worry for two boys she loved from the bottom of her heart.

The rain had increased in its fury. Darkness had descended almost completely. And in the calming yellow light of a cosy nook in the Jaisingh home three women tried valiantly to give warmth and hope and succour to a shattered fourth. Zoya's brave face, Maya's solid strength, Tilly's infectious optimism – they were trying it all. But

Rekha was sinking into heretofore unplumbed depths of misery. All those years of controlling even a slight spontaneity in expressing her emotions with the inner warning voice of "Melodrama, Rekha" seemed to have been defeated by an even louder voice that said, "Let it all out, Rekha!" And the woman oscillated wildly through various stages of grief. There was anger, denial, bargaining, guilt, depression, all following one another in tumultuous disorder. It was frightening to see her like that. And Tilly had begun wringing her hands in despair verging on panic when Rekha's loud sobs were interrupted by the sound of a phone ringing, "We found them, they are fine" Anay's voice was thick with emotion as he passed on the best news possible to his wife.

It was about another couple of hours before the police, the doctor and the neighbourhood watch left. At around 9:00 in the night there were only Rekha, Anay, their respective parents and Rekha's friends and their respective husbands. The close group huddled together over a comforting dinner of dal khichadi and papad that Laxmi Tai had put together and listened as Anay sat down to narrate, for the nth time that evening what had happened.

"It's just unbelievable!" his voice was tired and exhaustion seeped through every pore of his being, but this story had to be told, his people needed to hear every little detail.

"They were playing chess in my study...

"I told you they'd be playing chess! I knew it... but since when are they playing in your study instead of the attic?"

"Hush, Rekha, let the poor man speak!" her mother admonished.

"So... they were playing chess, in my study – they've been doing that these past few months -" Anay kept his expression carefully neutral, "when Mrugank heard a kitten mewling somewhere. Immediately he sprang out of his chair, upsetting the chess board, which upset Rishu. But they were soon both looking for the kitten. So they ran down, followed the sound and ran out just outside the boundary wall. And then they did the most inexplicable thing – they played with the kitten on the footpath, and then followed the kitten as it ran away from them. I will never understand why they didn't just pick her up and bring her home!"

"And then, Rishu told me, a pack of stray dogs appeared, so Mrugank grabbed the kitten and both the boys fled. Again, why would they do that! They love dogs, dogs love them... but both of them started running, the dogs were running after them and it was a Sunday afternoon, so no one on the roads... and before they knew it, they had slipped into the back garden of the derelict bungalow at the far end of the society."

Meghna Jaisingh gasped audibly, "It's such a scary place. All those broken windows and the ivy creeping up the walls. I've been saying for ages that something needs to be done about that place! Those Thakurs just disappeared one day... overnight they were just gone..." she let her tirade stop lamely as she looked around at the people around the room, every one of whom was clearly waiting for Anay to continue.

"Ma, maybe we should have listened to you long ago. Because the boys saw some extraordinary and terribly dangerous stuff going on there. They let the kitten down as soon as they realised the dogs were no longer following them. But the poor thing was so frightened it scampered up the tallest tree it could find. And then, Rishu tells me, kept crying, as if wanting the boys up in the tree with it. They called out to it. They looked around for help. But there was no one. So, Rishu decided to climb the tree to try and bring the kitten down."

Rekha looked like she was going to throw up. "He's terrified of heights. My baby boy. What a mad thing to do. And how brave." Her eyes once again filled up with the tears that had never really left them all evening.

"And then he fell. From a higher branch. Until another lower branch caught his fall." Anay's hands trembled as he ran them over his tired face, trying and failing to cover up the terror of a father at the fate that might have befallen his first born. "We were lucky. Really lucky. He broke an ankle, not his head or neck or back. But he was in terrible pain. And by now Mithu was crying, he was so scared that poor child. He couldn't find his way home, he couldn't leave Rishu...". Tilly left her chair and went and sat on the arm of Rekha's chair, and put her arm around her old friend in an old, much repeated gesture of love and support when it was needed most.

"Rishu was incredibly brave. He was in so much pain, but he didn't so much as whimper. By now the kitten had joined him on his branch and he was trying his best to comfort Mithu... but that was around the time that the men came."

What followed was fifteen minutes of hushed silence as Anay took them through the incredible story of how the old Thakur bungalow was now a haven for drug addicts and dealers; how Rishabh had realised quickly that these were not people they could trust, and how he had encouraged Mrugank to climb up into the relative safety of the tree until the men went away.

"Papa will soon be here, looking for us. I'm sure he has realised we are missing. You mark my words, Mithu, he'll be here before we know it" the 12 year old Rishabh Jaisingh had whispered encouragement to his frightened, worried 10 year old brother as he himself stoically battled the pain of a broken ankle. Everyone in the room marvelled at the quiet courage of both the boys. And at the same time shook their heads in disbelief at the absurdity of it all.

The strange men had milled about silently in that deserted backyard for what seemed like forever. The rain began to fall, it began to get really dark and both the boys had begun to get very scared.

"I don't know how I never thought of looking in that damned place! And I don't know how they didn't hear us shouting! We kept shouting out their names! Of course, Mithu told me that he thought he heard some voices a couple of times, but the men were practically under their tree then, so they sat in silence, my poor children."

"Tell me again how you found them" Rekha sniffed through a clogged nose.

"I don't really know. We had looked everywhere else, the police teams were saying that they had not intended to run away, so it was unlikely that they had hopped onto some vehicle of their own accord" once again the horrible realisation of what might have been swept across the already ravaged face of Anay Jaisingh, and he stopped short, waiting for his constricted throat to open up again. His father went and put a comforting hand on his shoulder, and Bruno left Meghna Jaisingh's feet to nuzzle him. "I don't know what we would have done if someone had actually kidnapped them, Papa." "Don't even think about it, son. They are back, they are fine, thank God!" Sr Jaisingh stood tall and rock solid behind his beleaguered son. The same pride and courage on his face as was seen on Anay's.

"That's how Rishu must have looked as he comforted my Mithu on that tree today. They all look the same. My poor Rishu, he is such a sensitive boy... will he grow up to be like these two? Strong, but distant?" Rekha thought to herself miserably.

"I was simply calling out their names" Anay's voice shook her out of her reverie "when all of a sudden I heard Rishu's voice calling back, 'Papa, Papa, we are here'!"

"I brought all three of them down, carried Rishu to the car. And called Rekha. And after that, all of you know what happened."

"Rishu is to have a cast for 2 months. No surgery required, thank God." Rekha's mother was dabbing her eyes as she spoke.

"But, beta, why did they run after the kitten in the first place?" Rekha's Dad asked.

"Oh... I forgot to tell you, did I? They wanted to surprise Riva with a kitten..."

It was now Tilly's turn to cry copiously, "My darling, darling, darling boys! Bless them. What pure gold they are, these children..." she babbled to a comprehensively touched room.

"They've called the kitten Rio. But I think it's a girl kitten... she's sleeping next to Mithu." Anay said with his first real smile of the long evening.

"I don't care if it is a girl or a boy or a half girl and half gargoyle. If my boys have decided its name is Rio, then it is Rio!" Tilly's flashing eyes dared anyone to challenge her. And the mood broke. Although it was still raining and very dark outside, it felt like dawn had broken.

Everyone was talking at once. The relief, the gratitude was overwhelming. They were all talking over one another, across the room, when Rekha said in a small voice, "Mom, can you send all my stuff over when you get back to your place?"

At first, no one heard her. So she repeated herself. This time, much louder.

For a moment there was complete silence.

And then Rekha Jaisingh's mother replied, without batting an eyelid, "Sure."

Chapter 26

"So, you've gone back to Anay's place?" Gajju's eyes were fire when they looked at Rekha across a small table at the New Coffee House.

She wasn't aware of the bristle in her voice when she answered, "Yes, I've gone back home."

They seemed to be meeting more and more often nowadays. Sometimes over coffee, sometimes just for a walk, sometimes for dinner. Gajju had been telling her stories from his world. It was an exquisite, exotic world. The long nights he spent under the stars somewhere in the Sahara just so he could he get the perfect shot of the moving dunes as the first rays of the sun turned the black sand to pink gold; the time when he was in Kenya and had seen a giraffe give birth; his thrilling assignment with the Indian Army when he had been taking photos of the daredevilry of the commandos and he had been half hanging out of a helicopter to get the angle he wanted and had almost fallen out. Her heart had been hammering wildly when he had told her that last story. Her knuckles clutching her glass of wine - they had been at dinner at a swanky Italian restaurant - had turned a ghostly white around the fine stem. She had actually felt sick, like she was going to throw up on the damask laid out in front of her. Gajju had noticed. So he had moved on quickly to another story – a funny one about a dog chasing him up a tree after he had tried to take pictures of her cute new pups in a posh suburb of New York.

Raghu Kaka had continued to ignore them. He'd been getting increasingly more unfriendly every time that he saw just the two of them together at the New Coffee House. And Rekha, although she would never admit it to anyone, knew exactly why. So that day, when Gajju stepped outside to take a work call (it was too noisy inside to talk work with a Japanese client) Rekha called out to Raghu Kaka, "Kaka…!" And almost sullenly he sauntered over and said, "More coffee? You've already had 3 glasses… but, whatever, you know what is good for you and what is not…"

"Kaka…" Rekha's voice faltered, her eyes lowered. "I only wanted to thank you for coming home to see Rishu and Mithu. They really loved the idli sambar you had packed for them." "Got it from home, not from the restaurant kitchen" he gruffly replied. "I know, Kaka" Rekha's eyes filled with tears "thank you so much!"

"Don't thank me… maybe I shouldn't have given you that damned photo…"

Before he could say anything else Gajju was back. Raghu Kaka gave him a reproachful glare and asked him, "When are you going back to your fancy America-Shamerica?"

"Why would I go back, Kaka? I'm home for good…"Gajju answered

………

"He's home for good?!!" Zoya almost yelled.

It was a busy Monday morning and Zoya and Zaid were at work, together, trying to make up for lost time. The team was in, the place was buzzing with the familiar energy that had been missing in the four plus months when the brother and sister had been at odds. But Zoya's voice rose over the buzz as she heard Maya's news. She took in the startled expression of the people on the floor and hurried back into her own cabin, continuing in a quieter but hardly less indignant voice, "And what does he intend to do here? Take pictures of the Aga Khan Palace? Who does he think he is fooling? Can Rekha not see what he is trying to do!!!"

"I know..." Maya sighed, sounding more than a little resigned. "I don't understand Rekha right now. She's chosen to go back to Anay's place; yet she's hanging out all the time with Gajju. I mean, it's so obvious, right? She can't not know how he feels about her! And she practically told us the other day that she was in love..."

"Yeah! What was that! What were her exact words – 'I think, finally, I'm beginning to understand this whole love thing'. What does she think she is doing! My God, I really, really, really don't want to go all judgemental on her... but I think she's enjoying making Anay miserable" Zoya was breathing fire.

"You think that's what she's doing?" Maya's voice was surprised.

And the surprise in her voice made Zoya stop short.

"Isn't that what she is doing? I mean, I thought it was obvious..."

"Really?"

"I think so... see, when I was mad at Zaid, my whole life was all about making him see how much he had hurt me."

The usually highly insightful Maya Wagh had hung up the phone after that conversation with Zoya's casual observation nagging at the back of her mind. Over the past couple of months Maya had grown more and more restless. And a terrible thing was growing silently inside her. Resentment. She didn't hate her husband, she resented him.

Every morning when he left for work, she felt a bitterness in her throat when she said to him, "Have a good day!"

And then there were the children. And the house. And her in-laws. And her parents. And her friends. And the problems of the various maids and drivers and watchmen. So many people. And they all gobbled up her time. Everyone seemed to be so involved with their own little dramas that no one noticed the cracks appearing inside Maya.

People living on fault lines know that feeling. When the earth trembles and everything sways. If they are very lucky, the tremor passes after causing nothing more than a few moments of heart-stopping terror. If they are not, then they face devastation.

What is true of the earth, is true of her people. Fault lines sometimes develop where the person was once whole and unbroken. And then all bets are off.

What does it take for us to be torn into such seismic disorder, teetering on the verge of cataclysmic upheavals? And how come no one notices? Walk around the unbearable chaos of Delhi, and you won't for a moment guess that you are on anything but stable ground. But that's not true. Delhi sits on three major fault lines and a major quake could flatten the beating heart of a nation.

"Why has this crust fallen apart!" Maya cursed silently under her breath. She had been working on a simple Vicotria sponge when she had made that call to Zoya. "How can I be so stupid? How can I mess up a basic Victoria sponge? And I think I want to bake for the rest of my life?"

She was berating herself viciously, but silently, when Shaila Wagh sauntered into Maya's beautiful sunlit kitchen and tapped her daughter lightly on her shoulder.

"Ma!" Maya whirled around and almost dropped the bag of icing sugar in her hand. "What are you doing here on a Monday morning? Aren't you supposed to be at that awful kitty of the truly terrible Wagh tribe?" Maya had never really forgiven her father's extended family for not standing up for her mother against her virago of a grandmother.

"I bunked" there was a naughty twinkle in Shaila Wagh's kind old eyes.

"Ma!!!" Maya groaned. "Who uses the word 'bunked' anymore? Where are we? In the 1980s! Ma, seriously..." she ended lamely, half laughing, half aghast.

Shaila serenely draped her silk ikkat duppatta around one of the many elegant chairs strewn around that tastefully done kitchen, turned to face her daughter with her hands on her hips and a broad smile on her lovely face and said, "No more cheek from you, young lady. I will say what I want. I'm too happy to be here instead of in the middle of that coven of witches to care which decade I'm living in..."

"Now come on, make me a cup of that masala tea of yours, and don't tell me you've polished off those amazing ginger cookies you made last week. Although with those two boys in the house, I don't expect anything to last for more than a couple of hours. Honestly, Maya, the stuff you bake is impossible to resist!"

It's a thing. A Mom thing. Or at least, it's a good Mom thing. Good Moms know exactly what to say and when. Shaila Wagh had dutifully attended the Wagh Women kitty for at least the past 25 years. Every third Monday the women of the Wagh family got together at someone's house for a morning of pure misery. The rules were very strict. All the food had to be home cooked. The home had to be spotless. Everyone had to come dressed in their very best. Sometimes, they even had a theme. Like that horrific year when they decided to dedicate every kitty to a particular weave of India. And Shaila had lost it when she had heard the youngest Wagh Woman declare pompously, "Next month we should all wear a Karavati from Vidarbha! After all, there is more to our weaves than the Paithani!"

Shaila hadn't even heard of the Karavati, let alone possessed one. She had come back home fuming, and hadn't realised that her tyrant of a mother-in-law had entered the kitchen where she was quietly ranting to her daughters. The next week, a package had arrived home from the dry-cleaners. Senior Mrs Wagh had been haranguing one of the poor maids about the right way to pick methi when one of the drivers had brought the plastic bag into the house. "Shaila" she had called out imperiously "take this into your room."

"What is it, Aai?"

"Do as you are told."

There had been the customary burning at the edges of her heart, but Shaila had done as she had been told. She had opened the package to find the most exquisite saree she had ever laid her eyes on. Stunned, she had walked back into the living room to ask her mother-in-law "Aai, what is this?!!"

"A Karavati. It's my mother's. Keep it. Give it to one of the girls one day" she hadn't even looked up from her newspaper to answer her daughter-in-law.

"It's beautiful... but why?" Shaila's voice had been filled with awe.

Both Maya and her sister Mandy had been in the living room then; both had unselfconsciously drawn in their breaths and waited for what they had known would be a whiplash of an answer.

But that day, Aaji had surprised everyone. "Wear it. I was never beautiful enough to drape it. You are. Go show those women what real beauty looks like." And with that she had folded up her newspaper with a crisp snap and barked out some instruction to the gardener who had come in to tend to their vegetable garden.

Maya didn't know why she had thought of that hazy memory, but she asked her mother, "Mom, you remember that saree Aaji gave you? The Karavati? You still have it? Did you wear it?"

"Of course I have it" Shaila's eyes moistened and her voice softened. "That was her most precious gift to me; after your Baba, that is..." The sadness lingered on in her voice.

"I don't know how you do it, Ma. She has always been so evil to you. And you never retaliated. You were always so kind to her. Even now, after all these years of living with her, you've never once spoken of how horrible she was to you. And no" Maya gestured to her mother to stop her before she could even open her mouth. "Ma, no... please don't start. Don't tell me how she isn't really all that bad and how she meant well. She was a monster! And Baba... oh my goodness, don't even get me started on how he absolutely deified her. Ma... how can you be like this? How can you not let it bother you?"

This was not a new conversation. Shaila had heard it all before. From both her daughters, but even more so from Maya. Mandy hadn't been that keenly observant. Privately, Shaila had always thought that her younger daughter was the luckier of the two – Mandy didn't feel as deeply as Maya did; she loved and lived with an easiness that was somehow missing from Maya. Maya had always been outraged at the way she had been treated by her mother-in-law. But Shaila had always chosen to head Maya off, distract her, pacify her and sometimes even share a little mischievous gossip with her every time that she brought up the topic.

Today, however, with a mother's unerring instinct for what she believed her child needed, Shaila Wagh sat back in a comfortable chair in her daughter's kitchen, and told her the story of her relationship with her mother-in-law.

"I was a young bride, Maya bala" she began, that old term of endearment rolling off her tongue with an old, old ease. "You've heard from me so often what it was like back then – the huge family, your Baba's unquestioning adoration of his mother, your Aaji's dictatorial nature... But you know, when I think back, I think she was just very lonely."

"You have got to be joking, Ma! Please don't tell me you are going all Dr Phil on that old devil" Maya scoffed, the rebellious eleven-year-old never too far below the surface when it came to the tumultuous and tenuous relationship with her paternal grandmother.

Shaila put up a restraining hand, smiled a sad little smile and continued, almost to herself, "No... think about it. She was only 13 when she got married. She was Aba's second wife, his first wife died after being married to him for ten years. They say Aba never ever really got over her. And maybe, at some level I understand that too – they were both 16 when they got married, it was a love marriage, which in itself was a huge rarity in those days, and then they went to college together, they practiced law together. I think she had some sort of cancer that killed her. But, whatever, she died, he was heartbroken at 26..."

"How come they didn't have any kids?" Maya asked the question that had been taboo in the family, no one was allowed to discuss Aba's first marriage.

"I don't know, but I think that was part of the problem – she died because she had some sort of cervical cancer or something. I only know that Aaji was chosen by Aba's parents. She came from a village back home, she was considered to be 'good and healthy'; they had had enough of their son's strong-headedness. The whole – you did what you wanted and see where it got you, so now you do as we tell you – routine. I remember, once, just after I had got married, one of your Aaji's aunts-in-law had cackled within my hearing – 'Moru Anna should never have got married to this one, but what to do, that first one died, and without any children; he had to have children, no? But what a let-down! That one was so beautiful, and this one – dark and flat-chested. And after so much of a fuss she could only give him one child. Poor Anna!' Women can be so evil, Maya. What a mean thing to say, especially in front of a new daughter-in-law!"

Maya sat in round-eyed wonder. She had never thought of her Aaji as anything but draconian and in control. For the first time she felt stirrings of something other than anger and grudging respect for the most overbearing presence of her childhood – and it tasted like empathy.

Shaila in the meanwhile continued "I know one thing for a fact – your Aaji loved your Aba with a desperation that was completely out of her control. I have seen how her eyes used to follow him as he went about his daily business, how she would hang on to his every word. And your Aba, I feel, never even realised it. He died completely unaware of how much his second wife adored the ground he walked on. Aba's heart died with his first wife. Or maybe he was always like that – head in the clouds, oblivious to the world around him. I have no way of knowing. But I saw that he always kept a picture of his first wife in the old drawing room, in his copy of Hamlet. Romeo and Juliet would have been too obvious, maybe. And that big picture of hers on the wall, next to the pictures of his parents? He always personally dusted all three pictures himself, even after he grew old and it was difficult for him to get up on that rickety chair to reach the pictures. Once, I remember, your Baba offered to get the pictures fixed lower on the wall so that he could reach them. And he had replied, 'Shekhar, they can't come down to me, I have to go up to them'. Your Aaji had been in the room then. I will never forget the look on her face. She looked like all the life had been sucked out of her. I don't think he even noticed. And that was pretty much her whole life. A thin, dusky woman fighting a lonely, hopeless and utterly pointless battle against a ghost and a memory."

"Now you are just romanticising the whole thing, Ma..." Maya's voice was hushed and lacking in conviction as she tentatively broke into her Mother's musings.

"I don't know, bala" Shaila sighed into her masala chai. "Maybe I am... but it mustn't have been easy for her. You know how obsessed everyone in the clan is about fair skin and green eyes. Aaji wasn't dark by any stretch of the imagination, but she wasn't fair. Imagine how much grief that would have caused her back then. She used to tell us these stories of how, in her time, people in Pune would put up notices that went 'Please don't bother to walk up the stairs for a conversation if your daughter / the bride-to-be is not fair skinned'. She used to say it lightly and scoff at it, but I always saw how hurt she was. And remember how proud she was of your Baba's skin! Even when the two of you were born, she didn't ask whether the baby was a boy or a girl, she only asked, 'is it fair?'

She was always extraordinary in her own way. She turned all her energy into the kitchen. Her kitchen garden was legendary. And her food was manna from heaven. The only time that Aba would notice her was at the dining table. He loved the food she prepared. He refused to eat anything that was not prepared by her. Towards the end he would insist that she sat and ate with him. That was the happiest I have ever seen your Aaji.

Anyway, too much of that old biddy. Tell me about your next dream recipe" Shaila smiled warmly up at her daughter. Normally, Maya would have rushed into a detailed description of whatever new concoction was swirling around in her head. But today she hesitated and asked, "Ma, you really think he noticed her cooking?"

And Shaila Wagh, once again with the unerring instinct of a

mother replied, "Men are strange creatures. They don't really know the right things to notice. Your Aba definitely noticed her cooking. But she wasn't an artist. She was just a sad woman in love. And she would have been happier if he had noticed the dimple on her cheek."

Maya sighed heavily as she shut the lid on the airtight container of ginger cookies "Yeah, maybe she was just stupid. She should have been happy that he noticed her food."

And Shaila Wagh's eyes grew a little older with worry as she saw the struggles of a grandmother live on in the battle of her granddaughter. As that August morning drizzled its way into a sleepy afternoon, Shaila Wagh sent up a little prayer to the God of Happiness, "Give her what her heart longs for, dear God; or give her heart new eyes!"

Chapter 27

(AUGUST 24 2016)

They had all given up. Somehow, it had all failed. The big dream project. The Party. Looked like it was not going to happen. For the entire month, all four women had simply stopped exercising. It was either raining too much, or there were meetings, or Rekha was hanging out with Gajju, or Zoya was travelling or Maya was travelling. For an entire month – nothing.

"It's all because of that shopping trip" Tilly grumbled. "We jinxed ourselves. And all that food that you keep dishing out to us, Maya! How are we ever going to get back on track" she ended with a cooing sound. Lately it had been impossible for Tilly to stay in a bad mood. And Rio was to blame.

Riva and Rio were inseparable. The kitten had been vaccinated and groomed and handed over to Riva immediately after Rekha's boys had returned home with her. And it had been love at first sight. No one could keep the two apart. Riva had even taken Rio to her school one day! She had begged and begged and begged Tilly to bring Rio along. So, with permission from the angelic Principal of Riva's pre-school, they had pulled off a 'bring a pet to school' day. It was complete chaos. The dogs and cats did NOT get along. But the children had had so much fun! One half of the bungalow in which Riva's pre-school had spread itself had been given over to the dogs, the other half to the cats. And it was quite fascinating how the little children had simply blossomed in the presence of these pets.

"The best part was when the kids who had started off being afraid of the critter people just crossed some sort of internal threshold and started enjoying themselves. There was in particular this one little fellow called Aryan. He had been whimpering and hiding behind furniture. And he screamed when our tiny little Rio walked straight up to him. But Rio is an angel. She just stood there, stock still, and turned the megawatt power of her kitten eyes on that boy. In no time at all he was scampering around the place with Rio in his pocket, making friends with all the other cats! He didn't quite manage to make friends with the dogs... but I think the world just found another old cat lady. Except she's trapped inside the body of a very young boy whose chin dimples when he smiles..."

Tilly kept up this monologue, unmindful of the highly amused looks on the faces of the adults gathered in her quirky, fun, cheerful drawing room. Unmindful, because she hadn't even seen them; she had eyes only for Rio who was doing unimaginably cute kitten stuff to entertain herself. The fact that Tilly was riveted and fascinated and completely in love was incidental for the kitten-in-command.

"Cats are amazing creatures" Anay remarked casually. "Dogs, they are just goofballs of love, and they love everybody. But you should watch out for cats. If a cat loves you, then you must be really, really special."

"Did he just say 'goofballs of love'?!!" Zoya, who had been increasingly more and more her old self, shrieked from the other end of the room where she had been rifling through Tilly's collection of old photographs. "My, my, Mr Jaisingh! What are you? A hippie at heart? How come we never got to see this side of you, huh?"

Anay blushed slightly at the ribbing and sent a quick glance in the direction of his wife. Rekha, however, seemed withdrawn; she was chewing on her lower lip, staring at her phone. And Anay's smile vanished; his eyes resumed that haughty, distant look that his rivals in the business world had come to fear.

"She seems to be doing that a lot lately" Maya remarked quietly to Tilly. Tilly looked up long enough from Rio's antics to look at what Maya was saying. She too saw it. Rekha, sitting in the middle of loved ones, yet withdrawn into some unreachable corner of her own self. Rekha, staring at her phone, oblivious to all else.

While everyone else fidgeted nervously and seemed at a loss to handle the sudden awkward silence, it was Zoya's mature, worldly wise husband Asif who smoothly pressed a drink into Anay's unresisting hand and guided him onto Tilly's terrace garden. "I'm not the kind of chap to normally notice such things, but even I have to see that this place is like something out of a fairy tale! I don't know how our mad woman Tilly manages to do these things, but she can add a little bit of magic to almost everything she touches..."

Maybe it was the quiet assurance in Asif's voice, the unhurried pace of his conversation, or the whiff of some indefinable flower that hung lightly in the damp air; whatever might be the reason, the tightness in Anay's chest slowly but surely dissipated, his breathing returned to normal and he even found himself relaxing into an intelligent conversation about the Game Theory and its relevance to their respective businesses.

"What are you guys talking about?" Tilly butted in, Rio firmly in place in the front pocket of the ridiculous apron she had taken to wearing. Her reasoning, "What can I do if I was not born a kangaroo?" It was that typical Tilly brand of unreason that had had all her friends and family falling under her spell for as long as anyone could remember. And today was no different. She plonked herself and her precious Rio on a toadstool that she had fashioned out of an abandoned tree stump from the University and effortlessly drew Asif and Anay into an uproarious conversation about circus tents and how she had always imagined that the Big Top was actually the petticoat of some giant woman; stolen from her by mischievous imps. Now, there was nothing really funny about this. Especially since it came from a grown woman who had no business talking about giants and imps as if they were real. But Tilly had this gift – she could make the impossible seem normal; she could make two men who were serenely discussing advanced economics participate vigorously in a conversation that was sublime in its absurdity.

Rekha, however, remained hopelessly unaware of any of this.

She had drifted off silently into Tilly's bedroom which was populated by the kids who were engaged in a boisterous game of speed chess. It was a silly game, invented by the two oldest children – Maya's firstborn Tuhin and Rekha's older son Rishabh; and it involved all the chess pieces talking (yelling) loudly at one another and generally behaving in a most undignified manner on the chess board. Rekha slunk into an overstuffed armchair in the farthest corner of Tilly's room and curled into herself, pretending to be interested in the game, but actually far, far away in her own mind.

It was Anay's casual remark about cats that had set her off. She'd never been able to bring herself to really love another cat after Mowgli. So she hadn't been paying too much attention to all the silly banter around Tilly and Rio. But Anay had said something that had made her catch her breath. "You should watch out for the people who cats love" he had said. "They are the ones who are special…"

And her mind had whirred back to the days of college. Those long hours of watching Mowgli watch Gajju as if he were the only person on the planet. Those blue eyes never strayed too far from Gajju's face; every time he spoke, it felt like Mowgli was listening. He would sidle up to Gajju, rub against his legs and generally behave extremely clingy for a tom cat. "That cat is not normal" she would tease Gajju. "He is just an old puppy! Next thing you know he'll start wagging his tail and barking at other cats. And postmen. And milkmen." Rekha remembered how much she used to laugh at her own silly jokes about the love affair between Gajju and Mowgli. But Gajju would never laugh at his Mowgli. He was seriously, steadfastly in love with that cat. And that cat was in love with him. "So, now what? Just because that blessed cat loved him, and because Anay says that cats only love very special people, does that mean Gajju is special? What rubbish! Anay thinks he knows everything. Who does he think he is? Making statements like that and making them sound as if they were gospel truths?" And just as she would be building up a head full of steam about how annoying and presumptuous and smug Anay was, an unbidden memory would sneak up. Gajju laughing with his head thrown back and the sun catching his shiny hair, Mowgli riding on Gajju's shoulder as if he belonged there, Mowgli and Gajju sauntering side by side down the long driveway that led away from the Main Building of the college, Gajju with his hands in his pockets, whistling his tuneless tunes, Mowgli matching his pace, looking equally at ease with his place in the world.

"I think I am going completely crazy. I can't go on like this. I have to do something. I have to stop!!!"

Rekha stood up with a jerky movement and almost fell over onto the children's chess board. Ruffling the tousled curls of Zoya's Samar and murmuring a hurried, "Enjoy your game, bachcha party!" Rekha almost ran out to join the rest of the gang.

"People! Anyone wants to play Antakshari?"

No one responded. Because no one noticed. Everyone was too busy having a really good time. And Rekha felt her sense of desolation and disconnect deepen. It was like she was an onlooker at a film set. Even worse, it was like she was an outsider.

The occasion for the impromptu dinner was a typical Tilly non-occasion. The house had been decked up in candles and crazily patterned cushions and throws and rugs. Chintzy florals and big, bold stripes sat comfortably together on her random collection of seating options – an oversized sofa here, an old trunk there, low chairs, high stools. Everything about Tilly's home was a statement – and that statement was Tilly. Not that she ever set about to make any statements. She didn't need to. Tilly was one of those forces of nature, making her presence felt simply by existing. Today she had invited some of the people she loved most on the planet to a "Welcome home, Rio" party. And while she claimed that it was Riva who was most in love with the precious kitten, the kangaroo apron gave her away completely.

"She needs a man in her life" Maya was startled by the quiet murmur of Arvind's voice in her ears. There had been a strange new dynamic developing between the two of them. Maya had found herself increasingly resentful of her fulfilled husband, so she had been withdrawing from him more and more, almost but not quite without realising it. The thing was, the more she withdrew, the more he seemed to want to get closer. Quite literally. "Why does he have to sidle up to me like this? Breathing heavily onto my neck like some lust-struck teenager? What's the matter with this man?" Maya thought all of this, and said none of it. For a brief moment her jaw clenched and little white spots appeared at the corners of her tightly pursed lips. But years and years of training in the tradition of women who managed to conquer unruly emotions took over, her jaw loosened up and she asked instead, "Tilly? Why do you say that? She seems perfectly happy to me..."

"I don't know. I just thought she seems lonely..."

And just like that a hot flare of anger ripped through Maya's hard won composure "Not everyone needs a man to feel fulfilled. And what's the point of having a man in your life if he is blind to what makes you happy? Tilly has something no man can give her – she does what she loves and loves what she does. Just, just... stop." Arvind had reached out to put his hand around her waist and draw her closer to him. Normally, she would have given in to the unspoken demand of his hand, knowing what was to come later in the night. But lately, she had found herself resisting more and more often. After that first time when she had sent him off to bed alone she had never outright refused him sex. But she had found these other ways of resisting. She would purposefully stand as far from him as possible in public gatherings, she'd move her shoulders just enough so that it would be impossible for him to slip a casual arm around them, she'd suddenly be hugging one of the children so that Arvind couldn't hug her when he left for work. Little acts of rebellion. Some things never change. There had been that eleven year old Maya who had stuck out her lower lip and devised small ways of rebelling against the unrelenting control of her grandmother. And there was this Maya who continued to orchestrate little rebellions. Except, this time, the enemy was within. Not that she knew that, of course.

Tilly had seen that little interlude between Maya and Arvind. She couldn't hear what they had been speaking about, which was a good thing of course, or she wouldn't have been quite so considerate towards Arvind. But she saw Maya push his encircling hand away, she caught the anger in Maya's flared nostrils and the quick hurt in Arvind's retracted hand.

A word that she had used earlier in the evening strayed back into Tilly's head "Have we all just jinxed ourselves? It seems like yesterday when everything was absolutely perfect. And in the space of a few short months everything feels like its falling apart. As if the Anay and Rekha thing was not bad enough, now what's up with Maya and Arvind! And to think we've called her P Reks for so long. Perfectosaurus Reks – what a joke, she's such a mess. Thank God Zoya's fixed that whole Zaid issue, though. It would have been too much if that were still festering!"

The evening smiled and laughed and sang on. But the pieces didn't fit any more. The edges were jagged, and the patterns made no sense. It was like someone had taken a well settled jigsaw puzzle and not simply messed it up, but added new pieces to it, changed the frame, thrown away the old one.

There was no going back to how things were. There never really is. But that evening, as Tilly watched over the ebb and flow of life, love and laughter passing between her closest friends, an unbidden lump formed in her throat and something stung her eyes.

"Is the Party over? Is the party over? Thank God" she said for the second time that evening "thank God for Zoya. And her family. May they always stay happy and together."

There was a loud uproar from the children's room. Someone had managed to kill someone else's queen; and some kids found something about it very funny.

The adults too joined in in the general ruckus, with Zoya and her older son Sikandar doing a little victory dance. Tilly's sombre moment passed; the party came back to life.

And then Asif died.

He collapsed in the middle of Tilly's dining room. One moment he was laughing and joking and helping himself to a slice of pizza. The next moment the plate had slipped out of his hands, he had fallen to the floor, and died. Just like that.

For a split second no one reacted. And then everything moved as if in a Tarantino movie. Split screen, fast, dark, incomprehensible.

Within 4 minutes of his collapsing they were inside the Emergency Room of the hospital that Tilly's apartment block shared a common wall with. Anay and Arvind were superhuman in their strength and agility. And in their presence of mind. They didn't waste a second trying amateurish CPR. The moment they realised they couldn't find a pulse, they carried him out of Tilly's first floor apartment and rushed into the hospital next door.

But the doctors confirmed that his heart had simply stopped beating.

In the span of a few seconds, Asif Quettawala, 45, successful lawyer, great husband, extraordinary father, perfect son, perfect son-in-law, exemplary friend, and an exceptionally good human being was snatched from the world. In front of the disbelieving eyes of the three people who lived and breathed because of him.

In the span of a few seconds, Zoya Quettawala died too. Only, her breaths kept coming. And she didn't know why.

Chapter 28

(August 31, 2016)

"She hasn't said a word to anyone except the kids. She won't talk to anyone. She won't cry in front of anyone. Please, Anu, please tell me what I can do to help her" Zaid wept uninhibitedly into the bosom of his wife and his dearest friend Anu. He had maintained an outward composure for far too long now. But the dam had been breached after he had seen Zoya hum quietly, holding Asif's picture close to her heart. He had walked into her room tentatively, hoping she would speak to him. But the only acknowledgement that she gave of his presence was that she stopped humming. She continued to sit with Asif's picture hugged in an embrace, rocking back and forth as if comforting a distressed child.

No amount of loud crying could have undone Zaid as much as the heart-rending calm of Zoya's countenance. There was desolation in her quietness, far beyond the reach of tears, far beyond the comfort of shedding them.

"There's nothing, nothing, nothing that is left for her, for us. Asif is gone, Anu. He's gone. My Asif is never coming back, Anu!"

Zaid cried like a little boy. He cried till he was exhausted. And then he slept. For the first time in a week, Zaid slept.

It was early in the day. The boys had gone to school. Zoya had dropped them. She had hugged them tightly to herself, as if willing some courage and strength to pass between their skins. Whether from her to them or them to her though, she wasn't quite sure. And as she had let them enter school she had said to them, "We love you. Dad and Mom, both of us, we love you."

Anu covered a sleeping Zaid with a thin sheet and looked up to see Zoya standing in the doorway. Zoya silently motioned for Anu to follow her, and she did.

It was over a cup of tea that Zoya had made for them in the kitchen that she uttered her first words to an adult in a week, "I have nothing to say."

And Anu simply sat there, one arm around the young woman she loved as if she were her own sister.

"Do you want me to wake Zaid up?" Anu asked gently, after a while.

And Zoya who had reverted into her open-eyed semi-comatose state came back to life. She grabbed at Anu and said with something close to panic in her voice, "Anu, please! Please! Not Zaid. I don't want Zaid." There was something fierce, almost feral about her when she repeated, "Not Zaid. He is the last person I want just now."

Anu felt pain sear through her body like a hot rod, pain for her husband, pain for her sister-in-law, for the young family ripped apart by a violence not of their doing. And she wanted to scream. But she forced herself to remain calm, "Whatever you need, babe. Absolutely anything you need."

"You know, I don't have a problem with going to sleep. I have nothing against it. I only try and stay awake because it's the waking up that I can't handle" Zoya spoke into her mug of tea.

She looked up for a moment and saw the question on Anu's face. She didn't have the strength for an explanation, but she sighed heavily, took a deep breath and with a visible effort tried one, "When I sleep, I forget, Anu. It's those few moments of transitioning between sleeping and fully waking up that I can't face. For just a few moments as I am struggling to wake up, I think he is still here, that I have to tell him about some ridiculous dream I saw or that he has to drop the kids to school and I have to wake him up so that he doesn't get late. For just those few moments, I forget, Anu. And then I remember. I can't face waking up every day, Anu. I never want to sleep again."

The tears were flowing freely down Anu's face. But Zoya remained dry eyed.

For the rest of the day, Zoya did not utter a single word to anyone other than her children who came back from school in better shape than anyone had anticipated.

It was around 7 in the evening when Tilly got up and announced to everyone, "I'm getting her to talk. I don't care what happens."

Everyone had been coming to Zoya's house every day for the past week. The house was constantly full of people. Zoya's parents, her in-laws, Asif's younger brother and his family who had flown in from Singapore, Zaid, Anu, their kids, and all of Zoya's friends and their families – everyone was there. And yet, none of them had been able to reach Zoya. She had shut herself off from the world and no one could seem to find a way in to the maximum security prison that she had locked herself into.

But today, Tilly had made up her mind that she was going to succeed or die trying.

So she took the young Rio in her hands for moral support, straightened her shoulders and marched into Zoya's sanctuary. She entered without knocking, prepared to do battle with her dear friend if needed. But Zoya surprised her with a wan smile. She took Rio into her hands, buried her face in her soft fur, took a deep, deep, breath and said to Tilly, "Is everyone here? I have something to say..."

And then Zoya spoke. She spoke as if every word was costing her; as if every sound escaped her after an enormous internal battle. But she spoke.

"Thank you for being so patient with me" she began. Her father and brother almost stood up to protest, one could almost see their "We love you, what has patience got to do with this, we are here for you" outpourings forming in their mouths; but their respective wives restrained them and both kept a vice-like grip on their respective men for the rest of Zoya's monologue.

"I have nothing to say" Zoya continued, unaware of the brief moment of melodrama that had just unfolded. "Which is why I have said nothing for these past days. But I love all of you, and I know you love me; and I know that I owe you an explanation. Not only of the past few days after Asif decided to die" Asif's mother quite understandably bristled at this and almost came to her feet in outrage, but Asif's brother Hussain had his mother tucked into his arm, so he managed to quieten her down. "Not only since Asif decided he had had enough" Zoya continued, "but also of the days to come. I have nothing to say because I don't have the words. I don't know which words can be used to describe what I feel. What was between Asif and I was between only the two of us. I don't know what to say about that thing we had, that life we had, that 'Us' that we were, that will have any meaning to anyone else. Maybe it will, but it won't mean to anyone else what it meant to us. So, what's the point of talking about it? And, there are no words. I have no words."

Zoya was becoming more and more agitated as every impossible word made it past the barrier of her lips. Many people in the room were crying silently. Zoya's mother's white duppatta was soaked through with tears. But Zoya went on, "I am in so much pain that I cannot tell you. Every breath feels like my insides are on fire. I don't think this is going away anywhere, anytime soon. For a couple of days after he died I thought I should die too. But I am not going to. Not if I can help it."

Asif's mother could take this no longer. She pushed herself out of her younger son's restraining arm and staggered up to her feet. "He did not decide to die. How dare you say things like that! He wouldn't have died if he could have helped it."

Hussain stood to stop his mother. But she held up her own hand imperiously, drew her tiny self up to her full height and marched straight out of her dead son's house. As she closed the door silently behind herself, it felt like she was walking out of her dead son's widow's life. Hussain followed after her, but no one else moved.

"I am not going to die. But I have no idea if I will ever live again. I have no plan. Except that for the sake of Sikander and Samar I am going to focus on doing what needs to be done. One breath at a time. I cannot bear the pain. But I don't see any other way. I will not complain about the pain. But please don't expect me to be better. I can't bear to see the worry on all of your faces. You have all done so much for me and the kids already. I am going to ask you to do one more thing – for the foreseeable future, I am going to ask you to not ask me how I am. Understand, for my sake, that nothing makes sense to me, every breath is torture, and I don't see this getting any better. I'm sorry that I'm repeating myself. But I've thought this through in all the time that I haven't spoken to anyone. And you know what, Zaidu – I'm not going to be turning to you. No, don't look like that. I love you more than you can ever know. But I've just realised something. These past few months it has been like life was showing me some secret, but I refused to see it. And my blindness caused me to lose both of you – both you and Asif. For months I had lost you. But life gave us both another chance. I have no chances left with Asif. And I feel like it was all my fault.

I lived my entire life in the powerful shadow of the two men who loved me, honoured me, protected me beyond belief. And I feel that I should have stepped out of that shadow to discover my own strength on my own. But I didn't. So God almost cut down one tree, and completely destroyed another.

I am nothing without you and Asif. And now Asif is gone. I can either cling desperately to the comfort of your shade, or I can step into the sunlight. I don't want to lose you too, Zaid. So, please, please, Zaidu, understand what I mean.

Today, I am nothing. But for the sake of Sikander, Samar, Asif,

Zaid, and all of you; but also for the sake of Zoya, I am going to change that. I don't know how. Except that I am going to do it one breath at a time."

And then Zoya went into her own room, quietly locked the door and cried the loud, racking, painful tears of those torn beyond repair.

When she emerged out of her room a good two hours later, assorted children were running around the house, the elders were having a quiet dinner, but a couple of smiles floated around the house.

Asif's portrait hung on the golden highlight wall in the drawing room. And under his ever-watchful eyes, his flock started to regroup.

One painful breath at a time.

Chapter 29

(September 1 - 3, 2016)

"Remember, we're supposed to be losing weight…" there was a little hint of humour in Zoya's shattered voice as she looked up from the gateau that Maya had insisted she eat. "I don't know why I made this… too much Harry Potter in my life because of the kids I guess… even I have started believing that chocolate makes you feel better…" Maya's voice trailed off.

She had felt more than a little lame. Truth be told, she had felt like a criminal. She had gone to bed the previous night with just one thought in her heart – "Tomorrow I'm baking that gateau that Pierre sent me the recipe for!" Pierre T (she didn't even know his name) was one of her many new friends on Instagram. She had started uploading pictures of her food on her insta page on a whim. And Tilly had taught her to use hashtags. Within a few months her page – ItsMaya – had become something of a sensation. She had followers from all over the world. And trading recipes had become one of Maya's most favourite things to do. After Asif's death she hadn't checked her page even once. But after Zoya had spoken last evening Maya had felt a sense of something loosening up inside the tight knot that she had tied her heart into. She had gone back home, her eyes swollen, her feet aching, but with a sensation of some light breaking through the darkness. She had made herself a cup of her favourite jasmine tea and retired to a corner in her large kitchen. There had been something indefinably therapeutic for Maya in the simple act of sitting on the floor. She had always felt most comfortable sitting cross-legged on floors. Her earliest memories were of catching suspended dust motes in the slanting ray of sunshine that would reach the cool floor of her maternal grandparents' cavernous kitchen back in the village, while sitting on the floor, waiting for the rest of the household to wake up. That day, as she had sunk down gratefully to the cool marble of her own modern kitchen, her eyes had welled up at the memory of the kind, quiet face of her maternal grandmother sitting by her side in that long-ago kitchen, telling her some silly story about a cow that ran away and the dog who simply wouldn't stop pining until she was found and brought back home. They had had this ritual – they would be the first to wake up and share a morning chat. Maya had always treasured that little slice of the morning. Every vacation she looked forward to sharing the silence and the rising sun with her beloved Mothi Aai.

Maybe some things stay with us forever. In our muscles.

It was muscle memory, then, that had led Maya to her favourite spot in the kitchen. And for the first time in forever she had looked at her Instagram page. That's when she had spotted the message from Pierre. He had sent her what he called his secret recipe for 'the world's most divine chocolate gateau'. It wasn't purely an act of generosity. She had first sent him her recipe for her signature carrot, beetroot and ginger cake. But she had forgotten how much she had wanted his recipe for the gateau after he had posted pictures and videos of what he had called a 'gateau gala'. The videos had been amazing. You could almost see the silkiness of the texture as guests cut through the sumptuous layers, you could see the layers spring lightly to the touch... the glistening, moist, delicious gateau with its rich fruit and cream had made Maya's heart do funny things. And she had been waiting for that recipe.

Now, she had it. And she had gone to bed clinging the recipe to her heart. She had woken up really early in the morning and rushed downstairs to her kitchen. There had been no other thought save her gateau for the entire time that she had been in the kitchen. Her hands had worked with a mind of their own. Her heart had skipped along. And without even noticing it, a little tune had found itself to her lips and escaped in the form of a whistle. Some people hum. Maya whistled. Another thing that her draconian paternal grandmother had never understood or forgiven.

After the gateau had been perfected, her heart had plunged down into her stomach, though. "What a terrible person I am! Look at me, whistling! I have to take this to Zo... how can I think of baking when she needs me...!"

Zoya's little smile as she ate that gateau, however, made Maya breathe a little easier. And in the minutes that followed, she felt like something changed. They didn't speak much. But whatever little they spoke of, it felt something close to normal. The kids' school. Rio the kitten. Professor Kadam from Tilly's days at University. Marie biscuits and how there could be no legitimate reason for their existence. Small, unrelated, unimportant conversation. But it felt like the world was tilting back into something resembling normal. And in the center of it all was the gateau. Zoya had reached out for a second helping. Then a third.

"Maybe that Lupin fellow is right. Maybe chocolate does help in fighting Dementors" Maya had thought silently to herself as she hovered watchfully over the fragile form of Zoya.

Zoya had lost weight dramatically. Her clothes hung off her, her skin looked like it someone had stretched it tight across her fine cheekbones.

"The thing about newspapers is that we are used to reading them. It's just not the same –reading the paper and browsing the phone…" Zoya was talking about another meaningless thing, whether newspapers would survive the digital age when Maya suddenly broke in, "I'm sending you food."

"What?" Zoya was sufficiently startled for a moment of genuine animation to touch her face.

Maya flushed deeply before saying, "Zo, it's the only thing I can do. And I don't know why, but I have to do it. For as long as I think it needs to be sent, I'm going to send you something I cook, every day."

The old Zoya would have laughed at this, she would have said something witty and got up and gone and hugged her friend for her stammering sincerity.

But the new Zoya simply said, "Okay."

And that was that.

Then there was Tilly. She did something completely out of character. She appointed herself as the morning walk companion of Zoya. Every morning, after the kids left for school, Tilly would be at Zoya's place. "I'm putting on all this weight. Can you help me shed it, Zo? I need you to come for a walk with me in the mornings. You know I'll never go out on my own… you know how I am about mornings and waking up. Asif" her voice nearly caught here, but she soldiered on "Asif always teased me about how I should be banned from mornings…"

Zoya noticed the tremble in Tilly's double chin. But she let that be too. Zoya was learning quickly to let some things be. She gave in to Tilly's blatantly connived plea for help. That it was such an obvious lie is what made her give in.

"Tilly is trying to pull off a Maya, Asif… imagine!" Zoya smiled into her mirror as she brushed her hair to head out for a walk with Tilly. She had suddenly become aware of a constant, unbroken conversation that she seemed to be having with her dead husband. He was her reference point, her sounding board, her confidante, her lover, her friend. And she had begun to realise that she wasn't going to let anything as paltry as death get in the way of that. So her conversation continued, "It's insane that she thinks that I believe her for a moment. I mean, it's not even as if we do anything like walk. We just stroll about peacefully, and then head over to the Uni canteen for chai… But why am I bothering to tell you all of this. You already know, don't you? You're up there, watching. And I'm blabbering away like a fool. Damn you, Asif. Just… damn, damn, damn you!" Her beautiful eyes filled up with water as she yanked hard at a particularly tough knot in her hair. The knot remained, but she ended up pulling out a clump of hair.

She looked at the knot in disgust. And anger. And something approaching hate. "Some knots cannot be untangled, they have to be yanked out and thrown away. What am I going to do with this knot in my heart? And my belly? And deep inside my bones, Asif? Can you even hear me, dammit!!!"

Zoya didn't even realise she had yelled out that last question. Tilly was at her door like a flash. And as she saw Zoya doubled over her dressing table, her body glimmering with an aura of visible pain, another piece of her heart broke. But she was made of sterner stuff than that – she would not let Zoya know anything of her own despair. She walked silently over to where her broken friend stood, gathered her in her arms as if she were gathering scattered bits of the wind, and led her gently out into the gloomy September day.

The one person who was conspicuous by her absence in the days that followed Asif's death was Rekha. She had been the one person that everyone had been counting on. And for the first couple of days she hadn't left Zoya's side. But after the funeral she had turned up increasingly rarely. She texted Zoya all the time. She kept telling her how much she loved her. But she did not come to visit.

"All she does is cry." Maya said to Arvind that evening.

"That's to be expected... Don't be so hard on her, Monu."

"Why is it to be expected? I can't believe you are saying this... How selfish of her!" Maya bristled in indignation.

"Selfish? I don't understand you women... she supposed to be your best friend, and this is how you speak of her!"

"You women? What do you mean by that!"

Their voices were rising by the second.

"Look, you can think what you want, but I believe Zoya deserves better than that..." Arvind was brooking no argument from his wife.

"I agree... that is exactly what I've been saying! How can she be so selfish? Zo needs us...!" Maya was now standing with her hands on her hips, her eyes shooting fire.

"What are you saying? Who is being selfish? Aren't you speaking about Zoya?" Arvind's bewildered expression might have been funny had Maya not begun to look like a thundercloud.

"Do you ever pay ANY attention to what I'm saying? I've been talking about Rekha all this time!" Maya spoke through clenched teeth, her voice taking on a dangerous calm.

"Oh! How was I supposed to know!" Arvind bewilderment turning to amusement until a cold look from his wife stopped it midway and it froze into some sort of tragi-comic snarl.

"By listening."

Maya wasn't one for dramatic flourishes. But her exit with a softly, but firmly closed door behind her left Arvind feeling like she had slammed the door in his face. And he should have followed her out. He should have gone into the kitchen and made her a cup of tea. And chatted with her and gotten her to laugh over the silly misunderstanding. But he didn't do easy. He had never gone after Maya. Literally, metaphorically, anything. A silly misunderstanding wasn't likely to change what felt like a lifelong dynamic. So, Arvind didn't follow Maya to calm her ruffled feathers. And Maya didn't expect him to.

Chapter 30

(September 5, 2016)

"You have taught me everything. Happy Teachers' Day." The text on her screen made Rekha's eyes water. Again.

She was completely exhausted.

She had never cried so much in all of her life. And she had been crying quite a bit in the past few months.

"It all started in February" she thought to herself. "And now this is September. Six months. All I've done in these past six months is cry. And Asif! Asif dead! I don't know how to handle this, I really don't. I know he wasn't my husband. I know this is about Zo and about little Samar and Sikandar. But how could he die! It's NOT fair!"

That voice in her head had been droning on and on like a broken record. And she had no idea how to get it to stop.

"I haven't been able to pull myself together to go see Zo... but I know she'll understand. And I know I'll figure out whatever it is that I'm trying to figure out. Then I'll go see her and I'll apologise and I'll explain it all to her!"

Anay walked past his beloved wife. And he wanted to reach out and he wanted to tell her that everything was going to be fine and he wanted to mean it. But he walked past her. And Rekha miserably read cold stiffness in his receding back where there was none.

"Anay..." she called out to him, unsure of why she did, unsure of what she wanted to say next. But he turned around as if whiplashed. And before she knew it, she blurted, "Could you take the day off?"

He simply dropped his briefcase where he was standing and said, "Sure."

They spent the whole day together that day. Doing nothing much. The Ganesh festival was usually a huge celebration in the Jaisingh household, because it was Rekha's favourite festival of the year. This year they had quietly installed the Ganesh idol the earlier day. The electrifying festivity of every year was missing. But the house still felt special. There was a calming, benevolent presence in the house. And as Anay and Rekha worked silently in the vegetable garden picking out fresh *durva* for the pooja, as they ate a peaceful lunch before the boys came home, as they discussed what should be prepared for the *prasad* in the evening (they agreed on ras malai, a first, who makes ras malai as prasad!), it was as if some great sorrow was being vanquished.

'They don't call him 'sukhakarta, dukhaharta' for nothing" Rekha's mother told her husband after she got off the phone with her grandson. "Anay took the day off. And he and Rekha 'hung out'. Mithu was telling me! Thank God... the girl seems to be seeing some sense finally!"

Rekha's mother had never castigated her. But she had never been able to fully support her daughter's decision to move out of her home. "What could she possibly be lacking!" she had constantly wondered. To her and her husband's credit though, they had never made Rekha feel unwelcome. Rekha's father had remained steadfastly optimistic. "She just needs some time. We've always expected her to be strong and sensible. And she has never disappointed us. So maybe she is being unreasonable, but it's Rekha. She'll figure it out. We simply have to give her time; and a place to anchor down in when there is a storm…"

Rekha's mother had rolled her eyes privately at the storm metaphor. She thought it was excessive. But she had played along. For a while. When she had noticed an increase presence of Gajju in Rekha's conversation she had been alarmed. "What does she think she is doing? And why is that fellow back again? Doesn't she remember how badly he had treated her!" she had said on more than one occasion to her husband. One day she had even plucked up her courage and called up Maya. But Maya had reassured her, "Don't worry, maushi. Rekha is a good, responsible girl. Let's give her some time…"

That time which everyone had wanted to give Rekha seemed to have come to an end today. And Rekha's mother sent up a prayer of fervent gratitude to Ganpati Bappa.

Back in the Jaisingh household though, nothing dramatic happened. In fact, nothing much happened at all. So Anay could not quite explain why he felt like an enormous weight had been lifted off his shoulders and his chest. When the family gathered around Bappa for the evening aarti, he couldn't explain why he felt like everything was right with his world.

As for Rekha, ever since Anay had uttered his simple 'Sure' in response to her request to take the day off, she had not looked at her phone even once. It was only as she was tucking the children in for the night that she realised she didn't even know where her phone was. "Good night, babies..." she whispered softly as she switched off the lights in their room. "Good night, Ma..." her boys sleepily murmured back. As she softly closed their door behind her she stood undecided for a split second. Just for a split second she almost chose to go looking for her phone. But then she chose differently. With new found purpose Rekha Jaisingh turned her back on her phone, on Gajju, on Zoya, on her other friends, on her parents, on everybody else in the world and walked into a peach and white bedroom where Anay waited. Quietly.

And she sat herself down on the corner of her large bed and asked Anay, "Why did you look happy when I said I wanted a divorce?" Now, we have to feel for Anay. He was almost happy. And he had watched Rekha entering their bedroom with something approaching hope. If he had been hoping for a passionate ending to a peaceful day, then this question was enough to douse any glowing embers. So, there was an understandable slackening of the jaw when he heard Rekha's question. His customary reserve deserted him and he said, "What? Are you mad? I was happy? Are you mad?"

And Anay Jaisingh did something he had never done before. He stormed out of their bedroom in his immaculate pajamas, didn't even bother to slam the door on his way out, grabbed the keys to his car and drove off into the night.

It should have scared Rekha. It should have upset her. It should have made her feel anything other than relaxed. But as she watched her husband drive roughly out of the gate, Rekha Jaisingh's shoulder's relaxed. She padded to her side of the bed, laid her head down on her pillow and closed her eyes on a day that should have made no sense and no difference, but it did.

In the final moments before she slept, she missed her phone. She wanted to send out an urgent text. She struggled against the impulse. She almost won. She almost nodded off to sleep. But she couldn't. She dragged herself out of her comforting bed and roamed through the house, looking for her phone. She found it finally in the seam of the sofa that she had been sitting on when she had asked Anay to stay home that morning. There were a million messages on it. But she had eyes for only one name.

"Zo" she typed, "I've been a bitch. Coming to see you tomorrow. I love you..."

Chapter 31

(September 8 - 13, 2016)

"It was extraordinary..." Zoya said with a faraway look in her eyes as she ate the warming soup that Maya had brought over for her.

"It's just a simple goulash..." Maya replied, blushing slightly.

"What?" Zoya looked at her, confusion writ clearly on her wan face. And then she smiled a tight little smile. The old Zoya would have laughed aloud, but even a smile was a positive sign for this Zoya. So she smiled through the fog of her persistent pain and said, "No, sweetie! I mean the soup is fantastic, as always, of course. But I wasn't speaking about it. I was speaking about P Rex. I meant to tell you about her visit the other day... You know, that day, when you made me pumpkin cake." Maya couldn't help feeling a thrill that Zoya remembered days by the food she had prepared, but immediately she felt remorse and heartache – that all Zoya had to hold on to for now was the food she had prepared. "You're not listening, Maya..." Zoya's deadened voice broke through her reverie. "Sorry, Zo... what were you saying?"

"I was saying, Rekha came over the other day and it was the most extraordinary day I've spent with her in a long time."

"Why?"

"Well, for starters, she didn't cry. You know how she has been for the past many months – all moody and thunder cloudy... She wasn't like that at all. She was calm. And supportive and sensible and wonderful. It was like P Rex was back. I wonder what happened. I don't know what has changed. But I'm glad it has!"

Zoya went back to her soup. (No one but Maya would call it a goulash.) And Maya watched her eat in companionable silence. She allowed her mind to wander. And as it often did when it wandered, her mind went to the new recipe she was trying out. People might speak in the same languages, but they think in languages of their own. The mind has its own grammar. Colour and light are the grammar of the painter, music is the grammar of the singer or the pianist. For Maya, her grammar was food. She didn't have to try to think about it; she thought in it. A beautiful day was a lemon meringue day for her, a rainy day was a chicken soup day or a rajma chawal day. Today had been a goulash day. Zoya had sounded feeble on their first morning phone call. It was a typical rainy day in Pune. And normally, Zoya would have been in top form – the rains were her favourite time of the year. But the clouds and the constant fine drizzle had deepened the despair of her friend's shattered life. And Maya had known that lifting her out of that deep pit would require more potent magic than could be contained in a simple chicken soup. So she had thrown herself into the preparation of the goulash. At the end of her endeavours she had achieved a thick, nourishing, flavourful, heart-warming concoction that had Zoya visibly reviving with each spoonful. When Zoya had asked for a second helping Maya had felt almost gladiatorial. "I'll defeat you, you just watch" she seemed to be saying to the pain that plagued her friend. "I'll feed her and she'll be strong and happy and you will lose and she will win and we will win and take that..." she seemed to feel.

In the very worst time that Zoya had faced in her young life she had that one thing going for her - she was surrounded by people who not only loved her deeply and wished her well; they actually plotted and strategized and devised ploys to defeat the things that threatened her well-being. Zaid and Anu were holding up the work end. She hadn't been to office since Asif died - and it did not matter one bit; things were being more than taken care of. Tilly and Rio were a constant presence in Zoya's life. Tilly, in fact, had done a typical Tilly thing and managed to convene a meeting of everyone that was important to Zoya when Zoya had gone to pick up the kids from school. She had taken to doing that in the past few days - she would first pick up Riva, then hang out with Riva and Rio, then pick up her own kids, a couple of times she had even picked up Maya's and Rekha's sons and all the children had spent the rest of the day together. Something about getting into the car, driving off to the schools, waiting for the boys and Riva to come out the gates, getting them into the car, driving them back and seeing them off safely into their waiting homes seemed to be giving her a sense of purpose. It was important to her - being personally responsible for her children and for the children of the people she loved. So she did it...

It was on one of those days that Tilly had managed to get everyone together. "I know it's early days. But I've thought about this. I've thought about nothing else. And I want to know if you guys are going to be with me on this..." Tilly was uncharacteristically nervous as she spoke to the small collection of people around her. To the question on most faces she answered, "This..." gesturing helplessly with her hands, including all of Zoya's home in their sweep, settling finally on Asif's photo in the drawing room. "...this mess that has become Zoya's life. I've been thinking...".

"Speak, Tilly. It's okay. We're all listening." The return of P Rex had not gone unnoticed by others either. The calm in her voice, her steady eyes, her composed aura was having a soothing effect on everyone. Tilly felt it too, and she took a long, steadying breath before she continued, "I think we should all forget that Asif is dead." There she was, Tilly saying something so outrageous that no one quite knew how to react. Hussain, Asif's brother who was still in India, looked around to see if their mother had heard Tilly. Mercifully she hadn't, or Tilly might not have been allowed or able to continue. And that would have been a great pity, because what Tilly was about to deliver was a piece of sheer genius. "So, here is the thing. And this is not only for Zoya. It's for all of us. It's for Samar and Sikandar. But most importantly it's for Asif. Asif did not deserve to die. But he did. And that makes me sad and miserable and, I have to be honest, it makes me so angry, I could kill him were he not already bloody dead." Tilly's eyes flowed over and she didn't bother to wipe away the tears. "But you know what, before he died, he lived. And I'm saying we should just forget that one moment when he died and continue like it never happened."

She glared defiantly at the room through her tears, waiting for someone to shut her down. But no one did. She could see that they weren't totally with her yet, that they couldn't quite see where she was going with all of this, but they trusted her enough to let her continue. She could almost hear Maya thinking to herself "Go, girl, make your point, we'll catch up..."

"And I'm not a fool. I'm not saying we should pretend that everything is fine and that he, that bloody so and so Asif, has gone on a vacation or anything stupid like that. I know he's gone. And that he's never coming back. But, I'm saying 'gone' doesn't have to mean 'dead'. He cannot die. Not until there is even one of us left who will keep him alive. Look at it. Zoya, the kids, Asif's mom, everyone needed him. For that matter, Zaid and Anu and their kids and all of us, we needed him too. It's our turn now. Asif needs us. He needs us to keep him alive. And if we insist on treating him like he were dead, we are all letting him down!"

There was the beginning of a new understanding on the faces that surrounded her. Rekha sat visibly straighter. Maya had a smile through the tears in her eyes. Zaid had stopped clutching his head. Tilly continued, "Do I mean that we set a plate for him at the dinner table? Certainly not. I mean that we keep his spirit alive. I'm not stupid. I'm not one of those guys who thinks we should have kept the corpse..." Panic was creeping back into her voice and she was beginning to lose steam, she looked around the room a little beseechingly when Rekha, calm and poised and collected, gathered her pallu around her shoulders, walked over to where Tilly was sitting, sat down gracefully next to her, took her hands in her own and said, "I'm asking Zoya today if I can take some of Asif's shirts back home with me. I mean, he's not going to be needing them, and Anay always said that Asif had fantastic taste."

And just like that, another little bit of the mountain of grief that had descended upon that group after Asif's death crumbled and fell into dust.

It was a process. The healing, the letting go, the moving on. And it wasn't easy. It would be many, many months before Zoya would give Rekha those shirts that she had asked for. But a beginning had been made that day. And it was Tilly who put it best when she told Asif's enraged mother, "Auntyji, we are not betraying him. We are not leaving him behind. We are learning to live with him, in spite of the fact that we can't see him anymore. We are moving on, with him, Auntyji. Not without him. Why should we bury him and mourn the moment he left us when we can choose to make him and his spirit a part of our daily life? Please forgive me, Auntyji... but we don't see God, do we? And yet, he is a part of our daily life! Asif is no God, but there is no reason we should allow something as insignificant as death to stop him from being alive."

<center>~~~~~</center>

"We shouldn't allow something as insignificant as death to stop him from being alive??? She said that?!! Mad woman she is! But... that's Tilly for you! Why haven't we all met up yet? I mean, I keep asking you when we can all meet and you keep avoiding the question, Re. In fact, you don't even meet me anymore. I can't tell you how happy I am to finally see you today, it's been weeks..." the petulant note in Gajju's voice escaped before he could cover it up. Rekha noticed. She simply behaved like she hadn't. It was an old habit with her, one that she didn't quite know she had. Even all those years ago, when they had been in college, she used to do it. Gajju would say or do something that felt off colour and she would pretend that she hadn't noticed it. They walked next to one another that day, talking about Asif and Zoya and all that had happened after his death. Rekha had carefully not mentioned the day that she and Anay had spent together. In fact, she hadn't spoken about herself at all. It had all been about Zoya. And about how all of them were working together to somehow survive this complete disaster.

To be fair to Gajju, he had listened with all his heart. Like he really cared about Zoya. And maybe he did. He had texted her a few times, he said. But he hadn't gone and met her. In fact, although he kept pestering Rekha about meeting the others, he hadn't actually contacted anyone directly, let alone gone and met them.

"So why haven't you?" Rekha turned her now calm eyes on Gajju's impassioned face.

"Sorry? Why haven't I what?"

"Why haven't you just gone and met the others? It's not like you don't have their numbers or don't know where they stay..."

He stood still in his tracks then, that tall, incredibly good-looking man, his stubble growing endearingly on a still strong jawline, his camera slung permanently across his broad shoulders, and he crinkled his eyes out of old habit. In a moment Rekha was transported back to their days lounging about the college library and canteen. She remembered in particular that one day when she had asked him why Mehdi Hassan and why not Jagjit Singh and he had squinted up into the sun and thought for a long moment with his crinkled eyes and replied, "I don't know. The heart has its reasons..."

It was like the intervening seasons had never happened. The sun was the same, the set of his jaw was the same, the eyes still crinkled up, and he still replied, "I don't know." She waited for the rest of the sentence. But it never came.

~

Into the slowly recovering clan there was the intrusion of a surprise visitor. Sarika reappeared. Slimmer, but not much slimmer. Still dressed in clothes that crumpled like sack cloth all around her. Still wearing four shades of dull brown. Still unglamorous. But completely changed. She walked differently, she held herself differently and in spite of the sombre situation that she had walked into, she positively glowed from within.

After she had met everyone and hugged Zoya and held her close and listened with growing horror to the story of how it had all happened, she said simply, "We are here for you, Zoya!"

Almost no one caught the pronoun. Except Shaila Wagh, Maya's mother who had also come along that day to spend time with Zoya. Across the big, comfortable room, the elderly Shaila Wagh's eyes met Sarika's soft brown eyes and Sarika smiled imperceptibly, with an even more imperceptible nod of her head.

A little later, as they all huddled around saying their goodbyes for the day, Sarika found herself standing next to the gentle presence of Shaila Wagh. Hesitatingly she reached out to her, and whispered, "I wanted to tell them today, but maybe tomorrow I'll text them. I'm pregnant. And so happy!"

Chapter 32

(September 25, 2016)

It had taken a couple of weeks, but by now everyone knew that Sarika was pregnant. The girls had all met at Zoya's place the earlier day.

"It's a month already! I don't believe how quickly time has flown!" Mitali's generous lips quivered through a thick layer of nude lipstick. "I've been sending you healing, Zoya. You and the kids. How are you feeling, my dear?"

Zoya simply smiled in answer. Mitali immediately turned to the sack that she carried and the movement was not lost on Tilly who was hovering like a helicopter parent around Zoya. She knew that expression, she knew what was coming next, and she was not having any of it. Fixing a bright smile on her face and forcing a vice-like grip on Mitali's ample arm she trilled, "Mits! Did I show you Rio's new blue ribbon?" It wasn't easy, pulling a determined Mitali off her target, but Tilly was something of a virago herself when it came to protecting the people she loved. When she deemed that they were safely out of earshot Tilly whispered fiercely, "Leave her alone, Mitali. Do NOT give her any talismans or stones or powders or candles. Not today. Just leave her alone!" Mitali's big eyes widened in shock. She had never faced the wrath of Tilly, had never imagined that one day the full power of that dynamo would be turned on her. "But I was only trying to help..." she murmured weakly. "Not like this. And not today. Give her whatever it is that you wanted to give her if she comes asking for it. But today, leave the southwest corners and north eastern water bodies alone." "You don't have to be so mean about it..." Mitali's big eyes filled up with the easy tears of self-pity. But Tilly had already moved on. She had spotted Asif's mother heading towards Zoya and SPG had nothing on her when she was in bodyguard mode.

That's when Sarika had spoken to Mitali. "Hi..."

"Oh my god! You are here! I didn't see you! You had almost blended into the wall!"

Sarika was too used to this to mind even otherwise. But now, she didn't even notice the implied 'what are you wearing, you poor drab soul'. She was too busy being happy.

"How are you, Mitali?" she asked, and where there used to be shyness and even diffidence there was now a distinct serenity in Sarika's voice.

The self-declared savant in Mitali was too wrapped up in being hurt over Tilly's brashness to notice. So she continued in the slightly patronising tone that they all had perfected when talking to Sarika "How was the break, dear? Hope you are looking for another job now? After all, for how long can you go on like this, na!"

"Like what?" Sarika asked mildly. To a perceptive listener that would have sounded like a Socrates using his method of question after question to reveal that the answer lay inside the seeker. But no one was listening. Everyone was gathered around Rio and her new blue ribbon. Outside the kitten coterie Mitali replied, "You know what I mean... like this... alone, not settled, no job... you know!" Mitali was flustered for the first time. But Sarika wasn't. Her voice was kind when she answered, "I don't want a job. And honestly, I don't need one. My work keeps me busy. And it pays pretty well..." "What work? Surely you can't be serious about pottery!"

Sarika almost laughed aloud, "No, no. I'm not serious. I'm having far too much fun to be serious about it."

And then she told her, "Besides, I can't engage myself in a full-time job anymore. I won't be able to manage it. Being a single mother is going to be my biggest job for the next few years."

And that had done it. Everyone knew in a matter of hours if not minutes.

"Girls, can we meet tomorrow at NCH?" Roopa had texted.

"Let's meet at my place. Sarika, what do you feel like eating? Or is it too early for that question?" Maya, unsurprisingly had answered.

And then she had turned to Zoya who she had been sitting next to. "I'll pick you up, Zo? You should come... you need it."

"Nah... not sure I want to leave the kids alone. It's a holiday tomorrow..." Zoya's trailing voice had said what her words had not. "It's too early. Asif's been gone only a month. It's too late. I'm never going to be happy again. I can't bear to talk about new life when my life has ended. I hate myself for not being able to feel happy for Sarika. But please, Maya, I can't do this."

Maya Wagh was not the daughter of the extraordinary Shaila Wagh and the granddaughter of two incomparable grandmothers for no reason. She heard every word that was never uttered by Zoya. She had squeezed her dearest friend's dried out hand and said simply, "I'll send you the bisi bele bhat. And will bake chocoloate cupcakes only for you. Everyone else is getting sabudana kheer." The gross injustice of that culinary diktat had made even Zoya almost laugh. And for the kind-hearted Maya, that had been enough.

So, it was with something akin to mischief that she cooked the sabudana kheer the next day. Everyone was so used to her complex, exotic, unique desserts that no one was expecting what Tilly immediately and vociferously denounced as 'sick food' from the magician Maya. "What have we ever done to you, Maya? I'm going to call you MeanMaya now onwards. For the rest of the day. Okay... once. But seriously... sick food???"

"You mean food for the sick, young lady... no?" Maya tossed back a friendly laugh.

"No, I mean sick food. And I'm complaining to Zoya!"

"Oh, she got chocolate cupcakes..."

Ordinarily that would have caused a storm. But not anymore. Now Tilly just sobered up and gave Maya a brief one-arm hug before whispering into her ear "Saint Maya, not MeanMaya..."

Mitali had forgiven Tilly for her slight of the earlier day. Or maybe she was just in too much of a hurry to hear Sarika's story to let anything like a silly woman snapping at her stand in the way. So she almost physically herded them all into Maya's comfortable family room, got everyone settled and commanded, "Tell!"

With so many pairs of eyes trained on her, the old Sarika would have receded further into herself. But this Sarika seemed to have found an unshakeable equanimity.

"There isn't much to tell, actually. I fell in love. He was married. He loved me, he said. But he couldn't leave his family. It took me a few years to figure this whole thing out. But when I did, I told him I wanted to have a baby with him. And that was that. I will never see him again. He will never be a part of this baby's life. But I got what I wanted. And I'm happy..."

The ground seemed to shift from under Tilly's feet. Her head swam and she felt like she was going to faint. She didn't, of course. But she swayed for a moment. And held on to Rekha for support.

"I don't believe this" she said through clenched lips. "It was so simple. And I never saw it. And now, it's too late..."

It was the first time ever that Tilly had spoken about her time with Prof Aman. Her best friends had always suspected, there had been plenty of gossip, plenty of conjecture. But Tilly had never breathed a word about the greatest love of her life.

But hearing the simple Sarika speak and watching her glow with the benign happiness of having what she wanted had completely undone her. She could not bring herself to pretend to be interested in Sarika's story. In fact, she wanted to cover her ears and run away. "Surely, surely, surely it cannot hurt so much after all these years. Is this how Zoya feels, like her insides are ripped out! How dare I presume that I can help Zoya heal? Pain like this, surely, it can never go away!" She was gripping Rekha hard now, and until her own knuckles hurt from the effort she didn't notice the welts that were rising on Rekha's hands. Rekha, however, did not make a sound. She simply let Tilly hold on. It's the least she could do, she thought, after the past many months of letting Tilly and her gang pick up after all her own melodrama.

"You met him at your college?" Roopa was amazed.

"And he was younger that you are?" Mitali couldn't get over the delicious scandal in the story.

"And what about his own kids? He should have thought of them..." Rashmi's maternal instinct extended to all children, not only his own.

"Yes to all three of you" Sarika replied. "He teaches Sanskrit. He is 8 years younger than I am. And yes, he not only thinks of his children, he loves them; and his wife is a lovely girl."

"But then... how?" The unasked question quivered in the air and sank into oblivion because no one dared to ask it in the face of the glares that Tilly was directing towards them all.

Chapter 33

(September 26 and 28, 2016)

"How did we all get to this point?" a puffy eyed Tilly asked herself as she looked into the mirror, getting ready for another day at work. "All we wanted was a Diwali Party; and to lose some weight. We haven't really exercised in forever. I have put on weight, instead of losing it. And that is in spite of all the morning walks I do with Zo. Zo is so thin that we're all getting worried. No one knows what Rekha is all about. Maya seems okay, but then, I don't know... And most days I don't even want to go to work."

That last thought struck her like the proverbial bolt of lightning. She saw the widening of her own eyes in the mirror and caught her breath for a moment. Slowly, as if in a trance, she got up from her stool at the mirror and plonked herself down on her bed. Almost without conscious thought she took off her long earrings and undid the knot that she had severely tied her hair into. For the rest of the morning, she did not move. She switched off her phone, she sank back into the mountainous pile of cushions on her bed and lay motionless.

"For what felt like the first few hours my heart was hammering wildly in my chest. Could have been only for the first few minutes, though,

I don't know. But eventually, I calmed down. I concentrated on my breathing. And for the next few hours all I did was force myself to breathe in and out. Could have been minutes though. I didn't check." Tilly was talking to Maya and Rekha in the park outside her house. She had called them and asked if they were free to catch up. Maya was in the middle of a baking a batch of macaroons that she was gifting to a relative to celebrate a new pregnancy. Rekha had planned to catch up with Gajju for coffee. So, obviously, they both told her they were free.

"I'm done. I quit. I sent in my resignation a couple of days ago and I don't care that no one is accepting it. I. Am. Done."

"Okay…" Maya waited for her to continue.

And Tilly knew that she had done the right thing in getting these two girls to hear her out before she spoke to anyone else.

"I wish Zoya were here too… but I don't want her to think of all this right now. She has too much to handle" Tilly said, almost to herself.

"Wish granted, Tilly" smiled a voice from behind her.

"Zo!!!"

"I called her… " Maya smiled by way of explanation.

"I came…" Zoya hugged the three girls one by one before they ended up in a rather embarrassing group hug.

"Thanks, buddy. I know this is so small compared to what you are handling. And you still came…" Tilly's voice was small.

"The small stuff I can handle, Tilly. And after Asif I have realised that nothing is small. Or big. It's what it is, in the moment... Oh my god. This is what I am most afraid of..." Zoya groaned a little.

"What???" all the three asked in unison, clearly alarmed.

"Stop! Don't be like this... like I'm going to implode or something! I'm afraid that I'm going to end up like this terrible widow bua from old Hindi films, where all she can do is go around giving gyaan and mop her eyes with the corner of her white palla and talk about how her dear departed husband used to say this and that..." and before the disbelieving but relieved eyes of her best friends Zoya laughed her first real laugh in over a month. The tears that rolled down her cheeks as she laughed were what Tilly poetically called 'brass tears' – alloys made out of joy and pain and relief and sadness and a tiny bit of freedom. As the setting sun glinted through the liquid amalgamation of many emotions on Zoya's upturned face that is exactly what they looked like - molten brass.

"This Tilly should be an artist. Maybe it is a good thing she has quit that rubbish job of hers" Rekha thought.

"So, any plans now?" Zoya knew exactly what kind of question to ask Tilly. She wasn't foolish enough to ask – 'What plans now?" Because that was just the kind of question that would get Tilly's back up and send her off into a completely unnecessary tirade about why life needed a plan. So she simply asked if Tilly had any plans.

Both Rekha and Maya noticed her deft handling of a prickly issue and they exchanged a quick glance. Things were looking better and better.

"No. Not really. I'm going to ask Baba if he can help me out financially. I know you guys could have helped too" she looked up from her shoes for long enough to smile quickly at her three best friends before continuing, eyes firmly fixed on her pink running shoes, "... but Baba is selling off some old family land back in the mountains; and I've asked him to hand over my share if he could."

"My brothers' wives aren't thrilled, of course. They think the land belongs to the men of the family. I told them it belongs to the Chowdharys. And that I was still very much one. And that I would continue to be one even if I did get married or something. That hasn't gone down too well. But I don't care. Then they also said I should at least wait till my Baba passes away before I claim a share. To which I told them I wasn't a vulture, thank you very much. And that I had made a simple request to my father, and that if he felt it was okay, he would accede to the request and that if he felt otherwise, he would not and that was that."

As she paused to take a breath the others couldn't help grinning at that typical Tilly outburst.

"Any particular thing you need so much money for?" Rekha picked up the tactful thread that Zoya had introduced.

"Not really. I own the house. I'm paying EMIs on the car, but have enough to cover the final payment on the car – so I effectively own that. Got rid of the driver last month, as you girls know. Riva's fees are taken care of for this year. So, no. No. I don't technically need the money for anything immediately. But I want it." And here she looked up from her shoes again and looked straight into the waiting faces of her friends. "I want it to buy my freedom."

"And not freedom from, but freedom to. I want to give myself the freedom to do what I really care about. All these years peddling lies about people who had the money to buy the media – it has made me sick. I thought I was only doing a job. But I could never make my peace with PR. I mean, what was I really doing? Planning intelligent and creative ways to spin a story so some capitalist could make more money by buying himself, and yes, it was mostly him and not her, so by buying himself an image without ever having done a thing to claim the image? Making polluters look like philanthropists, making money-grabbing schemes sound like social welfare initiatives? I don't blame them. I blame me. I couldn't do it anymore. I couldn't peddle any more lies, spin any more tales. And so, I quit.

And Zo, I think Asif had something to do with this decision. He taught me that we don't have forever. That all we have is the present moment. He taught me that a life well lived is one that is lived inside love. He died a fulfilled man, Zo. A happy man. I want to die happy. So, I not only quit, I quit to do something that I really, really care about.

I'm setting up a day care" and here she paused long enough to take in the looks of shock and horror on her friends' faces before she continued with her trademark impish grin "for dogs and cats and any other pets!"

"No. You cannot be serious!" Rekha clapped her hands in an unfamiliar expression of spontaneity.

"Well done! I love the idea!" Zoya's animation was touching.

It was Maya's stunned expression that went unnoticed though. She recovered quickly enough to gloss over the moment. But there was definitely a moment when her heart leaped into her mouth. She didn't ask herself why. She would do that later. For the time being, she focussed on being happy and excited for her friend.

"What a Tilly thing to do! When did you come up with this idea? For how long had you been thinking about it, you cow! You didn't breathe a word!" Maya beamed.

"Speaking of cows, I'm going to have a shelter for retired cows. I hate the dairy industry. What's this rubbish story about 'the cow is our mother, she gives us milk'. The poor thing does no such thing! She produces milk to nourish her calf and we turn her into a milk producing machine! That is simply not done. Imagine what it must feel like... to be kept in milk constantly because some spoilt brat somewhere must be given his glass of Complan before school by a doting mother who doesn't care that another poor mother has been kept in distinct discomfort so that her own pampered, entitled little devil can turn his nose up at a glass full of her – cow, not mother – of her lifeblood..."

She did this. And her friends knew she did this. She blabbered when she was nervous. And you could always tell how nervous Tilly was by the number of punctuation marks she missed in her diatribe. Because that is mostly what it was – a fairly irrelevant rant. So, did she care about the unfair treatment of the milch cow? Sure. Did she think the problem was entitled and pampered children of over-protective mothers? No. But Tilly had a penchant for the dramatic that would reveal itself in the funniest of ways.

And this was funny. Because she spent ungodly amounts of time trying to get both her daughter and her cat to drink milk. Rio was such a funny creature. She nibbled at carrots and ran away from fish and lapped up curd rice. Arvind had explained it to Maya as being 'the law of madcap magnets'.

"There is no such thing! You are so making this up..." Maya

had laughed through what had become her almost permanent substratum of resentment with her husband.

"No, I'm serious! Madness is magnetic. See how you and I have stuck to one another through the years..." he had smiled in reply.

"We are super boring. We are not mad!" Maya had been too surprised to remember to be resentful.

"I used to think so too, Monu. But I think we're both a little mad..." and he had sauntered away, hands in his pockets, whistling a tuneless tune.

"Since when does he whistle, and since when does he walk like that... like he was 20 years old and in a black and white romantic film set in Rome!" she had wondered to herself as she had stared at his retreating back in amazement.

That incident flashed past Maya's mind's eye as she watched Tilly fidget with her watch and her phone and her dupatta, still bright eyed with nervousness.

"Are you going to stop twittering like a sparrow and tell us more about your brilliant, mad idea, Tilly?" Zoya said with something that sounded like the return of Field Marshall Zoya.

And Tilly stopped fidgeting only to jump up, leap across to where Zoya was sitting and give her a quick hug. She scurried back to her place on the old wooden bench that they had now occupied and said, "Okay, deep breath, Tilly. See, the reason I'm freaking out a little is that I have no clue how I am going to do this." To the anticipated declarations of support and outpourings of advice she raised a hand and continued, "No, no, don't tell me I can do it, and I will figure it out. That I know. I mean, I don't have a venue, I don't have a vet on board, I don't have volunteers, I don't have clients... Dear God, what have I done!"

"So, here's what I think, Zoya brought out a tissue paper from her tote – she had gotten used to carrying them nowadays – and looked around inquiringly for a pen. None of them had one, so Tilly simply walked up to a group of elderly men who were out on their evening walk and returned with three pens.

"You didn't have to borrow three!" Zoya laughed.

"I didn't! Borrow them, that is. They gifted me these pens." Tilly didn't find it at all strange. People just did things like that for Tilly. If she needed a lift, 5 people would offer her one, if she needed change, the office boy would move mountains to make sure she got it. It was inexplicable, until you saw how easily she gave. On that evening in the park if those elderly gentlemen had asked her for a pen, she would, in all likelihood, asked why they needed one and then gotten herself invited over for a cup of tea to discuss the viability of the insurance policy that the gentleman had needed the pen to sign on in the first place.

But today she was the one receiving help. And Zoya was making a list.

To – do:

1. Get a place
2. Get vet/s on board
3. Get volunteers to sign up
4. Get clients

"See? That's how simple it is." Zoya said with a very mic drop expression on her thin face.

"Not funny!" Tilly rolled her eyes.

"I agree. I'm very serious. It is as simple as that. And let's make this happen. What say, girls?"

Chapter 34

(October 2, 2016)

They hadn't met for the past ten odd days. And Gajju was beginning to get sick and tired of waiting.

"I'm thinking of taking up a new assignment. In Ghana, Raghu Kaka…" he said to the old man who had stopped at Gajju's table to clear away his third glass of coffee that afternoon.

"Good. You should. When are you going?" Raghu Kaka asked with a barely concealed edge of anger in his voice.

"Kaka, why have you been so angry with me? Why is everyone so angry with me?" the puzzlement in Gajju's face and his voice would have been endearing had it not been for that constant undertone of petulance.

Raghu Kaka simply smiled, patted the younger man on his broad shoulder and said, "Talk to Rekha."

"But that's all that I have been trying to do… she just doesn't seem to want to, anymore!" he was still handsome enough to draw admiring glances from the women sitting in New Coffee House as he raked his hands through his greying hair in an age-old gesture of frustration.

"Then listen to what she is saying by refusing to talk to you..." he was a busy man, Raghu Kaka, he didn't have the time to waste chatting with only one table. There were other stories waiting for him at other tables. There was that old customer of his who was giving up medu-wada sambar for idli chutney because her husband was having his third extra-marital affair and she thought it was all because of her weight; there was the old couple who had come to share a mango milkshake in honour of their first date here; there was happiness and heartbreak and drama and romance and some robust arguments over politics; there was so much he had to address. Raghu Kaka bustled away like a Mother Hen on wheels. And Gajju sat back. Moody, withdrawn, staring at nothing with unseeing eyes when the girls all walked in.

Rekha hadn't noticed him; she was trying to adjust her dupatta that was made of some insanely beautiful peach fabric. "Or maybe it's insanely beautiful to me" Gajju thought to himself, his heart thudding almost painfully in his chest. "I can't believe I walked away from her all those years ago. No sunset in the Kalahari can make up for all that lost time. And now, is it too late..."

The despair in his heart couldn't be masked by the effusive grin that he tacked onto his face as he stood up and held his arms akimbo in a way that took the girls back 16 years. "He's just the same" Maya thought to herself. "Recklessly, dangerously handsome. Which man his age can carry off a lemon yellow linen shirt and duck egg blue trousers!"

While some junior waiter pulled their tables together to fit them all in Gajju walked over to Zoya and pulled her into a bear hug. He whispered something into her hair that made Zoya smile through the tears that came all too easily to her eyes. And that tender moment undid Rekha. All her hard-won poise shattered and she felt her treacherous heart begin to hum once again in that old, familiar traitorous tune. She wanted to turn back the clock. She wanted to forget her husband, forget the past fourteen years; and God help her, but for a terrible, terrible moment she wanted to forget her children and run into the waiting arms of a man she had loved like she had never loved anyone else.

It took Raghu Kaka to bustle into the centre of the little group to break the spell.

Because that's what it felt like to Rekha – like someone had slowed time down magically; like the world had fallen silent and like there were only the two of them, standing apart, but falling headlong into one another.

"Melodrama, Rekha, melodrama" another old, familiar voice spoke up in the poor woman's head. But it was weak. Where once that voice had a steady, steadfast, almost stentorian ring to it, today it was quaking and wavering and barely above a whisper. So, she ignored it. It was easy for her to do so. And pretended to busy herself trying to find a chair that was furthest away from the table fan that was playing havoc with her hair and her filmy peach concoction of a dupatta.

"I've been wanting to come and see all of you for so long now... but Madam" he said the word with so much emotion in his voice that Tilly said later that she wanted to fan her cheeks with a dainty Japanese fan, it was that hot "Madam has kept me at arm's length."

"That's just stupid" Tilly said with trademark candour. "You could have called us, come over, met us, done whatever... what could Re have done if you had just bypassed her?"

"But why would I want to bypass your Re?" once again that voice, that young twenty something speaking in the voice of a gorgeous thirty something.

"Are you kidding me?" Zoya exclaimed to Tilly as they drove back home a good three hours later. "That poor man doesn't stand a chance!"

"What are you saying, Zo? She was melting all over him like vanilla ice cream on a sizzling brownie. Pun fully intended!" Tilly retorted.

"Exactly!"

"Huh? So how does he not stand a chance?"

"Not him, duffer! Poor Anay Jaisingh seems out of contention..." Zoya finished with a heavy sigh a sentence that she had started with a broad grin. "Asif always said that Anay is a man in love, but also a man who is competing with a ghost. I don't think Re ever got over Gajju. And maybe, you know, maybe it's best if they just got back together..."

She wrung her hands uselessly and couldn't stop herself from exclaiming, "What a terrible mess! Can't people just see what a waste it is to live without love! I mean, what's the point? You only get one chance. And this is how you throw it away? What colossal stupidity?" the tears were rolling down her cheeks again.

And Tilly wanted to reach out and comfort her friend. But the words stuck in her throat. She wanted to give Zoya's limp hands a reassuring tug but she couldn't. Her own hands were gripping the steering wheel as if their life depended on the contact. She grit her teeth against a surge of emotion that was threatening to overwhelm her. They drove to Zoya's house in a heavy silence; both of them lost in their own worlds. And terrible worlds they were – filled with ghosts and clouds; dense with what-ifs and why-nots; dotted with regret; disfigured by loss.

It was Zoya who broke the silence. With the characteristic empathy of a broken soul she read the pain in Tilly's dry eyes. And as she turned to exit the car she simply leaned across and gave Tilly a one-armed hug. "Let him go. You cannot rewrite the past. And with him there is no future."

With the finality of her own words ringing in her ears she wearily climbed up the stairs to the home she had built with her Asif. "I'm not ready, Asif. I'm not ready to let you go. I don't think I ever will be. I think I'm going to die like this – having this interminable one-sided conversation with you. I don't really want to talk to anyone else. You are enough."

As she let herself in through the front door the laughing voices of her children greeted her. And a small smile broke through the layers of her grief.

"They're okay, Asif. We'll get through this. They're okay."

It was just after she kissed her boys good night that night though that she remembered why they had met in the first place that day – they were supposed to have had a brainstorming and strategic planning session on Tilly's hare-brained business idea!

"Maya! I'm so sorry to have woken you up... were you sleeping?"

Maya smiled into her phone and made no comment on the inverted logic of the sequence of Zoya's questions. Instead she simply asked, "What's up, Zo? You okay?"

"Yes, yes... it's just that I completely forgot why we had all met up today! You think you can whip up a sabudana khichadi breakfast and get the gang together again tomorrow?"

Maya didn't think twice. She pushed Arvind's hand off her and almost ran down to her kitchen. She soaked the sabudana, texted the rest of the gang and was happily planning a surprise sweet potato pudding to complement the khichadi when Arvind walked into the kitchen.

She was whistling as she jotted down ingredients for her pudding. Her rounded tummy was resting comfortably against one of the platforms made of some upscale Italian marble. She looked pretty. But more than that, she looked happy. Arvind almost broke into her reverie but at the last minute he decided against it.

He stepped back into the shadow of the corridor that led upstairs from the kitchen and walked back to a bedroom that felt strangely cold.

Downstairs Maya continued whistling. She had noticed her husband stepping in. She had relaxed when she had seen him stepping out. It had all been there for Arvind to see – in the set of her shoulders and the rigidity of her spine. But she knew he wouldn't notice. He never had. And now she wasn't sure she needed him to. She had her friends, she had her cooking and she had an Instagram page. She glanced at it again, that page of hers. ItsMaya had just notched up a whole new bunch of followers. And that had brought her tally up to a cool 51k followers. "Not bad, Maya madam, not bad for a woman who does nothing much except have fun cooking and baking and plotting the downfall of Arvind Desai..."

That last thought physically shook her. Her phone fell out of her hands and the screen cracked. It was as if the splintering of the screen mirrored something splintering in her soul. She clutched at the cold Italian marble under her slightly trembling hands and thought, "This is not who I am. This is not what I want. I have to speak to Mom!"

Chapter 35

(October 4, 2016)

But that had been easier thought than done.

First of all, the gang had readily agreed to meet for sabudana khichadi at 8:30 in the morning the day after the tumultuous and eventful NCH rendezvous. The breakfast had spilled over into late brunch and early lunch with everyone feeling the need to cling on to one another.

"Did you girls manage to put together that business plan for Tilly? I could help if you like..." Arvind had been getting increasingly more solicitous in the past few days.

"We're good. Not to worry." The more caring Arvind got, however, the more Maya seemed to want to pull away from him. He was getting a little alarmed. And it didn't help that his mother would every once in a while, sweetly suggest that maybe she was spending too much time with all 'those friends' of hers. "I think they are too bindaas and too uncaring about things like family and responsibilities and things like that. Don't you think so, Aru? I mean, look at that Tilly – she never seems to have a care in the world and she's always roaming around, no husband, no nothing. Zoya, poor thing, was the most sensible of them all, but now what can we expect out of her? I can understand why she is drifting about, no husband to go back home to. But shouldn't she be more hands-on with her kids? And don't even get me started on that Rekha! What a perfect life! And what a mess she has made out of it!"

Arvind's mother might have continued in this vein had Maya herself not entered the drawing room, a plate of chakli in her hand. "I'm trying this new baked chakli and I'm making it out of only millets – here, taste some!"

"It's brilliant, Maya! But then, I was just telling Aru what a fantastic cook you are…"

And it was to his great credit that the said Aru had the grace to blush at the blatant lie.

Not that Maya cared too much nowadays. There was a time when her mother-in-law's pettiness would have stung her. But lately there had been this thing growing inside her. She was scared by it, and when she allowed herself to think about it, she was appalled by it – she was becoming increasingly more furious with her husband.

"Am I going mad?" she asked herself for the umpteenth time as she wandered back into her kitchen, that plate of baked chaklis carrying nothing more than a few crumbs now. Arvind had been almost effusive, by his admittedly low standards, in his praise of the savoury goodness of the Diwali staple. "You should note the recipe down, Maya! This is really good!" he had said as he had polished off his third chakli. And Maya had had to physically grit her teeth to prevent a retort from escaping her lips.

"How can he not know that I have every single recipe meticulously written down? All the versions, everything that went right, everything that went wrong, dates, times, quantities, ratios, ingredients, options for ingredients... how can he not know? And he isn't even on Instagram! What kind of an idiot is he?" she fumed silently as she went about scrubbing her kitchen into a state of spotless loveliness.

"A hard-working, highly motivated, highly intelligent, deservedly rich idiot..." the unfailingly just voice that was Maya's gift from her mother answered. And she stopped in the middle of her vigorous scrub down; her shoulders slumped a little and she breathed the long, calming breath that was once again part of her inheritance from her mother.

"Maya, seriously, get a grip" she scolded herself. "And talk to Mom!"

So, the next day, when Shaila Wagh saw her firstborn sitting at her dining table, her chipped cup of warm milk in her hands, she knew something was troubling her child. But she wasn't the legendary Shaila Wagh for nothing. She didn't go for the tactless frontal assault. Instead, she went for her tin of homemade nankhatai. And set out some of the buttery goodness on an old and old-fashioned bone china plate that had delicate pink roses along its scooped edges. The plate brought an immediate smile on Maya's face.

"Maaa! How many times have we told you to get rid of these hideous plates! Who uses this anymore! They are soooo..."

"Tacky!" both mother and daughter said in unison. And then they laughed.

"I love them" Shaila said. And Maya covered her ears in mock despair saying "No, no, no... I don't want to hear that story of how your parents bought these plates for you from some rundown store in Tulshi Baug because they thought it was where all of Pune shopped... I've heard it a million times, Ma! The plates are hideous..." Maya trailed off as she dunked the nankhatai in the warm milk and ate it with a contented sigh. "That is so good, Ma! And to think you've never given me the recipe for this!"

"You've never asked. But if you are asking now, I can give it to you. You probably never needed the nankhatai before this..." and deftly she brought the conversation to where Maya needed it to be.

But Maya didn't leap at the opportunity. She sighed at it. And continued to stare into the depths of that old, chipped cup as if the sugary dregs it now contained held answers. With a visible effort at gathering herself she said, "Mom, I don't know what's happening to me. Remember you used to tell us about this Fernandes family that you knew?"

That threw Shaila Wagh off for a moment. Normally she knew more or less where conversations were going, but this detour caught her off guard. So, she repeated, "The Fernandes family? You mean the nice Goan family who were our neighbours when I was newly married? Claire Aunty and Flory and Fiona and their eight or nine brothers?"

Maya nodded her head in agreement before she continued "Remember how you used to tell us that they were all fantastic people, and very talented and all, but that they all had one finger on the self-destruct button?"

Shaila nodded the affirmative in increasing bewilderment as Maya went on.

"I think I must have found my self-destruct button, and it certainly feels like I have one finger permanently on it. I can't shake the feeling that I am suddenly going to do something very stupid and that it will all blow up in my face..."

Shaila waited for her daughter to continue, although her heart had begun to hammer against her ageing chest.

"I think..." and Maya faltered. But she drew herself up straighter in the chair that had been hers since childhood, looked up to look straight into her mother's eyes and allowed her worst fears to come tumbling out of her mouth "I think I hate Arvind."

And for a moment she thought her mother would faint, or the world would tilt, or something terribly dramatic would happen. But nothing did. After the smallest of tremors in the hand that held a nankhatai Shaila Wagh recovered. And gazed placidly on at her daughter, as if she was waiting for her to continue.

Maya, however, looked at her mother with puzzlement. She had said out loud what was to her the most terrible thing she could say, and her mother hadn't even blinked!

"Ma! Did you hear what I just said??? I think I hate Arvind!" Maya said with a distinct edge of panic to her voice.

"Of course I heard you child... but surely that is not your 'finger on the self-destruct button' thing. Or is it?"

"Mom! I hate him! Isn't that just the end of everything?" Now the panic was unmistakable.

Imagine her surprise when she saw her mother smile a broad smile at her and say, "You want tea? I'm making ginger tea for myself.

Want a mug?"

"Mom, aren't you listening? Of course you are. It's just that nowadays you are reading all this romantic, mushy Nora Roberts and Denise Whatshername and Gloria or Gladys or whatever and you think you know all this relationship crap..."

She subsided into a rebuked silence as quickly as she had when she had been a sassy child, trying to badger her mother over some silly trifle. All those years ago all Shaila Wagh had needed to do was direct her trademark narrowing eyes towards her daughter; all these years later the eyes were still in play, except the narrowing had now been replaced by the slight arching of one eyebrow.

"I'm sorry, Ma... it's just... I don't know what's going on, I don't know when I started hating him, I don't know why I hate him... it's quite horrible, actually!"

"Have you spoken..."

"To any of my friends?" Maya interrupted. "No... I don't want to speak to them about this... not when I don't even know what's going on..."

"No, child. You are jumping to too many conclusions today. Let me complete my question – Have you spoken to Arvind about this?"

The question startled Maya who answered almost too quickly, "Of course not, Mom! This is not his fault! He has done nothing wrong! What can I say to him?"

"Hmmm... so... how much do you hate him?"

"What?"

"You heard me... how much do you hate him?"

"Ma... I don't know... I don't what you mean, I don't know what to say..."

"You are such a smart girl, Maya... answer a simple question – how much do you hate Arvind?"

"I don't know" the answer was a perturbed sigh, more than it was a sentence.

"Come on, bash up some ginger for me... I need that cup of tea."

The next half hour was bizarre for Maya. She had gone to her mother with the expectation that talking to her would clear her head and that her unfailingly dependable mother would talk some sense into her. But nothing of the sort happened. Shaila Wagh made two cups of stellar ginger tea and chatted about nothing with her daughter.

Maya couldn't believe what was going on. By the end of a long, meaningless anecdote about how her grandfather hated coriander Maya had had enough. She slammed her long empty mug of tea down on the bamboo coaster and said angrily, "Mom, you want to tell me what's going on? I come to you for help, and what are you doing?"

"Why, I am waiting, beta... I asked you a question that you haven't answered!" Shaila answered with mock surprise in her gentle eyes.

"What do you want me to say, Ma!!!" Maya flung her hands dramatically in the air and leant back in her chair to stare at the old cream ceiling. And spoke to it. "I hate him when he leaves for work, so busy and important and focussed. I hate him when he comes back home – fulfilled and waiting to start another day. I hate him the most when he tries to get close to me and pretend like he understands... Oh, I don't know what the matter is with me, Ma!!! I hate feeling like this!"

"So, you don't want him to go to work?"

"What? No! Of course not! He should work...why shouldn't he work?"

"I see... you just want him to be miserable doing what he does?"

"No! How can you say that? Why should I want him to be miserable?"

"Then you don't want him to get close to you?"

"Ma! You are just doing this to irritate me, aren't you?"

"Not at all, beta. I'm just asking... "

Maya slammed her tilted chair back onto the kitchen tiles with a loud slam. She shook back her unruly hair, slammed her hands on the table and said, a tad too loudly, "Fine! You want to know what is really bothering me? Fine! I'll tell you! He doesn't even know me! He thinks I care about his stupid business. I don't! I couldn't give two hoots about square feet and landscape and mergers and acquisitions and stocks and investments. I DON'T CARE! And he doesn't even KNOW!" Maya was pacing up and down the long kitchen now, her voice rising with every agitated utterance.

"He LOVES his work. At least that's what I think. But then I think he is INCAPABLE of LOVING anything. Other than that photo that he still keeps with him, I don't see any signs of deep, passionate LOVE in him. And I HATE that. I HATE that he can live so happily without LOVE! What kind of a man is he! He doesn't even KNOW that I LOVE food and cooking and he hasn't even seen my Instagram page and he thinks cooking is my HOBBY! I HATE HIM! He doesn't even KNOW...!"

Maya had never allowed herself to get into such a rage. Not once in her life. But this thing had festered in her for too long and Shaila Wagh sat back quietly and watched the infected pus of festering feelings flow out. She didn't ask her to quiet down. Shaila had few regrets in life; but she had never quite forgiven herself for teaching her daughters to lower their voice because that's what her virago of a mother-in-law had decreed as a rule for the Wagh women. But her mother-in-law was in an upstairs room, and Shaila Wagh had in any case grown enough to decide that decibels were not a threshold for women not to cross. So, she let her daughter raise a little bit of hell. And she watched on calmly.

"I mean, just YESTERDAY, he had the bloody gall to tell me to WRITE DOWN a recipe for baked millet chakli! How can he NOT KNOW that I make copious notes, of EVERY SINGLE RECIPE. EVER!"

"Why should he?" Shaila asked quietly.

Maya spun around on her heels as if she could not believe what she was hearing.

"What!!! What do you mean by 'why should he know'? Why shouldn't he? I know everything about his stupid work. I know what meetings he has to go to, what deals he is working on, how the stupid, stupid share market is performing... I go to his office for all the poojas; I know EVERYTHING about his work. How can he not KNOW ANYTHING about mine?"

"Your what?"

"My work, dammit, Ma!" Maya was spluttering in anger by now.

"Is it? Is that what it is? Your work?"

Maya was about to respond angrily when she caught sight of the slight smile playing on her mother's lips... and she slumped into her chair, all the fight drained out of her in one single moment.

Clutching her head in her hands she said, "I don't really hate HIM, do I, Ma? I am so MAD at him!"

"At him?" again there was a gentle teasing in her mother's voice.

"You are evil, Ma. Evil. And genius. How do you do this? Of course I'm not mad at him. I'm mad at ME! How have I NOT KNOWN anything about what matters to ME! Just look at me, Ma. This privileged, loved, pampered even, respected woman in her late thirties. And I haven't had the courage to follow my heart, my love, my passion! What a weak, pathetic woman I am!"

At this point Shaila Wagh got out of her chair with a small wince, her old knees had started bothering her, and walked over to her dejected daughter and folded her into a gentle embrace. "Don't be silly, Maya. You are a brave, beautiful, passionate woman; an artist who has finally woken up to her calling..." Gently tucking her daughter's wild hair behind her ears in a long familiar gesture she sat down next to her and continued "I've been watching you for the past few years, and wondering when you would reach this point. Your heart is in food. And it is YOUR JOB to follow your heart. Your husband might understand or he might not. He might become your greatest advocate or he might not. He might enjoy your food as much as you enjoy cooking it for him or he might not. But this is not about him. This is about you. And no, you don't hate how he can work without love; you hate how you can love and not put that love to work for you. Maya, you don't hate Arvind. It's even worse – you resent him. You resent the fact that he enjoys his work, that it fulfils him; that he has a sense of purpose, and that he has it all; work, family, love, wife, friends, everything. But you are too fair and just a human being not to see that that is not his fault. Those are the choices he made. And they have worked out very well for him. Make your choices, Maya. Commit to your purpose. You don't need anyone to tell you this. Not me. And certainly not Arvind Desai."

And then there was silence. For a long time, Maya Wagh sat in her mother's kitchen till a rumbling in her stomach told her it was way past lunch time and that she was suddenly ravenously hungry. Almost on cue her mother materialised with a plate of grilled cheese sandwiches in her hands. They had always been Maya's band-aid food. Her grandmother had rationed cheese with an inexplicable miserliness; and she had frowned upon extravagances like white bread. But Shaila had always managed to whip up a grilled cheese sandwich when her Maya had needed one. And today was definitely a grilled cheese sandwich day.

"I know what I'm going to do, Mom. I'm setting up a business. And a chain of cake shops. But first, I'm setting up a school – India's first school for home bakers. And I'm going to teach underprivileged kids – young men and women both – to bake. I'm going to make this world a happier, better, sweeter place, Ma; one cake at a time.

But first, I'm going home and apologising to Arvind. I was not being fair. And he deserves better..."

Shaila Wagh was proud of her daughter that day. But she was also a little worried. "What if Arvind is just completely insensitive to what Maya wants? I know I told her that she doesn't need him to acknowledge her path, but surely he should have known by now! Dear God... I really, really hope he sees her passion and that he supports her. I don't know what she will do if he is blind to her!"

Mothers are like that. Strong and scared at the same time. Giving their children wings and then praying for kind winds. That is exactly what Shaila Wagh was praying for as she watched her beautiful daughter drive back into her life – the blessing of kind winds beneath the wings that she knew her Maya had just discovered.

Chapter 36

"I'm not going to fund you." Maya had not forgotten her husband's first reaction when she had told him of her dreams.

"But I never asked you to fund me... how dare you presume something like this!" Maya's anger had been swift and sure. But Arvind hadn't reacted to her anger. He had simply held up a hand and said, "Monu, listen!"

It was the 'Monu' that had done it. She had simmered down enough to let him continue.

"This is your big break, Monu. This is your dream. And I will not stand by and let you take it lightly. You are not going to run this as if it were some whim. At least not if I can help it. Not on my watch. We get one life, Monu. We should spend it doing what we love." It was only Shaila Wagh's upbringing and Maya's innate sense of self-worth that had allowed the moment to pass, because as he had spoken about love, his eyes had strayed unselfconsciously to the desk in which Saira's old picture still sat. But they hadn't lingered there. And he had continued, "Put your skin in the game. Take on the risk of losing. I'll help you with a business plan, if you will let me. I'll get you the best finance options. I'll be the guarantor for your loan. I'll just not give you the money..."

Maya had turned away from him as he spoke. She had waited for him to talk about her food, to mention the magic that lay in her hands. But she had waited in vain. Behind her turned back Arvind had continued to speak. Excitedly. He had grabbed a pen that had been lying around and started scribbling something on a newspaper that he had been reading. "Here" he had announced triumphantly to her turned back. "See, I've even got your basic business flow structured and put on paper! Look na, Monu! It's looking good!"

And in the softening of her spine Maya Wagh had accepted an apology that was never going to be offered and forgiven a man who was not even seeking her forgiveness. He had noticed none of this, of course. In his mind he was being the most supportive and encouraging partner possible. And maybe he was. But that morning had made one thing crystal clear to Maya - her husband was never going to see her as an artist, he was never going to love food in the way that she did, he was never going to understand how food and cooking made her happy. In that moment she had had a choice to make - to be angry at the man who was blind to her art, or be grateful for the man who celebrated her purpose. She had chosen the latter. And the volcano that had been building up inside her had subsided quietly. Sure, she was a little singed and a little burned up on the inside. But no one knew. The surface remained whole. And life had gone on smoothly.

"I didn't actually press that self-destruct button, then!" Maya thought to herself as she drove to the first meeting with the bank that she had applied to for a loan. "That Fernandes family would have turned out so different if they had just taken their fingers off that button. Dangerous button it is. And I have to remember to stay far, far away from it. I would have risked everything. And for what! Arvind is a good guy. And he doesn't look down on me for being all googly eyed about my business, so why should I judge him for not being googly eyed about his... This whole thing about being passionate is overrated. But, wait, has he just channelled all his passion into sex and have I not realised it? Maybe I've just taken it for granted that all men are like that about sex. Maybe they aren't as interested after all these years. I should ask the girls..."

And then it struck her – her girls were the last people she could ask about men and sex. Tilly was Tilly. Rekha and Anay were a huge question mark. And Zoya... dear God, it wasn't even two months yet.

"Why are you looking like you have seen a ghost?" Tilly's impish voice jerked Maya out of her reverie. They were both applying for business loans on the same day. Arvind had worked tirelessly to help both of them create rock solid business plans. And the numbers too were looking good; which was all credit to Zoya. Zoya had thrown herself into the number crunching for both of her friends' new businesses. She had had only ten days to put it all together, but she had delivered.

"Asif would have been so proud of her" Maya muttered wistfully as she collected the papers from her car and prepared to walk into the bank with Tilly.

"Is. Asif IS very proud of her. We are sure that wherever he is, he is proud of her..." Tilly's plan of keeping Asif alive included many and constant corrections in the usage of tense. She would come down strongly on people who referred to Asif in anything but the present perfect tense.

"Yes ma'am! He is indeed!" Maya smiled a sunshine smile as she walked purposefully towards her future, Tilly in tow. And if Tilly faltered a little as she took the first flight of stairs up to their meeting, Maya either didn't notice or, if she noticed, she made no comment.

The meeting went better than expected. And both the women emerged a couple of hours later feeling like their lives had just gotten a whole lot more complicated. It is one thing to dream a dream; it is completely another thing when the dream has mortgages, interest rates and repayment schedules attached to it. It feels more real. Which is not necessarily a good thing.

"We haven't signed anything yet. But it already feels so final!" Tilly said later that day as they huddled over chai and samosas at Zoya's place.

"And that's a good thing, right?" Zoya asked mildly.

There was a tiny pause before Tilly shook her curls and said "Yes. Yes, of course. It's a good thing!"

Zoya wasn't going to let that pause slip. But she wasn't going to bully her friend into speaking either. "She'll tell us if she wants to. And if she doesn't, then I'll ask her in a few days. But not now. Everything needs time. Even Tilly and her madcap decisions." Zoya's new awareness of Time with a capital T had changed her in subtle, yet important ways. She didn't look at the phone when she drank her morning tea. She didn't read a book, read the newspaper, switch on the TV, talk with anyone. She simply drank her tea. She breathed slowly. In the first few days that had been because even the simple act of breathing had hurt. But now, her body had a new rhythm. And that rhythm was slow, deliberate. We hear of people who suffer some terrible brain damage and they have to relearn simple tasks like eating, or wearing their clothes. Zoya had become like that. She was relearning her entire life. Not that she thought of it like that.

But Rekha did. Rekha with her piercing awareness of emotions, her frightening clarity on love and longing, her heightened sense of life and living; Rekha saw the recalibration of Zoya. "You can do it, Zo!" she often silently egged her friend on. "You can find a new person inside that debris, you can build that new person, you can be that new person. You are not the pieces, Zo. You are the hand that brings those pieces back together. You are painter, you are the potter, you are more than your sorrows, Zo!"

She said none of this out loud. And yet, Zoya seemed to hear it. She leant more and more on the Rekha that had finally resurfaced in their lives. She went for her morning walks with Tilly a few times a week, she gratefully ate the food that Maya continued to send her. But she shared her silences with Rekha.

The human being is a strange creature. It thinks of itself as being defined by its five senses. And yet, it is more than the limitations of its sensory organs. It cannot see love, it can feel it. It cannot touch loss, yet it experiences it. It hears things that are never said, it says things without ever uttering a word. And yet it lives blissfully unaware of its extrasensory blessings. Until something comes along that shatters the illusion of limitations – something like tragedy. When everything breaks, a new awareness is born. And Zoya and Rekha were bonded by this rarefied awareness of the broken.

"So... are you going to talk about it, Re?" Zoya asked her later that day as they sat in the balcony, quietly watching the night steal the march on a valiantly struggling sun. Night came early nowadays. People ascribed it to October. And of course, it was. October, that is. But it felt strangely apt to Zoya. "I wonder what grief feels like on days when the sun keeps shining. Must be so irritating – all that bright sunlight and no darkness. This darkness is like a balm. It makes the grief more liveable." Zoya's mind often wandered off nowadays, so it took her a moment to realise that Rekha had answered.

"I have decided."

"You have? What? And about what?" Zoya asked calmly.

"I think I will always love Gajju. And I think I will always want Anay to love me. It's a mess. But this much I know – I am no longer going to live without love. I have spent fourteen years of my life not knowing if Anay loves me. And that is all I have ever wanted. I have wanted him to love me. I look around at everyone and I see how selfish I must seem. My life is perfect – the perfect house, the perfect kids, the perfect family, so much wealth and comfort; I know that from the outside I must seem like this spoilt, pampered creature who can't think beyond herself.

But Zo, I really can't. I feel that time is running out, it is slipping out of my hands. And that if I don't do something about it, I will lose my chance at happiness. And all I want is happiness. And I am going to stick my neck out and risk everything for it."

The sun had lost its fight against the night by now. The friends sat in darkness; neither wanting to switch on the light in the balcony; content in the shadows that were thrown by the light in the living room.

"I'm not sure I understand. But I think that you do." Zoya murmured. "So, what are you going to do?"

"I'm going to speak to both of them. The only thing left to decide is who do I speak to first – Gajju or Anay?"

She sounded calm as she said this. But Rekha Jaisingh was experiencing a veritable maelstrom of emotions inside her. She knew her life depended on that one call –Gajju first or Anay first.

Chapter 37

(October 16, 2016)

She hadn't slept all night. But that was to have been expected. Rekha Jaisingh had never felt more afraid in all of her life. To be fair, she had never done anything that demanded courage out of her. Her whole life had been laid out for her. First her parents, then her husband – she had been provided for, indulged, celebrated. It was to her great credit that she had remained humble and grounded and sensible through all that ease.

An easy life is not always a blessing. The soul needs its travails to grow. All the soft hands that had moulded Rekha Jaisingh had given her a cocoon, but she was not about to become a butterfly without struggling against the comfort. This was Rekha's struggle to become the person she desperately wanted to become. She was done with living in quiet comfort. She no longer cared about accepting gracefully all the many indulgences that life showered upon her. She wanted more. Not only for herself. But out of herself, out of her relationships. Rekha Jaisingh, poster child of perfection, wanted to feel something. Anything. Her lukewarm, perfect temperature life; her tepid, polite relationships; her glossy veneer of wealth; she was done with it all. Rekha Jaisingh, mother of two of the most gorgeous little boys on the planet had tortured herself for months with one question – 'how can I do this to my boys?' And today, Rekha, just Rekha, had finally decided that she could no longer go on like this; and more importantly, that she would no longer go on like this.

Anay was in office. Her boys were in school. And Rekha knew that she could not put it off any longer. One last time she asked herself who she was going to call first. But she didn't really need to, she already knew. Not that it lessened the panic in any way. There are the firemen who scale walls and rescue kittens out of burning buildings, the world watches on in awe as they risk everything to save a quivering ball of fur. And then there are the acts of incredible bravery that the human being commits in anonymity. Like picking up a phone and making that one call that could potentially spell complete disaster.

But Rekha made that call. In the deep, almost visceral knowledge that this is what constituted the act of burning bridges, she acted on the decision that she could no longer delay making.

And when that dearly loved voice answered, she said, "Gajju, it's me. I want to meet you. Can we meet in the University... 5 o'clock today?"

When he answered with a too enthusiastic "Of course, I'll be at the main building lawns from 4:30!" she smiled a 'Thank you' and cut the call.

It was the next call that was more difficult.

"Anay, can we go out to dinner tonight? Just the two of us. I want to take you to a place I like..."

Anay's response was less than enthusiastic. It was restrained and careful and there was a hint of something that Rekha did not want to identify as despair in his "I had a late meeting planned, but will 9 work?"

"It will. I'll come to the office, we can go from there…"

And so it began. The day Rekha finally grew up. The day she made the choice to claim her life, not simply let it lead her by the hand.

She spent the morning in a state of nerves, compulsively going over every corner of her little kitchen garden until she got on Laxmi Tai's nerves; enough for the otherwise patient and even indulgent Laxmi Tai put her hands on her generous hips and say, "I think you should sit in the upstairs verandah while I make you sandwiches with some mint chutney that I will make out of this beautiful mint that is growing so well… you hover over it any longer and it will wilt and die." The dialogue was delivered in a tone that brooked no argument, so a duly chastised Rekha wrung her hands in futile despair and slunk off to her own room; where she spent the day till her kids came back from school. She usually liked to be at home when the children came back. She liked seeing their rumpled uniforms, their socks falling around their ankles, their hair dishevelled and their faces reflecting what kind of day they had had. "I send them off with such neatly parted hair, I cannot for the life of me understand what they do to come back looking like hooligans" she had often laughed to her friends, in that way that only mothers have, when the words are of complaint but the tone is that wonderful maternal mixture of pride and love and gratitude and joy. She liked sitting with them and the family dog Bruno as they talked about nothing. Laxmi Tai would generally have a treat waiting for them by the time they got home, and every once in a while Rekha would add a little something that she had either bought or made to the table in their room. She was an adept cook, if not a great one. And it made her happy to make some fudge or dry fruit bars or even homemade jam sandwiches for her boys. But today she barely called out a "Hi there, babies! How was school?" before she hid under her blanket for a pretend nap.

A wide-eyed Rekha found herself in the University lawns around 4:45 that evening, though she wasn't quite sure how she had got there. When Gajju saw her walking up the steps to the gazebo where they used to sit when they used to come here, way back when life was magical his heart began its now familiar painful drumroll against his chest. By the time she smiled at him and came and sat down next to him, he was aware of the delicious sensation of the rest of the world melting away.

And when she said her first words, "Gajju, I love you…" he almost cried. He had put his entire life on hold, spent the past eight months in Pune, wooed the woman he regretted losing, and waited with growing desperation to hear just those words from Rekha. As he made to fold her in a hug, she raised her palm in that graceful way of hers and continued, "I have loved you for the past 16 years. And I have never loved anyone like I love you, I probably never will."

Something in her tone finally set the alarm bells ringing in Gajju's mind; his heart was still hopeful, but his mind registered the forthcoming 'but'…

"But, this is it. I am doing for you what you never did for me. I am giving you the dignity of an explanation."

As Gajju spluttered in helplessness Rekha continued, her voice like honey tinged with the acid edge of lemons "I love you. And that is completely irrelevant. I love you. And so what. I love you, Gajju, with the ferocity of a cyclone that has travelled stormy seas to finally meet the land that calls out to her. Passionate, but so destructive. When a cyclone makes landfall, na, Gajju, it destroys everything in its path. Have you ever photographed a cyclone, Gajju? I am told it's a beautiful thing. Terrible, but beautiful. I love you like that, Gajju. It's beautiful, but terrible. I love you, Gajju. No, don't stop me. Let me say this. Over and over and over again. Because I will never say it after this. Let me say to you all the love letters I never wrote to you. I want to tell you today how it felt to wake up after you chose to leave me. And no, don't tell me that you didn't have a choice... you did, and you made it. And I'm finally alright with it. Because you don't have to love me, it is enough that I love you. I love you, Gajju. But it's over."

He knew she had told me to let her speaking, but he couldn't stop the strangled "Why?" from escaping him.

Rekha continued as if she hadn't heard him "There were days when I would look at the breeze as it lifted the summer curtains in my room and it would physically hurt. Just looking at things that reminded me of you would hurt. And the summer breeze reminded me of you, the Pune rain falling in a fine mist against my face as I went to University reminded me of you. Onion bhajis reminded me of you, the stupid Govinda movies reminded me of you. Everything was you. I could literally not imagine living another day without laughing with you. I missed your laugh more than I missed anything else. When you used to laugh, it used to be like everything was fine with the world. And then I didn't have that laugh in my life anymore and it felt like nothing was fine with the world. I was just a child, Gajju, but it felt like the sun had gone out, like I had nothing to live for. Now that I look back on the years that followed your choice to disappear from my life, from what was 'our' relationship, I see that that is how the very young love - completely, unreservedly, foolishly. Yes, I was foolish, my dear Gajju. But I was also blessed. I have never known such highs of ecstasy, such lows of complete despair. After you left me, I continued to love you like only a mad woman can. I cried and despaired and I shattered. The piercing pain of your betrayal was almost as exquisite, perhaps even more so, than the joy of the few years when we were together. But then, the storm abated. The sharp pain dulled to an even throb, until one day it subsided into numbness. That gaping hole that you walking out had gouged out of my heart finally grew new tissue. The open wound healed, but I lost sensation in that part of me. And I lived in comfortable numbness."

She stopped there. Her shoulders sagged with the obvious relief of having said out loud at least a part of what she had held inside her for far too long.

"But I no longer want to live like that. I don't want the numbness, but at the same time I don't want the heady exhilaration and the plummeting depths. I have grown up..." and here her voice finally faltered. She could not bring herself to utter his name, so she left it at that. She knew only one way of uttering that name, and she could no longer say it. The name was a stranger to her all of a sudden, and she found its newly unfamiliar sounds impossible to utter.

He heard the absence of his name. And his heart finally understood what his mind had known for some time now.

"I have grown up" Rekha continued "And I want different things from life. I want honesty and trust and respect and yes, I want love, but I don't want a cyclone, I want a river. I want to nurture and grow and I want a garden. Gardening takes patience, you know. It takes faith and love and hope. But it also takes hard work. You have to give, without expecting anything in return, you have to get your hands dirty and your clothes messy. There is no glamour in gardening. And you have to be willing to deal with the weeds that will necessarily crop up, you have to show up and be there and generally feel like all you are doing is hard work and sometimes even after all the hard work your plants will shrivel up and die. But then there are those that actually grow. And you walk out one fine morning and a little bud is blooming in a quiet corner and you feel like life is beautiful."

Rekha was taken aback by the sudden tears that pierced her eyes, but she didn't bother to blink them back. They rolled down her cheeks, unchecked, as she looked at Gajju with eyes that were blazing like the sun setting on an ocean, fire and liquid all at once, "I want a garden, my dear friend. And that's not something cyclones are good for!"

Without another word she got up, smiled at a distraught man with boundless kindness, reached out and gave his hand a reassuring squeeze and walked away.

One part of her life was over. But a scarier encounter remained. And Rekha Jaisingh didn't know if she had it in her to say another word after the evening she had just had. She was drained, exhausted. And her real battle hadn't even commenced.

Chapter 38

(October 16, 2016)

She didn't second-guess herself that day. She had had more than enough of that in the past few months. So, when she felt that she needed to change after her final encounter with Gajju, she changed. She wore an old pair of jeans and a comfortable grey t-shirt. The t-shirt had mismatched buttons.2 black and one hot pink. She had sewed on the hot pink button when one of the original black ones had fallen off. She smiled ruefully as she remembered that wanton act of small rebellion. Of course, she had never worn it after the pink button revolution. "So typical of me – passive aggressive I think Zo would call this behaviour... Not a good way to feel about yourself. But" she saw her reflection give a little shrug "that was me. And I'm done with being that person. Here I come, Anay Jaisingh, imperfect buttons and all."

Which is why she was even more surprised when Anay smiled his quiet smile at her pink button as she entered his office and said, "Nice! It looks so nice on you!"

He didn't say anything else as his neat fingers swiftly cleared up the remnants of a long day from his desk. After a few moments of silence that felt oddly companionable to Rekha he looked up from his now tidy fiefdom and asked, "Where to? Should I ask the driver to bring the car around?"

Rekha hesitated for a brief moment before asking, "Would you mind driving? If you are not too tired, that is…"

"Of course not! You know I love to drive! And with you…" Anay let that sentence taper off.

So it was that Anay and Rekha Jaisingh found themselves in a long Audi in the middle of the old city area of Pune. It was almost 9:45, but the old city was still bustling, the streets were crowded, two wheelers zigzagged across the narrow lanes as if they had a mind of their own to make up for the minds that their riders clearly seemed to have left at home. The usually calm demeanour of Anay's face was broken more than once as he swore beneath his breath at some idiocy or the other of assorted bikes, scooters, autorickshaws and fellow cars. "Everyone thinks they are riding two wheelers! I don't think Pune has ever got out of the two-wheeler mind set! How can you think of weaving an SUV through two tiny lanes of traffic on a road that has clearly been built for bicycles… Insane!"

Rekha smiled secretly to herself as her husband's steady hands gripped the steering wheel tighter and tighter.

"You should park in that lane to your left. There's almost always no one here. It's a dead-end, so no traffic that uses it as a thoroughfare…"

"How did you know! What a great place to park. Never in my life would I have imagined that there is this quiet corner in the busiest part of town" said Anay as he guided the long car smoothly into the canopy of a banyan tree that looked like it could have been a thousand years old.

"This old bungalow here used to be the home of my music teacher."

"You learnt music?" Anay asked in surprise. "You never told me!"

"Oh… that's because I hated it" there was a laugh in Rekha's voice as she answered. And if the laugh sounded a little manic, she chose to ignore it.

"That old teacher of mine was the single most boring person I have EVER met! You know how much I love listening to classical music now…" If the vast expanse of the banyan had not been throwing such shadows on Anay's face Rekha would have noticed his expression, which said very clearly that he knew no such thing about her. But the banyan was doing what a banyan is supposed to do – create a play between light and shadow – so Rekha noticed nothing and carried on blissfully unaware, "But when I used to come to her, I would want to go to sleep! She made the notes sound like we were doing some sort of military drill; all do this and do that and hup two three four!"

By now they had walked up to one of the many bridges that straddled the river that split the city into two different universes. And Anay was wondering where they were headed. "Some sort of hole-in-the-wall joint on the other side, looks like. Ah well, Rekha has impeccable taste, so I wouldn't worry too much." He was strolling along, enjoying the mild October river breeze, his hands in the pockets of his Italian trousers, when suddenly, Rekha stopped. They were halfway across the bridge, standing on what would have been the middle of the river bed, when his wife of fourteen years suddenly announced, "Here, this is where we are having dinner tonight!" And then she simply walked to the stone balustrade that separated the footpath from the road and sat down on it.

Anay was genuinely perplexed. And if Rekha hadn't been so desperately afraid of what the outcome of their conversation might be, she would have laughed out loud. But frightened as she was, she couldn't supress the little giggle that bubbled out of her tight chest. "Come, sit. With your back to the road. The city looks lovely from here."

Anay meekly followed his wife's voice and sat himself down where she dusted a place for him to sit. He continued to have this bewildered expression on his face, though. So, she took some pity on him and reached across and undid first one and then another button of his crisp formal shirt that had remained unwrinkled from around 8 that morning.

"Maybe you could roll up your sleeves, stretch your legs..." Rekha waved her hands in what she imagined was a helpful gesture at groups of people who were doing the exact same thing across the length of the bridge on both sides of the road.

"Errrr... sure. I could do that..." Anay pinched the bridge of his nose in a familiar gesture and Rekha's heart almost leapt up into her mouth.

"What have I done? Am I completely insane! He is never going to understand. He hates being here... what was I even thinking!" she panicked.

Which is why she was more than slightly surprised when she looked up with terrified eyes into Anay's questioning face as he said "Where did you wander off to? You haven't heard a word of what I was saying, have you!"

If she had been even slightly less distraught, she would have heard the laughter in her husband's voice. But now she simply nodded her head mutely and listened in growing wonder as Anay said, "I was saying this is the nicest thing I have done in forever. I never realised how nice and refreshing it is to sit here and let the city sort of flow around us..."

He absent-mindedly put an arm around his wife's shoulders and she almost jumped. He couldn't not notice, and with a splintering feeling somewhere in the region of his heart, he hastily removed that arm. Only to have his wife clutch at it, and grasp it firmly between her own two hands.

No one else noticed. People were chatting happily around them. The traffic was quietening down. The chaat stalls were doing brisk business. And under a clear October night sky, nobody noticed the little drama that was playing itself out between two obviously rich people on a bridge full of stories. No one, that is, other than the ancient chai-walla whose business it was to spot the people most in need of his magic brew. He spotted that moment of a removed arm and grasped palm. So, he sauntered over to where the two sat, his ancient brass kettle in one hand, a couple of chipped china tea cups in another. In a city infamous for its lack of hospitality, there were these few characters, who went straight into the annals of 'Puneri legends'. The chai-walla on the little bridge, known to his legion of admirers only as 'Anna' was one of them. Gruff to the point of being rude, his uncanny sense of who needed his famous masala chai, who needed a ginger chai, who needed sugar free chai and who needed his strong chai was one part of his urban legend. The other was his chipped china tea cups. People swore that the same tea tasted completely different when drunk from any other cup. So, when he poured two cups of ginger chai and handed them over to

Rekha and Anay, they simply took them, almost in gratitude. Anay moved to pay him, but Anna waved imperiously to a young chap who shouted across the chaos, in chaste Marathi, "Drink now, pay later. What if you want more cups of tea? We can't keep taking money for one cup at a time..."

Anay smiled broadly at this little exchange and said to Rekha, "Nowhere else in the world but in our Pune, no? What characters...!"

"All I ever wanted was for you to be in love with me." Rekha blurted out her truth. The very baldness of her statement, the raw pain in her voice would have been enough to stop Anay in his tracks. But it was the sight of her large, liquid eyes that completely undid him. He made as if to speak. But with the slightest nod of her head Rekha stopped him.

"I thought I wanted a divorce. But all that I ever wanted was for you to be in love with me. And I heard it on Oprah once, it was Dr Phil I think who said it, that we can't confess each other's sins. I didn't understand it then; I think I understand it now. I've spent so much time blaming you silently; but I'm done with that. So, the reason I asked you out tonight is simply to tell you how I feel." She stopped for the tiniest of breaths before continuing, "I think I love you like Bruno loves Mama – without holding anything back. And I have waited all these years for you to love me like that. But you don't. And it has taken me far too long, but I finally accept that. You have never intended to hurt me. I know that. But you are so formal, so polite, so... so distant, almost... I know you won't remember this; but many, many years ago I had run into your study and given you a paper cone of salted peanuts. I will never forget the look on your face. You looked like a cat had offered you a dead mouse!" And for the first time Rekha laughed at what had once pierced her heart. "I never got you a silly gift after that..." That is when the tears came. But she blinked them back. She wasn't going to give herself another moment of indulgent self-pity. On that bridge over a dying river, a woman grew up and came into her own. She smiled through the tears that glimmered at the edges of her long lashes and said to the man who she wanted to spend the rest of her life with, "I love you, Anay Jaisingh. And perhaps even more than that, I respect you. I accept you for who you are. And I will never expect you to eat peanuts out of a paper cone."

For what felt to Rekha like a very long time Anay sat slumped, his head in his hands. He felt like he was fighting this colossal internal battle, but to any outsider he looked simply like a man who was sitting silently after a long day, slightly tired, but silent.

But there was a battle raging inside him – between the imperious coolness that had been his inheritance and upbringing and something else that he had never been able to quite identify. Under a star-spangled sky, in the heart of a city that was setting down to slumber, a man stood up on a bridge, reached into the right back pocket of his immaculate trousers, pulled out his slim elegant wallet and handed a folded piece of paper to the woman who was still sitting, not sure what her husband was up to.

"What is this?" Rekha asked, genuinely bewildered.

"4th of May, 2003. That was the day you got me the groundnuts. In this paper..."

"But you threw the paper away! I saw you!"

Anay nodded "I did. And then I picked it out of the basket and folded it and kept it inside my wallet. I've changed a few wallets over the years, but this paper has always stayed with me."

It was Rekha's turn to be dumbfounded.

"I'm a fool, Rekha. I don't know how to express myself. I've been taught to keep my emotions under control. You know how the family is. We are all like that. So, forgive me if this comes out all wrong – please don't even think of a divorce. You make my life feel like it is worth living. I can't bear that house without you in it. You and your bloody enamel tub and your vegetable garden and the way you giggle with the kids and your humming as you serve us food... I can't live without it, without you."

Rekha reached a hand out to her husband and pulled him to sit down next to her. "Pav bhaji or bhel?"

"Pav bhaji" he replied.

Chapter 39

(October 19, 2016)

"She took him where?!!" Tilly laughed out loud on the phone, completely unmindful of the glares that were being directed at her. She had come to her CA's office, something to do with some paperwork for her new business.

"Mad that woman is! But so good to hear they have finally put this madness behind them…" her pen hovered over the dotted line. And the laughter suddenly died out of her voice as she said, "Maya, let me call you back."

She put her phone face down on the table in front of her, picked up the little sheaf of papers that her CA had handed to her, leant back in her chair and began to carefully go through every word.

The diminutive Ashish Khare, her CA, cleared his throat and said, hesitatingly, "Madam, you only need to sign. These are only the papers for company formation. Nothing complicated."

"Uhhh… let me take these back with me. I'll drop them off tomorrow morning."

And before the poor man could get in another word, Tilly almost scampered out of his office, throwing a hastily muttered "Thank you, Ashish" over her shoulder.

She took an auto, headed straight to Maya's place, sat gingerly at her kitchen table and asked for nimbu paani.

"Classic Tilly. Nimbu paani on a mildly cool October afternoon. When everyone else wants a warm drink, she will drink a summer cooler..." Maya smiled to herself as she added finishing touches of magic to a tall pitcher of lemonade.

"Ummm... how do you do this, Maya? How does even your nimbu paani taste better than anything anyone else makes!"

There were a few moments of silence before she continued, "You are the absolute perfect person for this business of yours. Setting up a school for home-bakers, and then a chain of cake shops. No one can do this better..."

The many years of friendship told Maya that Tilly was on the brink of sharing what was bothering her. So, she simply waited. Until Tilly finally set down the tall glass that she had been staring into and said with a heavy sigh, "I think I need some more time on the day-care plan. Some more time to figure out if this is what I really want to do..."

Maya wasn't going to push it. She knew Tilly enough to trust that she would do things in her own time. And for her own reasons. So, when Tilly went on to ask her the next question, Maya just allowed her to ramble on, "Our Diwali Party is never going to happen, Maya, is it... So much has changed, Zo is thin but broken, you are slightly plump and happy, I am fatter and jobless. Re is doing better than most of us, thank goodness; considering she was a complete mess when our big plans started..."

"Remember that stupid shopping trip we all went on? I haven't even looked at those clothes again. How did we end up like this? But, on the plus side, you have a great business idea, I have Riva and Rio, Gajju is probably gone, Sarika is pregnant, nothing much is going on in the lives of the others…"

"And Asif… I miss him so much. I don't know how Zo manages to carry on. And it's not even like we used to hang out all the time, Asif and us, you know what I mean. It's just that he was always there. It's different with Arvind and Anay. Arvind did such an amazing job putting our plans together. And Anay is always so sweet. But Asif was like the elder brother to all of us. Never realised how much he meant until one fine day he just wasn't there…"

"Have you spoken to him recently?" Maya's quiet question took Tilly completely by surprise.

"Who? Asif? What are you saying?" the confusion on Tilly's face was almost comic.

But Maya answered the confusion with a look of pure love and a gentle squeeze of the hand.

"You've never told us exactly what happened. You never take his name. But you should know that we know. And if you ever want to talk about it, I am here for you. We all are."

"Aman. His name was Aman."

The woman who bristled at the use of the past tense when it came to a dead man, sadly slipped into it herself when she spoke aloud the name that had lived like a fiercely guided secret in her heart for over a decade now.

"And no... I haven't spoken to him. I never will."

The silence that ensued hung heavy. And Maya wasn't used to that. There were very few things on the planet that were difficult to discuss among the four of them. But the Aman story was a disturbing exception. Tilly had never spoken about it. All her friends knew were the whispers and rumours that had abounded in the years immediately following the scandal. Of course, there had been a scandal – young, beautiful student and married, handsome professor, delicious doesn't come in too many different flavours.

Her friends had always been upset that the stories that made the rounds in those days almost never varied from the 'loose-charactered woman who bewitched a poor, handsome professor and charmed him into betraying his wife.' Tilly had emerged from the affair with the 'house-breaker', 'marriage-wrecker', 'other woman' tags; while popular imagination painted Aman as the bewitched innocent and his wife Najma as the angelic victim.

And for all her firebrand ways, Tilly had never spoken up against what seemed to her friends as a clear and obvious injustice.

It was all old news though. So much water under that bridge. Maya cursed herself silently for having brought it all back.

"None of my business... I shouldn't have asked the question. What possesses me sometimes? But she hasn't been herself these past few days. Something is bothering her..." Maya didn't even realise she had started mixing a batch of chocolate chip cookies. Baking was her default response to almost anything. And to see her beloved Tilly look so sad qualified as a cookie baking stimulus.

"They were right, you know..." Tilly said quietly to Maya's back.

"Who were?"

"All of them. I had no business getting involved with a married man. His wife didn't deserve it. All those names they called me? They were right."

Maya was too stunned to respond. Uncharacteristically, Tilly took Maya's silence to mean her agreement. And before Maya could react, she gathered her things and made as if to leave.

She would have, if Arvind hadn't walked into the kitchen, whistling.

"Tilly! Just the person I wanted to see! There is this amazing piece of land that Cooper Brothers has owned for a while now. I spoke to their Chairman today. He wants to do some CSR, said his company could do with some good PR. I thought of you immediately! It seems like it will be the perfect place for your animal day-care. We should go and take a look at it immediately. He was super excited by the idea. I told him that we could have a section only for strays. That could be his CSR bit, and you could pay rent for the day-care area. So, win-win for both! What say? When should I schedule this visit?"

Even Arvind Desai, the man who was notoriously poor at reading body language and related emotional cues, could see that there was something amiss in the palor of the woman who stood mutely in front of him, her eyes two big rounds on a drawn face.

"What's the matter, buddy? All good with you?" Arvind's concern touched Maya in a way that his excitement about business plans never could.

"Come on. Sit down. We'll have some of Maya's orange shortbread that she baked yesterday."

"You know I baked orange shortbread yesterday?" Maya couldn't believe what she was hearing.

"Yes. Why wouldn't I?" Arvind didn't even look at Maya as he answered her, all his attention focussed on Tilly.

"Tilly, look, you have a great business idea. And what makes it even better is that you really care about these animals. So, what could be better than turning your passion into your business?"

"Thank you, Arvind! I've been struggling to say this myself. This is exactly what I am doing – I am turning my passion into a business. And I can't do it. I simply can't!"

"What do you mean you can't!" Maya and Arvind both asked questions that translated roughly into this.

"I mean I can't do it. Or maybe, more honestly, I don't want to do it. I want to volunteer with those who are already doing these things. Because that is what I want to do. I want to take care of pets, I want to foster them, I want to give. Without making a business out of it. One day maybe I will want to build an empire. Today, I just want to live…"

"Tilly! What are you saying!" Maya's perplexed spluttering would have had Tilly rolling in laughter on another day. But today was not another day. Today was the day Tilly had finally broken her silence on her own story. Today was a special day in the life and times of Tillottama Chowdhary. And she was not going to let anything stand in the way of what she perceived as leading a life that made sense.

Strangely, it was Arvind who seemed to understand.

"You follow your instinct, Tilly. Do what you think is right" he said, gazing intently at Tilly's broken, fierce face. Another man, or maybe woman, might have said 'follow your heart'. But Arvind Desai hadn't quite reached there yet. Not that this itself wasn't a long enough leap. Many days later Maya would look back at that kitchen table moment as the one in which Arvind Desai changed tracks. It was like watching a huge, powerful train, running at full speed; move smoothly onto a new track. Her father used to take her, when she was a little girl, to the massive train stations in what was then Bombay and ask her to observe how trains seemingly headed in one direction would suddenly veer off into a completely different one. She vaguely remembered him explaining something about railway switches and slip switches and crossover switches. She had never paid him any attention, she remembered. All she cared about was the batata wada that they would eat at Karjat, on the way back home to Pune, and the cheese toast they would buy on the Deccan Queen.

Many days later she would remember, with a sharp twinge of nostalgia the exact taste of the spicy treat at Karjat, and she would be filled with an almost unbearable remorse at a flavour that was lost to the mists of time. "How come they don't taste the same anymore" she would ask Arvind one day, many days later, as they travelled back from a meeting in Mumbai by the Deccan Queen. Neither of them would remember the last time they had travelled by train, both of them would spend the journey reminiscing about childhood journeys. And Maya would look back upon that day in the kitchen when Arvind changed tracks; like someone flipped a switch somewhere and Arvind moved onto a track which would change everything.

But that was still many days away.

Today, Arvind Desai brought the conversation around to Rio's latest antics and Riva's school and how kids grew up before we knew it. And Tilly visibly relaxed, one soothing moment at a time.

Maya, however, was completely flummoxed. She watched in growing exasperation as Arvind and Tilly talked about absolutely nothing.

"Let me drop you home." Arvind finally said to her, as darkness started to fall in the Desai Wagh kitchen.

Tilly hesitated for a small moment, before she said, "Thank you. That would be great!"

"Maya, coming?" Arvind asked his wife casually.

"No, you go ahead... I've got some baking to do... a new recipe I've been wanting to try out."

But neither Arvind nor Tilly was really listening. There was a cat video on Twitter that both were giggling about.

"Okay... you mind telling me what that whole thing was all about today?" Maya couldn't not ask Arvind as they settled in for the night.

"What?" Arvind asked back, absentmindedly fiddling with the TV remote that always seemed to have run out of batteries.

"Maya, get someone to fix this damn thing, will you? It's driving me nuts. How is anyone supposed to operate the bloody thing as a remote if you have to stand two feet away from the TV for it to work! Might as well manually operate the TV then…"

"Sure. Sure, I'll do that."

Just as he was dozing off her remembered the question that Maya had asked him. "What was that you were asking me about, Maya?"

"Nothing" was the answer of a face turned away and hidden in the shadows of a deep black night that seemed to have settled into the room, like a cat settles itself on a window ledge – silently, but splendidly, occupying only a part of the ledge, but owning all of it.

Chapter 40

(October 23, 2016)

Some things can never be unsaid. So Maya was relieved that she
hadn't said it aloud. But her honesty wouldn't allow her to forget
that the thought had flashed across her mind "What is it with
Tilly... does she have a thing for married men?"

Arvind had talked about nothing and no one else for the past few
days. It was beginning to alarm the usually stable Maya.

Even the kids seemed to have noticed. Just last night at dinner
Ayush had said, "Baba, please! We don't want to hear another story
about T maushi and her childhood in the hills! Pleeeeaaase!!!"

Tilly had been busy too. Though none of the girls knew with
exactly what. And that in itself was disconcerting. Tilly had this
almost compulsive need to share her plans, her schedules and her
whereabouts with at least one of her three best friends.

For the past few days, there had been only a few perfunctory messages,
and then silence. So, when Arvind announced at breakfast that day
that he and Tilly were catching up for coffee at the Marriott later in
the evening, Maya put down her mug of coffee forcefully enough to
spill some on her Kutchi embroidered coaster and asked, "Just tell

me will you – what is going on with the two of you?”

Arvind looked up from his mobile, surprised “You mean she hasn’t told you? I thought you girls practically lived out of each others’ schedulers, not that that mad woman would have a scheduler…”

The laugh in Arvind’s voice soothed Maya’s frayed nerves almost immediately. There was not a hint of evasiveness in him; Arvind Desai did not look like a man with anything to hide. “She is talented, but completely crazy. She needs someone to hold her together.”

And there it was again. That ugly monster.

“You girls are a great influence though. She keeps saying that she would have lost it long ago had it not been for all of you. And she seems to love you just a little more than she loves the others. But that might just be my imagination.”

And there it was again, a breath of calm.

Maya wasn’t used to such a see-sawing of emotions. She didn’t like feeling like this. And she was wise enough to know that she needed to get to the bottom of whatever was going on very quickly, and that the only way to do that was by waiting patiently for Arvind to tell her the story.

He seemed completely oblivious to the storm raging inside her, though. Because he kept scrolling through his Twitter feed. And when he looked up to ask for more coffee, he caught his wife looking at him, hands crossed, which even he knew was a sign of danger. It took him a moment to remember what might have upset his usually unruffled Maya, but then he remembered “Oh yes. Meeting with Tilly! She’s been away on this photography assignment for the big animal shelter in Pirangut… you know those guys with all the funding? The Kirtane's started it, but now it's grown into this international project. What is the name… aah – Santa Pawse. Very quirky name I always thought. Anyway, she's been away, shooting for them. Something to do with a calendar they are launching in New York, around Christmas. I mentioned that to Banerjee, you know him, CEO of Cooper. He said they also wanted to shoot a calendar – the forts of Maharashtra. Some conservation project they want to do. I told you they were really focussed on CSR this year. So, I called them both over for a cup of coffee. I told Tilly she should share her photos with him. Let's see how it goes… Mad woman that friend of yours is."

Maya sat at the table for a long, long time after that. Her coffee went stone cold. She neither heated it, nor did she pour herself another mug.

"All these years. All these years I've known Tilly. We've been the best of friends; I've seen her do impossible things for all of us out of the love she has in her huge heart. Not once has she done or said anything even remotely inappropriate. Just a few days of silence from her, a few mentions of her by my husband and I threw all of that away! I thought she has a thing for married men. How shameful, Maya. How shameful! You are such a hypocrite, Maya. All that talk about sisterhood, and those years when you were supposedly mad at society for labelling Tilly as the marriage breaker and the other woman… It took only a few words of not even praise, simply a few mentions from your own husband and you went straight and bought into the stereotype. I'm not sure how I can forgive you, Maya. There has to be something that you can do to set it right. You figure it out. You do what you have to. And grow up. Even if there had been something happening between them, the question you should have asked yourself is not 'does she have a thing for married men' but 'is Arvind forgetting that he is a married man'. You are such a hypocrite, and such a fake. Oh, I know it was just a stray thought. But how did you even allow such a thought to stray into your head?!! It must have been lying dormant, just under the surface, under the veneer of civilisation and wokeness. You are NOT woke. Not if you can believe such bull about Tilly, or for that matter any other woman... and no, it is NOT okay that you believed it only for a moment!"

The calm, equitable, composed Maya was seething. And it looked like she had no way out of the docks. She was the accuser, she was the accused, she was the judge.

How often do we do that? We berate ourselves with a harshness that we wouldn't dream of dishing out to another. We preach kindness to others, we often practice it too. But we are all too often notoriously unkind to ourselves.

Maya had learnt the art of forgiving others, even in the absence of an apology. She had learnt it from her mother. But she was not even aware that she needed to apply the same principles of love and largeness of heart to her own self.

She thought that it would be unfair if she stopped berating herself, if she went easy on herself. When in fact, nothing could be further from the truth. But, like far too many of us, Maya didn't know that on that October morning that was rapidly marching towards noon outside her breakfast table window.

She must have sat there for a good couple of hours. Doing nothing.

Just staring into herself. Wondering how to recover from a statement that had never escaped her lips, but one that she herself was finding it near impossible to escape from.

When suddenly, seemingly out of nowhere, Tilly materialised at her elbow.

"What was I thinking? Am I completely mad? They saw me taking a few pictures, so they asked me to show them what I had shot, the next thing I know is they are offering me an assignment to shoot their calendar for their New York fundraiser, and I said yes! I know NOTHING about professional photography… it's like I have this death wish, and I do stupid stuff just to shoot myself in the foot!"

And Maya smiled a smile that felt like the sun breaking through the clouds for the first time in forever.

"You do realise that you have not breathed a word about this to any one of us…" she left the mildly teasing question hanging.

"But Arvind knew! I received the call in front of him that day… when he was dropping me home! I thought he would have told everyone!"

At Maya's quizzically raised eyebrow Tilly laughed the long familiar Tilly laugh – head thrown back, hands on generous hips, curls dancing about her face.

"Oh, that Arvind of yours! How have you managed with him for all these years? Dense as the mousse I should never have attempted. But just as sweet, and a little addictive…"

She had wandered off to the ample shelves that held the most beautiful collection of biscuit tins she had ever seen. She peered into one after the other, before picking out a deliciously pink concoction.

One bite and she squealed "This tastes like bananas! It looks like strawberries! Maya, how do you do stuff like this! Just so yummy... But don't distract me! I came here to wail about how I have made the biggest mistake of my life and how I am going to fall flat on my face and how you have to save me from myself!"

"You want a smoothie?"

"Mayaaaaa! You are not listening! What have I done!"

"You have done the best possible thing for yourself. And I want to go and hug that person at Santa Pawse who spotted your talent and gave you this assignment..." Maya's voice was kind and gentle.

"So, you DO know! I knew Arvind would tell you!"

Maya didn't bother to correct her. There were more important things to be done.

"Listen, we should have that Diwali party."

"What? Why? What do we even have to celebrate?"

"Lots. We have lots to celebrate. Starting with us."

Epilogue ᦔ

They did have the party.

Anay and Rekha were the first to arrive, with their two darling boys and a dog called Bruno in tow. Anay had his hand around his wife's waist when they walked into Maya and Arvind's beautifully bedecked lawns. It didn't look like he was going to let go any time soon.

Then Tilly pranced in. Running breathlessly after Riva and Rio. She had presented her first set of photographs to the client. They had loved them. "They said my pictures told a story, and they could make people cry and laugh and fall in love. Oh, and I write a little story with every picture, just a couple of lines. They said that just completely blew the socks off the guys in New York. Who knew a hobby could make me money?" she had gurgled happily over the phone on a concall between the four of them a couple of days ago.

She already had two new assignments, had found three animal shelters where she had committed to volunteer for a day a week, and she was working on her coffee table book which she had tentatively titled 'Indrayani'. She told people that that was because she felt a spiritual connection with the river Indrayani along whose banks Maharashtra's great Bhakti movement flourished. It was only her closest friends who realised that it was also the name of her hostel in the University.

They never said a word about it.

Zo arrived late. She told her friends honestly that she almost didn't come. But her sons had opened her closet, pulled out the most mismatched outfit for her and said, "Let's go, Mama..."; which is why she came dressed in a slightly absurd pink - grey - peacock blue ensemble. But she came. And everyone who saw her enter the grounds that day, one son on either side of her, knew that they were in the presence of courage and character and something approaching heroism.

Her wounds ached with a raw intensity that day. The bright lights shone in stark contrast to the darkness that lived inside her. It was a contrast that was almost too much for her to bear. But she not only bore it, she welcomed it. Somewhere inside her bruised, battered heart, she knew that she had to keep moving toward the light. Even if it felt so much easier to succumb to the darkness. If anyone symbolised the spirit of Diwali in that intimate gathering, it was Zoya Quettawala. Her head held high, her fragile heart beating, her soul ripped apart by the absence of her beloved Asif, she walked into a party and gave her children the best gift of all - that of a mother who defeated the darkness by choosing light.

Rashmi, Mitali and Roopa couldn't make it. They said the whole gang should meet up in NCH next week for breakfast, it had been too long. Everyone had tentatively agreed.

Sarika came. But she left early. The baby was only a few weeks away and she wanted to take it easy.

Maya waited until the end of the evening to unveil the logo of her new business "Brown Sugar". When everyone asked her why the name, she replied with a laugh "It's my favourite ingredient in the whole world, and besides, like Arvind told me, it doesn't hurt to have a name that makes people do a doubletake!"

Someone was heard asking her, "Your insta page ItsMaya is doing so well. Why aren't you creating a business out of the same name?"

"That's just it. My business? It's not just Maya. It's so much more."

Shaila Wagh was seen smiling a quiet smile of maternal pride as she overheard that answer.

Rekha's fingers dazzled with two new rings. Her nails shone like pearls. She overheard Anay telling Zaid that his favourite food in the whole wide world was now officially pav bhaji.

No one wore the clothes they had bought for the party once upon a long ago. Zoya's were too loose for her. Rekha couldn't bear to use anything from those months. Tilly and Maya needed to lose some serious weight if they wanted to ever fit into those ridiculous ideas.

Raghu Kaka had sent sambar for the party.

Gajju was not invited.

Some things were truly over. Others were just beginning.

Wish To Publish With Us?

———⁓———

We are always keen to look at interesting new content across genres.
Please mail submissions to: **submissions@leadstartcorp.com**

Proposals should include:

1. SYNOPSIS
   A summary of the book in 500 – 1000 words. Please mention
   the word count of the manuscript.

2. SAMPLE CHAPTERS / POETRY
   A couple of chapters from the book; these need not be in order,
   just send the best two chapters of the book. Or a few poems if
   the same is a collection of poetry.

3. A NOTE ABOUT THE AUTHOR
   An interesting note about yourself (about 200 words).

4. ADDITIONAL INFORMATION
   - Target audience
   - Unique selling proposition
   - List of illustrative content (if any)
   - Other comparative titles
   - Your thoughts on marketing the book

www.ingramcontent.com/pod-product-compliance
Lightning Source LLC
LaVergne TN
LVHW041456170726
843492LV00005B/1253